'DOWNHILL'

by ANN THORSSON

16.02.2020

To Isabelle,

With my very best wishes,

Ann.

First published in Great Britain as a softback original in 2019

Copyright © Ann Thorsson

The moral right of this author has been asserted.

Typeset in Dante MT Std

Editing, design, typesetting and publishing by UK Book Publishing

www.ukbookpublishing.com

ISBN: 978-1-912183-97-5

To

My Three Vikings

and

a Wuffalo

ABOUT THE AUTHOR

Image: Gabriel Rutenberg Photography

Ann Thorsson was born in Chesterfield, England. She now lives in a house by the sea just outside of Reykjavík, Iceland, with her Icelandic husband, their two bilingual sons and a Siberian husky.

'Downhill' is Ann's debut novel.

TO THE READER...

Though the drama is centred in the area around the Derbyshire/ Nottinghamshire/South Yorkshire border, I have tempered the dialogue for ease of reading, particularly for those readers who don't come from this area.

For those readers who do, then I'll leave you to read it as you speak!

Enjoy!

Ann Thorsson

PART 1

CHAPTER 1

Sirens Are Screaming…

30.7.91

Ged steadied himself in the sheltered doorway of the now-closed-down Co-op Furnishings while he retched, the muted image of his reflection in the grimy glass retching with him. Sun-bleached posters ironically declared 'Everything Must Go!'. Just another sign of the times – Castle Ridge was slowly dying, a victim of the Thatcher-years economic downturn. Beads of sweat began to gather on Ged's forehead, dampening the front of his lank, black hair; his body burned like a Sheffield smelting furnace. The dull thump and drone of afternoon traffic pounded the road behind.

He heaved again, grabbing the door handle as agonising pain shot through his side. The acrid smell of warm lager, gut fluid and stale shop-doorway piss wafted up to assail his nostrils as the last of the Fosters and rancid Cornish pasty splashed across his old Hi-Techs and the bottom of his jeans. Ged wiped the dregs of sourness from his mouth with the bottom edge of his old and faded '83 Monsters of Rock tee-shirt – his 'honeymoon' tee-shirt, unconsciously muttering a silent apology to Meat Loaf. *Should've* *been Meat that headlined, not that tosser Coverdale…*He rinsed around his teeth and spat out a gobful of saliva mouthwash.

Gerald Alan Steele – even his name had a bit of an edge to it, Steele/ edge, gettit? Well, he used to think it was funny. The one thing that he never thought was funny was the piss-taking that he used to get at school and down the pit for his initials – GAS. Fart jokes about his name were only funny for so long. But you had to man-up and take it. He didn't miss being down the pit – that was one *career* he was glad to see the back of.

Step by unsteady step, Ged cautiously made his way along the High Street, his gait attracting the disapproving stares and comments of the afternoon shoppers. Well, bollocks to 'em – he'd just been offered a steady job at his best mate's coal yard, *and* had all his horses romp home on today's little bet. He felt as though his luck could finally be turning – *about bloody time!* Ged fingered the winning ticket as he reached into the top pocket of his shabby Wrangler jacket to get his ciggies. Maybe having a smoke would clear the sour taste from his mouth. A thousand volts of pain shot through his side. Okay, so maybe having a smoke was not the best idea right now.

Right now, he just needed to stop the world and get off.

Right now, he just needed to get rid of this searing pain.

Right now, he just needed to get help. *They* needed to get help.

It was the only option left.

The bookies' neon sign teasingly beckoned him to collect his winnings, but that would have to wait until tomorrow. Shaking, sweating, hurting, and with his mind set on auto-pilot, Ged slowly made his way towards Colliery Hill, the main thoroughfare intersecting the shops from the residential side of town, and headed for home.

As Ged's mind absently wandered through his default Meat Loaf song, he became acutely aware of life emulating art. Why did he feel so torn, so twisted? And why could he hear sirens screaming? *They sounded so real…* Nothing was making sense.

His reality was slipping away.

His heart was breaking out, flying...slipping away.

Life-was-slipping-away...

'Stand back, clear out of the way please. Does anybody know who he is?'

What the...? Noise. Hurts. Faces, lots of faceless faces. Pain, lots of pain...

'The van driver didn't stand a chance...'

'The daft twat just stepped out into the road...'

Shit, that hurts. That hurts a lot.

'I think it's... hairdre...'

Blood, mingled with other escaping fluids, leaked from his body, staining his clothes with wetness and sticky crimson. Despite the excruciating pain, Ged inwardly laughed to himself – he could feel his crotch getting warm. He realised he was pissing himself. *Not cool, not fuckin' cool.* Everything was escaping...blood, piss, life-fluids...

Gas was escaping. GAS... *Fart jokes...not funny.*

'Stand clear...pulse dropping...'

His subconscious began playing tricks on his mind.

Somewhere in his mind he thought he heard an ice-cream van.

Somewhere in his mind he thought he heard a squeal of laughter.

Somewhere in his mind he thought he heard a squeal of tyres.

Somewhere in his mind he thought he heard a scream of horror from old Mrs Jessop.

Somewhere in his mind he thought he heard their Jon say, 'It's okay, Dad, come with me. I'll look after you...It's nice here...'

Jon? No, no, Jon. I'm not ready yet...I want to stay here...with...

He felt the sensation of being gently lifted, urgent voices, rapid yet uneven movement.

Julie...William...I want to stay...I want...

Blackness.

The salon was fairly quiet, just one old dear in at the moment –Mrs Burgess, one of the regular wash-and-set crowd. Julie busied herself with her client.

Quiet was not good – it allowed too much thinking time. Radio Hallam hummed along in the background, giving out all the local updates and music – mostly Human League and Def Leppard, she noticed. She began mentally counting how many times she and Ged had been to see Leppard, allowing herself a half smile. *Back when we were young, and free, and...*

'Do you want me to cut any more off the top, Mrs Burgess?'

Snip, snip. Snip, snip...*happy.*

The inane babble from Mrs Burgess was starting to irritate Julie, price-of-strawberries this, and too-hot that. She wanted – nay, felt - the need to be alone with her thoughts. *So much had changed...*

Radio Hallam announced they just had time for one more record before the news, the strains of Dire Straits' *Romeo and Juliet* filtering through to Julie. She could feel her eyes starting to sting.

Snip, snip. Snip, snip. *We've already lost Jon–*

Snip, snip. Snip, snip. *I know I've gone too far this time – I've pushed the limit with Ged...*

Snip, snip. Snip, snip. She re-focused for a moment, blinking away tears.

'There, how's that, Mrs Burgess? It looks nice, doesn't it?'

And what about Will? No...no, I would never hurt Will.

Remote voices broke through the foggy jumble of her thoughts. Peering through moist lashes, her dark eyes connected with the owners of the voices, noting that they were wearing police uniforms. One male, one female.

'Mrs Steele? Mrs Julie Steele?' asked the female voice.

They asked her to sit down. They were very sorry, but...

The crash of scissors hitting the tiled floor provided a spontaneous metallic applause to Dire Straits.

CHAPTER 2

When Worlds Collide

1979

Jean Bryant sat at the kitchen table, china tea cup in hand. She closed her eyes and took a deep breath – oh, how she wished she could close her ears as well. The dull, rhythmic *thump-thump-thump* and guitar-whine of whatever rubbish Julie was listening to in her bedroom overhead reverberated down through the ceiling and echoed around the kitchen walls. All that money they'd spent on piano lessons for Julie, exposing her to all the classics, and here she was, listening to music that would damage her ears. What was music coming to? With any luck it was just one of Julie's many teen phases. Jean poured herself another cup of Lady Grey and sighed – it was getting harder by the week to keep control of their daughter. Goodness knows how people manage if they have more than one child – must be a parenting nightmare. Coping with one was bad enough. She'd already noticed pitying looks and whispered exchanges between the ladies in her WI group, looks that said "Poor Jean, can't do a thing with that wayward daughter of hers". And Frank was not much help, always at the office with some court papers to read through. And if he wasn't there, he was either at the golf course or the country club "networking", as he called it. Well, it was about time he started laying down the law to their daughter, and not just to the toe-rags he represented in court. He let Julie get away with far too much...*Why should it just be down to me to...*

Her train of thought was jarred by the clatter of something hitting a wall overhead. Jean sighed – *please, no...*she realised her hands were trembling, the fine china cup tinkling on its matching saucer. She couldn't deal with yet another confrontation.

The pearly-white smiles and lip-gloss pouts of Charlie's Angels reflected back through the dressing table mirror at Julie as she sat down to do her hair. She looked at the poster and mimicked the pose of Kelly, her favourite.

'I bet your mother doesn't nag you about how much make-up you wear,' Julie said to the poster, as if expecting a reply. She defiantly put on a slick of cola-flavoured lip-gloss then slowly began to unwind the heated rollers, gently teasing through the curls with her fingers before brushing her long dark hair until it looked full and luscious. Ugh! How she longed to be one of the Angels – anything to get away from this boring little village, and this boring little life. The Angels' lifestyle looked so much more glamorous and exciting than hers. *And I'm pretty enough to be an Angel.* Julie launched her hairbrush at the innocent poster, narrowly missing Farrah Fawcett's face. She pouted her lips and changed her pose in the mirror, her teen sensuality screaming to be noticed. *Or maybe I could be one of those sexy girls in a rock video, flirting around all the rock stars?*

Julie glanced at the bedside clock – just enough time to listen to one more track on her new Van Halen album before going out for the bus. She turned up the volume of the record player – *not too much, mustn't incur the wrath of Mother* – unconsciously wiggling her backside to the thumping guitar rhythm of *Runnin' With the Devil*, and began loading her handbag with things that she needed to sneak past her mother – make-up bag, studded belt, bangles, facial wipes, Polo mints. Everything she needed to rock it up then later eliminate the evidence. The version of Julie that went out through the front door in Shirecliffe was not the same version that would arrive at the local rock disco at the Assembly Rooms in Castle Ridge. That version would give the crusty ladies at her mother's WI group something to *tut-tut* about. She retrieved her hairbrush from its carpeted landing zone and dropped it into her handbag. *Time to run the gauntlet and get past Mother without being searched.* She ran down the stairs, grabbing her leather jacket en-route to the front door.

'I'm off into town then. Tell Dad he can pick me and Helena up in the Market Square at 11:00. Byeee,' she shouted, without waiting for a reply. And with a rattle of glass in the ornately glazed front door, she was gone.

The knot that was in Jean Bryant's stomach unravelled.

Just a little.

Beryl Steele sat at her kitchen table, chipped and stained tea-mug in hand – "Greatest Mum" was just visible through her nicotine-yellowed fingers. She closed her eyes and took a deep lung-full of cigarette smoke, exhaling a fuggy grey cloud around her. She coughed, her chest rattling deep within.

'And where are you two buggers off to?' she enquired, as Ged and his best mate Col grabbed their fake-leather jackets, ready to leave.

'There's an under-18 rock disco at the Assembly Rooms, so we thought we'd head up there. Any chance we can cadge some fags?' Ged asked, as he took one last look at his reflection in the mirror hanging over the kitchen fireplace.

'Aye, take these, there's four left.' She shoved the packet of Benson & Hedges in his direction. 'Do ya need any money for the bus, or for some chips?'

'Bloody 'ell, Mam, did you have a win at bingo?'

'Well, if I can't spoil me lad now and again. Here, take two quid,' she said, stuffing two crumpled green notes into Ged's hand. 'And make sure you catch the last bus, love – I don't want you walking through the estate late at night. And be quiet when you come in. Yer dad'll have just come home from working the late shift, don't forget.'

'Aye, okay. See ya later, Mam,' said Ged, giving her a clumsy hug.

'Tarra, Mrs Steele.' Col also gave Ged's mam a teen boy-hug in return for one of her play-punches.

'Aye, see ya later, lads,' said Mrs Steele, rasping her words. *Aye, they're good lads*, she thought to herself, as she poured another mugful of Tetley's and reached for a new pack of cigarettes.

The single decker bus pulled away sharply, causing Julie to lurch forward as she made her way along the aisle. *Arsehole bus-driver.* Her best friend Helena had gotten on two stops before at the far side of Shirecliffe, and had saved her a seat in their usual spot at the back. That way they were the observers, not the observed. Like a pair of magpies, handbags were soon opened to covet each other's donations to the evening ahead.

'Two miniatures of Bacardi and two of Smirnoff. I couldn't sneak any more than that from the shelves,' complained Helena, hoping that her friend wouldn't be too disappointed. Helena's parents, Sylvia and Bryce Blakeley, looked after Shirecliffe's thriving village shop and off-licence, which also housed a small Post Office counter. And much to Helena's embarrassment, her parents were one of those bouncy, tweedy, Barbour-wearing couples that did everything together and still called each other "darling". Even worse, they referred to everything with countryside metaphors. Her older brother, Geoffrey, had already "spread his wings and flown the nest", and was now a "fledgling" at Nottingham University, as they loved to tell customers. She lowered her voice. 'I overheard Mum whining to Dad about the off-licence stock being down so I had to be careful,' she whispered, in defence of her stolen goods. Helena nodded towards Julie's handbag. 'What did you get?'

Julie rummaged among her make-up and trinkets to reveal her booty.

'A can of Coke and a can of Lilt – useful as mixers for the booze. And… ta-da – a fiver from mum's fruit-shop takings. So we can buy whatever we want.'

'You didn't!' exclaimed Helena, shocked at her best friend's bare-faced nerve.

'I did. Mum's got money coming out of her ears at the moment, what with the summer strawberry sales and stuff. I'm pretty sure she won't miss a fiver.'

Ged winced as he felt the sharpness of Col's elbow dig into his side, causing him to slop shandy over his jeans. He put his glass down onto the table, and started rummaging in his jacket pocket for a tissue.

'What was that for, you twat?' he asked.

'Have you been listening to a single word that I said?' shouted Col, trying to compete with the thumping rhythm of the music.

'Er, about what?'

'I was asking if you'd signed up for the apprenticeship yet. At the pit? Forget it – you're not list-en-ing…' Col's eyes followed the direction of Ged's distracted gaze. 'Uff, she's hot,' he commented, 'I wouldn't mind giving…'.

'Fuck off, I saw her first,' grinned Ged, cutting off Col in mid-sentence.

'But..I...you…' Col struggled to find the words to defend his position as the teen ladies-man. 'Okay then…'

Realising that the female of the species was finally having an effect on his loins, and buoyed by a rush of teen-bravado, Ged stood up and strode purposefully towards this dark haired goddess rocking her stuff on the dance floor. It appeared that Col was no longer the only one that could charm the girls.

And there they stood, mirror-images of each other playing imaginary guitars, long dark hair swaying rhythmically, chugging their heads in unison to the twelve-bar riff of Status Quo. As the beat of the music and the pulse of the lights enveloped them, the heady cocktail of Ged's surging hormones and Julie's alcohol-fuelled abandon drew their divided worlds closer together.

But of course, life's never that simple.

Is it?

CHAPTER 3

The Morning After the Night Before

Julie picked up the simple but beautifully scripted note lying on the kitchen table. Her mother always wrote in ink-pen, be it a shopping list or letter of complaint. *'You're grounded for one week, young lady! Mum xx'*

'One week! B..but…Ugh!' Julie's protest fell on stony ground as she slapped the sheet of blue writing paper back down on the table.

Her father assumed a stern pose, much like the one he used in court, and swept up the note. He waved it in front of his daughter's face.

'What the bloody hell were you thinking? Where did you get the booze from? You're under-age, you know.'

Julie rolled her eyes. 'Oh, no…here we go…'

'Don't take that tone with me, Julie. Did you get it from Helena's? Surely they weren't selling booze at the under-18s disco?'

'Where is Mum anyway?'

'Gone to the wholesalers, then to her veg shop. And don't change the subject…' Frank Bryant softened. As hard as he could be in court, he could never be hard on his daughter. 'Anyway, your O-Levels start in a couple of weeks, so you can use the time to revise. C'mon, get ready and I'll drive you to the salon. It was really good of Aunty Betty to give you this Saturday job, so don't blow it.'

Julie hauled herself up from the kitchen table, her stomach queasy, her head light.

'By the way, who was the boy I saw you with last night?' Frank Bryant grinned at his daughter, then gave her a knowing wink.

*

Ged munched on his cornflakes, almost choking with embarrassment from the merciless teasing of Lynette and Sharon, his younger twin-sisters.

'Ged's got a girlfriend, Ged's got a girlfriend,' they sang in their eight year old twin-harmony.

He pulled a face, then humorously stuck his tongue out at them.

'How do they know?' he asked his mam. *Christ, it was impossible to have any secrets in this town...*

'Our Brenda and her mates saw you kissing some lass under the clock tower last night. Quite pretty, by all accounts...'

Ged felt a grin being framed by colour rising in his cheeks. His older sister never missed a bloody thing! Brenda was all-knowing, all-seeing – she would make a bloody good spy! He quickly slurped up the last of his cornflakes and milk before exaggeratingly looking at his watch.

'Is that the time? Gotta go. Helping Col and his dad at the coal yard this morning. See ya!'

Inquisition – avoided.

CHAPTER 4

Call Me

Mid-morning sun filtered through the slatted blinds, creating a horizontal ladder pattern of light and shadow across the classroom. The magnified heat burned onto Julie's bare forearms, and the bright white pages of her notebook reflected intensely into her eyes.

Mrs Craven's backside jiggled as she chalked up the notable Acts and Scenes that the class needed to revise for their upcoming 'O' Level English Literature exam. She turned to them, looking over her glasses.

'So remember, Shakespeare's words should not be taken literally – look for deeper meaning in your analysis. Revise the key scenes. Let's take another look at Act 2, Scene II for example.' A whisper of pages being turned echoed around the classroom. Mrs Craven continued,

'What exactly does Juliet mean when she's doing her classic "O Romeo, Romeo! Wherefore art thou Romeo?" bit?'

'She's asking where he is, Miss,' came one reply. Mrs Craven's face crumpled.

'Where is Romeo?' she asked, exasperated.

'Under Juliet's window, Miss.'

'Exactly! So, why would she be asking *where* he is when she's having a conversation with him? She's asking "wherefore", Derek, not *where*. Anyone else?'

No reply. Mrs Craven sighed, wondering why she had to explain this again, just before the exam.

'She's really asking "why". *Why* is he a Montague? *Why* does he have to be from a rival family? Look at the next line – it gives you a clue...'

Julie looked up from her book, catching sight of some sixth form boys playing rugby out on the field. Her mind distractedly wandered back to last Friday evening.

To when she'd had a little too much to drink.

To when she'd met Ged.

To when she'd had her first real kiss.

To when she'd giggled and given him her phone number.

Emotion-butterflies began to swirl around in her belly, and she felt her nipples stiffen slightly. Would he call? Anticipation turned to apprehension – what if he called and her mother answered? The butterflies turned to angry wasps, stinging her from within.

Pshsst. Ged cracked open the ice-cold can of Tizer and took a long, refreshing drink. The heavy burden of his school bag cut into his shoulder as it snagged on the handle of the shop doorway, causing him to wince. He put the change back into his trouser pocket, the coins being needed for a certain task. There was a telephone box on the way home. And there was a piece of paper in his blazer pocket that contained a telephone number. A number which could only be called between 4-6 o'clock – after school, and before her parents came home. Her specific instructions.

The rusty top-spring squeaked in protest as Ged heaved open the phone box door, the stale smell of cigarettes and piss causing him to momentarily pause from entering. He cautiously kicked some chip wrappers to one side before stepping in, unsure of what lurked beneath. Ged carefully stacked the pile of change on top of the telephone set, trying not to knock it over as he perched the can of Tizer and a Cornish pasty alongside. He looked at the number on the piece of paper, though he already knew it by heart. *Come on, come on. Be a man. Make the call.* Eight, two, six…slowly, he dialled the number, his finger following the arc of the dial with each digit.

'Hello,' came the hesitant yet hopeful sounding reply of a young female voice.

Bip, bip, bip, bip, bip. Ged's pulse-rate matched the speed of the *bips* as he shakily put the first of his coins into the slot.

'Erm, hello, Julie? It's me, Ged. You know, from Friday night…'

Ged put down the receiver, and took a deep breath. How could he – Gerald Alan Steele – be the luckiest git on the estate? He gathered up his empty can and pasty wrapper and stuffed them into his school bag. He looked at his watch. Shit, he was supposed to be helping Col and his dad down at the coal yard at six, and he'd still got to drop off his stuff at home and get changed. Shit, bugger, damn-and-blast it, as his late-gran used to say. Time to get his arse in gear – there'd be plenty of time for love-dreaming once he was in the privacy of his bed. He grinned, and winked to himself as he exited the phone box. His school bag no longer felt quite so burdensome as he legged it in the direction of home.

After disconnecting the call with Ged, Julie returned the receiver to its cradle and hugged the cushion closely to her, savouring the moment. She glanced at the hallway clock – still time to call Helena with an update before her mum came home.

'Hey, why weren't you in school today? I missed you. Had no-one to share all the gossip with,' grumbled Julie, by way of a greeting.

'Hi…Oh, that stupid horse of mine knocked me over trying to get apples out of my pocket. Twisted my ankle. Mum made sure that I spent the day revising instead,' Helena explained.

Unable to contain her excitement, Julie blurted, 'He called me…he called me. Ged called me!'

'Really…so what did you talk about, you and lover-boy?' Helena asked. 'C'mon, keep no secrets, tell no lies.'

Julie's voice turned gooey. 'Oh…Friday night, our taste in music, just anything and everything really. Oh yes, and I'm grounded. My parents blame you for the booze, by the way.'

Helena interrupted, eager to share her mutual misfortune.

'Yeah, I'm grounded too! For a whole week! My dad also figured out where the booze must've come from. He's well mad. The only place I'm allowed to go is up the field to Jasper. Anyway, carry on…'

Helena listened patiently while her best friend dreamily recounted the details of her conversation with Ged.

'By the way,' Julie continued, 'what are you doing on Sunday? There's the Summer Fayre at the Lodge Gardens, and Ged's asked me to go. Do you wanna come, and make a foursome with us and his mate?'

'Oh no, not the "foursome" thing, Jules. His mate's bound to want to hold hands or something creepy. It was bad enough being left alone with him most of Friday night while you were dancing with lover-boy. Besides, you know it's not my thing,' pleaded Helena.

'I know – I just thought…Shit – Mum's here! Gotta go – I'm supposed to be studying. I'll talk to you at school tomorrow…'

Julie, pen in hand, looked up from the strategically placed biology books spread all over the kitchen table, the picture-perfect image of a studious schoolgirl. 'Hi, Mum…'

CHAPTER 5

Summer Lovin'…

The Summer Fayre was already in full swing when Ged arrived at the gates to Lodge Gardens. He could see families enjoying the sunshine – children running around, stalls full of activity and hubbub, while a metallic megaphone-voice encouraged people to join in with the fun. Ged sensed Julie creeping up behind him, causing a prickle of anticipation to run up his spine. He turned, just as she pounced.

'Ha-ha, you don't catch me that easy, lady!' he teased, but let her grab him anyway, relishing the touch and closeness of her scented skin. She had a more demure, scrubbed-clean look today, just a slick of lip-gloss and smudge of eye-liner, quite unlike the panda-eyes of the week before. 'You look nice,' he continued.

'Nice? Plain Jane, more like,' she grumbled. 'Mum and her WI crusties are here with the "Afternoon-Tea" marquee, so I'm afraid you get the plain version of me today. She freaks if I wear too much make-up. Thinks it looks "cheap".'

'God knows what she'd make of our Bren, then,' laughed Ged. 'She's like an advert for Avon! Anyway, shall we go in? Promise I'll be on me best behaviour when I take you for a cream-tea.' He smiled, and made a "Scout's Honour" sign to his forehead.

'No way! I'm not going anywhere near that bunch of judgemental old bags! You can buy me an ice-cream instead.' Julie linked her arm into Ged's – a combined act of defiance and bravado in case she was spotted by her mum or someone she knew.

They leisurely ambled around the Fayre, soaking up the atmosphere and enjoying the first flush of each other's company. Julie found herself the recipient of a little teddy bear after Ged showed his prowess on the 'Hook-a-Duck' stall. This was just how she imagined romance to be, and so far, it was living up to her teen-dreams. Julie noticed a small, red tent with a garishly painted sign-board outside, which read "Let Psychic Kate Read Your Fortune – Palm Readings 50p". She nudged Ged in the ribs with her elbow.

'Hey, shall we go and get our fortunes read? See what the future holds for us?'

Ged looked at her, his thick, dark brows furrowed together. 'You don't really believe in all that spiritual clap-trap, do you?' He shook his head, bemused. 'Nah, what will be, will be. Anyway, I predict that in the very near future, we're going to be eating ice-cream...' He nodded in the direction of the Mr Frosty ice-cream van.

'With a Flake, raspberry sauce and sprinkles?' Julie asked, trying to hide her disappointment.

'If that's what my good lady wants, then yes, with a Flake, raspberry sauce and sprinkles.'

They grabbed themselves an ice-cream each and settled under the shade of an old sycamore tree. Julie busied herself with Ged's denim jacket, making a makeshift blanket for them to sit on. A long-haired, blonde Farrah Fawcett look-alike, wearing a white strappy mini-dress strolled past them, surrounded by her posse of giggling attendees. Her blue faux-satin sash emblazoned with "Miss Castle Ridge 1979" separated her voluptuous boobs. She fluttered her false eyelashes at Ged and blew him a kiss. He pretended not to notice. Ged already had the notion that Julie might have a jealous streak, so swiftly turned his attention to her so as to avoid any undue girl-on-girl confrontations.

'Col was really disappointed that your mate didn't want to come today,' Ged explained. 'He quite likes her, you know. Although he thought that she played a bit hard to get on Friday night.'

Julie licked her ice-cream, catching the drips. 'Well, I hate to burst his bubble, but she's not interested. She, er, bats for the other side, you see.' Ged stared at her vacantly, not quite understanding her meaning. 'She's not interested in boys. That's probably why she played hard to get,' clarified Julie.

'What, you mean she's a lesbo?' asked Ged, still puzzled. This was alien territory to him – not something that was openly discussed, but rather sniggered at round his way.

'Yes. But please keep it to yourself. She hasn't even told her parents yet. You'll just have to tell Col that he's not her type, or something.' Julie stared hard at Ged – a stare that said *I'll kill you if you say anything*.

'Okay, okay, I promise,' he said, slightly taken aback. He thought it wise to change the subject. 'So, what are your plans once you've done your O and A-Levels?'

'A-Levels? What do you mean?' she replied, counter-questioning.

'Well, surely a grammar school smart-arse like you will be staying on for sixth form, to do your A-Levels?' he teased.

Julie play-pushed Ged, almost squashing his ice-cream.

'No, actually. I'm just going to grind my way through these O-Levels before going to Tech in September. Mum's making me revise at least one hour a day ready for the exams. I swear I'll scream if I see one more poem by William Blake!' She rolled her eyes in protest.

'I quite like Blake's poetry,' intercut Ged. ''The Schoolboy' is my favourite – I prefer that one, rather than "Tyger, Tyger".'

Julie looked at him, her surprise clearly visible. 'You know poetry by Blake?'

Ged looked at her, quite crestfallen. 'Of course. We've been doing him in English O-Level too. Seems to be the year for studying stuff by blokes called "William". We read *Lord of the Flies* at the beginning of the year by whatshisname...' He tapped his fingers on his knee while he thought. 'William Golding. I *really* liked that book, very powerful.'

'So did we! Yes, it is a very powerful novel. Quite grim.' Julie took a lick of her ice-cream, just in time to catch a drip of raspberry sauce before it fell onto her tee-shirt.

Prompted by the bold line of liquid redness, Ged said, 'We had to recreate the "Kill the beast! Cut his throat! Spill his blood!" scene in class, to get a feel for mob-rule, and how frenzy can take over. It was a great lesson!'

'Hmmf, our English lessons are *never* that interesting or fun.' Julie thought for a moment in an effort to catch him out. 'Did you do any Shakespeare?'

'Yep, *Romeo and Juliet*. And no, we didn't recreate the balcony scene in class!' laughed Ged. 'Like I said, the year of the Williams. Sounds like your posh school did the same English Literature syllabus as our lowly comprehensive...' He pushed her gently, teasing.

Realising that her cheeks were glowing peachy-pink for having prejudged and misjudged him as an "estate thicko", Julie began wiping her hands in the grass to remove the sticky ice-cream residue, thus creating a time diversion in which she could steer the conversation back in her favour.

'Anyway, getting back to your earlier question, I'm going to Tech to train how to be a hairdresser. Both me and Helena. Then we can take over my Aunty Betty's salon once she retires – she's got arthritis in her fingers, you see. Aunty Betty only has a son, and he's not interested in becoming a hairdresser. He's training to be an accountant. That's why I have the Saturday job there, learning the business ropes,' she explained, her tone sounding slightly more superior than she'd meant it to.

'Hang on a minute – your mam owns the greengrocer's, and your aunty owns the hairdresser's? Any other relatives to add to the Bryant business dynasty?' asked Ged incredulously.

'They're not Bryants. They're from Mum's side, the Halliwell side. And, yes, my Uncle Jack owns the acres up the back lanes there.' She indicated with her thumb in the general direction of the fields. 'That's where Mum gets a lot of her stock from.'

'Wow,' said Ged, wide-eyed at Julie's family-business connections.

'Wait, there's more,' laughed Julie. She paused momentarily to flick her hair sensuously over her shoulders, not realising that her actions were causing Ged to have a physical reaction in his underpants. 'That's just on my mother's side.' She continued the breakdown of her business-family tree. 'Dad's brother Eric owns the electrical shop in the town centre, and their sister, my Aunty Babs, owns "Sparkles", the jewellers.'

'Christ, you're like the Castle Ridge Mafia. Let me guess, your dad is *the* Frank Bryant, from Bryant & Harding, Solicitors?' asked Ged, as he readjusted his position so that his tee shirt covered the slight bulge in his jeans.

Julie felt the colour rising once again in her cheeks, as she nodded her affirmation.

'Why do you say *the* like that?' she asked, exaggerating *the*.

'Let's just say he's well known round our way – saved quite a few of the crims and cons on our estate from doing time. Is there 'owt that your lot don't own?'

'Nein. Ve are planning ze mass takeover, ja...' joked Julie, in a mock-German accent. 'What about your family?' she enquired, genuinely curious to know more.

Ged pondered a moment, choosing his words carefully. 'Well, one's father is an underground technical engineer working for a national conglomerate, while one's mother and older sister specialise in fancy underwear. And I have younger twin sisters who are currently in primary education,' he clarified, in his best pseudo-posh voice.

'Oh. But I thought …' began Julie, puzzled.

Ged's face broke into a wide grin. 'Me dad works down't pit, and me mam and our Bren work at the local knicker-factory making undies for Marks and Sparks. And I'll be expected to join the family business – on father's side, of course.'

The air hung silent for a moment while Julie digested Ged's teasing.

'Ouch…what was that for!' he squeaked, the recipient of a lover's punch-tickle.

'For being sooo bloody funny, Ged Steele.'

And that's why I'm falling in love with you.

CHAPTER 6

Coffee, Cake and Dog Hairs

Christ, it looks like a bloody church jumble sale – Julie considered the pile of clothes strewn all over her bedspread, trying to decide what to wear for her first meeting with Ged's parents. Having read between the lines from the insights of family life chez-Ged, she deduced that a simple outfit of jeans and a skinny-rib sweater were probably the most appropriate.

Ged met her off the 82 bus, and held her hand tightly as he accompanied her through the estate. Stepping over landmines of broken toys, broken glass and piles of dog-shit did nothing to allay Julie's nervousness, though she endeavoured to keep their banter light and cheery as they walked side by side. Loose dogs and little kids seemed to be everywhere, wandering around like nobody owned them. *So, this is where the Montagues live...*

Ever the gentleman, Ged moved the broken gate to one side and proffered an 'after-you-my-lady' gesture as he ushered her through. Cracked pebble-dashing and peeling green paint greeted her eye. *Wow, the Coal Board certainly know how to look after their workers!*

The heady aroma of cigarettes, wet dog, and sweaty shoes assailed Julie's senses as she followed Ged into the kitchen. Her gaze was drawn towards a cloud of tiny black flies showing interest in a bowl of dog food, causing Julie's stomach to do an involuntary high-jump.

Ged's mam was busy putting a pack of Mr Kipling's "French Fancies" onto a plate while the kettle bubbled away on the grimy cooker top.

'Ay-up, love, tea'll be ready in a minute. Or would you prefer coffee? So, this is the lovely Julie that I've heard so much abaht?' Beryl offered a chipped nail-polish hand towards Julie.

A flicker of mild amusement danced in Julie's dark eyes as she shook his mam's hand – she felt sure Beryl was about to curtsey. 'Pleased to meet you, Mrs Steele.'

'Oh, call me Beryl – no need to stand on ceremony wi'me, love,' she rasped in a gravelly cigarette-voice.

'Pleased to meet you, er, Beryl,' Julie repeated, uncomfortably. It seemed a bit too soon to be so informal. *She'll probably be expecting me to call her "mam" and go to bingo with her next.* 'Coffee please, no sugar, just milk, thanks,' confirmed Julie.

Ged led her through to the living room.

'C'mon, Gyp, get off the sofa, we've got company.' He gently lifted the family's elderly Jack Russell, Gypsy, into his arms and carried her through to her cardboard box in the kitchen. 'She's on her last legs. She knows she shouldn't be up on't sofa, but we're a bit soft on the old girl. She's nearly thirteen,' he explained.

Julie smiled her acknowledgment towards Ged's soft spot for the family pet. She recalled her own short-lived experience of having a pet – a goldfish which her dad had won at the fairground. It only lived for three weeks. But in all fairness, she was only seven years old, and had no clue how to care for anything.

After quickly scanning the living room to assess Ged's homelife, Julie calculated that cleaning didn't appear to be high on his "mam's" list of priorities. *And why does he keep calling her "mam" instead of "mum"? It's so irritating!* She moved a pile of old newspapers to one side so that she could sit down on the sofa, only to reveal a grease stain, a patch of ground-in cigarette ash and a generous coating of dog hairs. Julie fleetingly wondered if Ged would notice if she were to put one of the newspapers back to sit on, rather than sitting on the sofa itself. And if he did, would he consider it impolite? She looked for an alternative, noting that the armchair looked even worse. Presumably Ged's dad resided there. She gave a cock-eyed smile to Ged as she slipped a newspaper back, only to realise that she was about to sit on some 'Page-3 Stunna' who was pouting her lips and thrusting her fake boobs.

Beryl came in balancing the plate of "French Fancies" and some mugs of coffee on a used-to-be-white-with-roses plastic tea tray.

'I didn't put any sugar in y'coffee, love.' She nodded towards the mug, as she placed it next to the overflowing ashtray on the coffee table in front of Julie. Julie's gaze was drawn to a crack on the side of the mug. On closer inspection, she realised it was a black dog hair...*Lord get me out of here,* she thought to herself, while smiling a polite *thanks* to Beryl.

Despite outward appearances, Julie found Beryl to be quite motherly once they got chatting. Beryl certainly liked the idea that Julie was going to train to be a hairdresser – such a useful profession. And it was wonderful that Julie was one day hoping to own her own salon – a subtle hint for a free cut and colour, if ever Julie heard one.

Julie heard the flush of a toilet upstairs, accompanied by a hacking phlegm-laden cough. She realised that it must be Ged's dad when she heard the clomping of boots coming down the uncarpeted stairway. George Steele, better known as Jud, welcomed Julie with an outstretched hand, the other firmly clasping a copy of *The Sun* (also open at the Page 3, she noticed). In the split-second of time it took to stand up and take Jud's proffered right hand, Julie realised that she hadn't heard the running of sink-water upstairs after the flush. Rank armpit odour and cigarette-breath almost stopped her from inhaling as she opened her mouth to speak.

'Pleased to meet you, Mr Steele,' she lied, followed by a surreptitious wipe of her hand down her jeans.

★

As she lay on her bed pondering her visit to Ged's, Julie wondered how people could live like that despite there being at least three wages coming in. She found it strange that the pub, bookies, bingo and cigarettes were prioritised ahead of wash-powder, shampoo, deodorant and furniture polish. Yet they appeared happy, despite all the shit. They laughed, they chatted, they all sat together at meal times (albeit on the sofa in front of the telly), but they had a strange kind of family *togetherness*. A world away from her own clinical upbringing where everything had to be just-so. Where everything was done for the opinion, nay *approval*, of others. Her world was stifling – *clean,* but stifling, nonetheless. And though she knew that she'd never be one of *them*, per se, she couldn't help but feel a pang of *something* – jealousy? No, that was too strong a word. Envy? Perhaps. But she nevertheless felt a pang of...*something*.

Her thoughts wandered over to Ged. There was something about him, something about his persona – a rough diamond waiting to be polished.

He wasn't exactly one of *them*, yet he wasn't exactly one of *hers* either.

A compromising blend of the two.

Montagues and Capulets...

CHAPTER 7

Salmon Mousse & Sherry Trifle

'**S**o when do we get to meet your young man? You've been hiding him away for weeks,' Jean commented as she and Julie did the washing-up together. She passed a glass to Julie, expectant.

'How do you know?' Julie asked. She felt colour rising in her cheeks.

'Oh, I have my ways – there's not much that gets past me, especially with all the shop chit-chat,' said Jean light-heartedly. 'Your dad mentioned it, of course. And a number of friends saw you walking around the Summer Fayre with a young man a few weeks ago. Quite a handsome catch, they tell me – despite his long hair. But then I suppose long hair is all the rage with young men these days.'

Julie couldn't help but raise a wry smile at her mother's comments, particularly over long hair. 'Gosh, you can be so straight sometimes, Mum,' she laughed.

'How about inviting him over for Sunday tea? I could make a salmon mousse with new potatoes and salad. And perhaps sherry trifle for dessert. Does he eat those kinds of things, do you know?' Jean enjoyed entertaining, and never missed an opportunity to impress.

'Erm, I think the closest that he's come to salmon is out of a tin at Christmas. And trifle is usually that packet Bird's Trifle stuff. I don't think his mum has either the wherewithal nor inclination to make things from scratch,' Julie explained, thinking back to the first time that she visited Ged's house. 'She doesn't have a cleaner to help her like you do, and I think she's too busy with work and the family to find time to do a lot of cooking,' she continued, suddenly feeling the need to defend Ged's "mam" and his family's lifestyle. Julie took another glass from her mother, blowing away the soap bubbles before drying it.

'Oh…' Jean's mouth formed a perfect O when she replied. She was visibly crestfallen by this revelation.

'But then again, Mum, he's always open to trying new things. Don't change your favourite menu because of that. And don't judge a book by its cover – he's not a total slob, despite his long hair,' laughed Julie, nudging her mum playfully. It was not often they engaged in such togetherness, and each relished the moment.

'Sunday tea it is then. I'm looking forward to it, Julie,' she said, as she dried her hands on her apron. 'I'll leave you to extend the invitation to your nameless young man…' Jean let this comment hang in the air.

Julie looked at her mother and blushed again. 'His name's Ged. Short for Gerald.'

'Well, you can tell *Gerald*,' Jean emphasised *Gerald*, 'that I look forward to meeting him on Sunday.'

Julie seized the opportunity to tease her mother over her preferred use of his full name. 'And does *Gerald* need to dress formally?' she asked.

Her mother screwed up her face and narrowed her eyes, realising the joke was on her. 'Of course not, dear. That's only for a formal evening dinner. Just tell him to brush his hair and wear clean jeans…' Curiosity was starting to gnaw at Jean. 'And what does your young man – Gerald – do?'

'He's going to start an electrician's apprenticeship soon, once college starts,' Julie explained.

'Oh, how nice. That's a wonderful career. Much better than working in the colliery. Which electrical firm is he going to be attached to?'

Julie couldn't help but smile as she replied, 'The National Coal Board…'

Jean looked puzzled. 'Oh. I didn't realise that they needed electricians in the coal mines...'

'Mum, this is 1979, not 1879! They use heavy machinery and lighting down the pit these days, not pick-axes, pit-ponies and candles. Yes, they need electricians. And yes, they serve a proper apprenticeship.' Julie shook her head, unable to stop herself from laughing. Her mother similarly saw the funny side, and joined in her daughter's merriment. Encouraged by their moment of mother-daughter togetherness, Jean couldn't resist trying to learn more about Ged's family, only to find herself squirming uncomfortably when she discovered the likelihood that her matching Marks and Spencer's undergarments had most likely been sewn by his mother's hand.

*

The 16:10 bus pulled up at the bus stop not far from Julie's house, allowing Ged to alight. His smile broadened when he saw Julie waiting to meet him – it helped allay some of his nervousness. Meeting parents was new territory to Ged, as was coming into Shirecliffe.

'Wow, you look smart,' said Julie, as she brushed his lips with a shy kiss. Ged had gone all out to impress, wearing a new white cheesecloth collarless shirt, black waistcoat, jeans without holes, and had even given his trainers a wipe over. They began strolling slowly towards Julie's house. Ged whistled as he took in the size of some of the houses in the village.

'Aye, I thought I'd better have a bath and dress up a bit if I were coming into Poshcliffe,' he teased.

'Poshcliffe? Is that they call us in Grim Ridge?' she counter-teased.

'Touché,' he laughed. 'Hey, do you like my smell? It's *Denim*. Our Bren gave me one of those gift set things for my 16th birthday this year. Said I was "man-enough" to wear it now that I'm shaving.'

Julie sniffed. The fragrance really did suit him – it was earthy, sexy. 'Do you know who you remind me of, wearing that shirt and waistcoat? Francis Rossi from Status Quo. You could pass for his younger brother!'

'I suppose I should take that as a compliment...'

Julie noticed that Ged was carrying something in a little paper bag, 'What'cha got there?' she asked, curiosity getting the better of her.

'Chocolates. Milk Tray,' he answered.

'Oh, that's really sweet of you...thanks,' she replied, cuddling up to his arm.

Ged looked at her, his dark eyes twinkling with amusement. 'They're for yer mam, not you.'

'Oh...Well, that's still really sweet of you. She'll like that. Anyway, here we are, chez moi...' Julie nervously led Ged by the hand up the short tree-lined driveway to the front door, white gravel crunching beneath their feet. The house was a rather grand old detached, mostly red-brick, with white stucco on the walls and cottage-style windows with bull's-eye glass. Red brick chimney stacks rose from each gable end, majestically crowned with tall pots. Golden and glorious honeysuckle grew on a trellis frame around the arched front door, its sweet aroma just starting to add fragrance to the evening air. The small front lawn was neatly mowed, and bordered with tall hollyhocks, cornflower and other cottage style flowers. Ged took note of the brand new white Range Rover parked on the driveway, alongside a little white Escort van with *The Fruit Basket* emblazoned on the side panels – he assumed they belonged to her parents.

'I bet you don't rent this from the Coal Board,' he laughed, slightly overwhelmed by the neat, well-kept surroundings of the property.

'Mum enjoys her garden, she's rather proud of it.' Julie could feel a growing sense of pride for where she lived. She found it hard to imagine what it must be like for Ged, living on the broken and uncared for estate day-in, day-out. 'Come on in. You'll have to take your shoes off, though.

31

Hope you haven't got holes in your socks or stinky feet,' she joked. 'We're here...' she shouted, as she led Ged through to the kitchen.

Her mum was busy chopping salad. She dried her hands, and came to introduce herself to Ged.

'Welcome, my dear. Nice to finally meet you, Gerald. I'm Julie's mother.' Her handshake was firm, yet soft and warm. She smiled warmly at Ged, and he relaxed slightly.

'Pleased to meet you, Mrs Bryant. And, erm, you can call me Ged. Me mam only uses Gerald when she's mad wi'me...' He really hoped she wouldn't keep calling him Gerald... He heard the rustle of a newspaper being closed and put down, then strident footsteps behind him.

'Ah, so this is our Julie's young man. Pleased to meet you, Gerald.' Julie's dad extended a hand out to Ged. He looked clean shaven, professional, even though he was in his Sunday casuals of beige slacks, and cream and beige checked shirt.

'He prefers Ged, not Gerald,' corrected Julie's mother. Ged smiled to himself – he'd already won over Julie's mum, and he hadn't even given her the chocolates yet...

'Why don't you show Gerald, er, sorry, Ged around the house, Julie? And you can make a pot of coffee, Frank,' instructed Jean, 'then I'll come and join you all in the sun lounge, when I've finished preparing the salad and put the potatoes on.'

After showing Ged around the house, Julie led him through to the sun lounge. They could hear hushed, whispered voices in the kitchen, assuming Ged was quietly being discussed and scrutinised.

'Tea is almost ready, let's just have a quick coffee while we wait for the new potatoes,' Jean announced, as she joined them. Frank appeared behind her, carrying a tray with cafetière and cups.

Conversation was light and friendly as they got to know their daughter's boyfriend. Both Julie and Ged started to relax and feel comfortable in the presence of her parents.

Jean looked at her watch, then to Julie and Ged. 'You two go through to the dining room, and Frank and I will bring the food to the table.'

Ged looked at Julie, puzzled. 'I thought you said that you had a maid who cooked, and then rang a gong when it was time to eat. "Dinner is served, M'Lady" and all that,' he hissed in a low voice, as they made their way to the dining room.

'Did I say that? Really?' Julie couldn't help but giggle – she didn't realise that Ged had taken her seriously. 'Sorry, no, we don't have a maid...or a gong...'

Realising that it had gone dark outside, Ged checked his watch – the digital green glow showed 21:45. The last bus through the village was due in fifteen minutes. Ged nodded his head to Julie, and stood up with the intention to leave. Julie rose with him.

'Well, time flies, and all that. I'd better be heading off – I don't want to miss the last bus. But thank you, it was nice meeting you both. And thanks for the lovely meal, Mrs Bryant. That was a wicked sherry trifle!' Ged could still feel the effects of the sherry running through his veins – he felt warm and sleepy.

Frank stood up to accompany his daughter and her boyfriend to the door. 'Would you like me to run you home, Gerald? Erm, sorry, Ged. It's no trouble.'

Ged had an unexpected panic attack – as much as he would love to have a ride in the Range Rover, this meant that Julie's dad would see where he lived. He suddenly felt very servile and humble. Their lifestyles were worlds apart.

'Nah, really, Mr Bryant. The bus'll be here in a minute. I'll be home in a jiffy. But thanks anyway.'

Jean began collecting up the coffee cups and putting them onto a tray. 'Well, I do hope that we'll see you again, Ged. And thank you for the chocolates. That was very thoughtful of you.' She tapped the half pound box of Milk Tray.

Ged smiled shyly. Mrs Bryant seemed quite taken with him.

Julie's parents moved to the front window, curious to watch Julie and Ged walk off the property. Jean peered from behind the net curtain.

'Seems like a nice young man. Thoughtful of him to bring me some chocolates, even if they are Milk Tray.' She laughed gently. 'I guess he doesn't know that I prefer Thornton's Continentals.'

'Yes, I got the same feeling. Very nice. And I certainly didn't recognise his face...'

'Frank!' Jean exclaimed.

'Just saying...' Frank held his hands up in defence, before pouring a glass of brandy for himself.

'Well, I just hope that our Julie doesn't take advantage of his generosity, like she does yours...' Jean moved away from the window, and smirked at her husband.

'Jean!'

'Just saying...' she retorted, as she headed into the kitchen with the tray of dirty coffee cups.

Ged waved goodbye to Julie as he made his way along the aisle of the bus to the row of back seats. Good, they were empty – he could lift his legs and lay out over the length of them. He took out his cigarettes and lit one, watching the stream of smoke rise into the air as he exhaled. The yellow glow of the street lights lit up the village as the bus made its way along the narrow main road. He noticed that all the little grass verges were neatly cut. Many had tubs or planters overflowing with colourful summer blooms just on the edge of finishing for the season. Some of the larger houses were protected by tall, neatly clipped hedges; others had little white fences, or open borders stuffed full of shrubs and flowers. The bus made its journey from the village, down the winding, aptly named Cornfield Lane, bounded on both sides by ripe cornfields. They looked like large black blankets in the darkness. He could see the street lights of Castle Ridge coming into view. The bus stopped a few times in the town centre and by the Market Square to let people on and off, before heading down Colliery Hill into the bowels of the Estate. Ged stubbed out his cigarette and rang the bell for the bus to stop.

Home Sweet fuckin' Home...

CHAPTER 8

Them and Us

G ed could see every light blazing in their house as he walked up the street. *Christ, it looks like bloody Blackpool Illuminations. No wonder they're always moaning about the size of the lecky bill...* He moved the rickety gate to one side, choosing to go in through the front door.

'Is that you, love?' It sounded like his mam's voice was coming from the direction of the kitchen.

'Aye, it's me.' He kicked off his trainers in the hallway and went through to the kitchen. Beryl was just putting a fresh pot of tea on the table, while his dad opened a packet of Rich Tea biscuits. Jud took a handful for himself before putting the packet in the middle of the table next to the milk bottle.

'Cuppa?'

Ged grabbed a mug from out of the cupboard and put it on the table with the other two mugs. 'Ta, that'd be great.' He sat down with them. 'Where is everyone?'

'Brenda's in the bath and the twins are asleep in bed. So, how did everything go at Julie's house? Is it posh, like?' Beryl asked, burning with curiosity.

Ged described his guided tour of the large house, the friendliness of her parents, and what they'd eaten for tea. 'And do you know, I swear her mam must've put half a bottle of sherry in the trifle. Bloody 'ell, I felt piss-drunk after I'd eaten it. It was right tasty though,' he laughed.

Beryl raised her eyebrows. 'Booze in food? Tch – it isn't even Christmas! How the other 'alf live, eh.'

'And that's not all,' Ged continued, 'her mam's got one of those fancy microwave oven things. She says that it cooks food in a jiffy.'

Beryl looked at him wide eyed then gathered her cardigan around her, as if in defence. 'Uff, gimme gas any day. Don't trust all that nuclear food that goes "ping" when it's done,' she said, exaggerating the "ping".

Ged dunked a Rich Tea biscuit into his mug of tea and left it in just a fraction too long. A chunk broke off and sank. Ugh, he hated the biscuit sludge in the bottom. He pushed his mug to one side. 'Her dad offered to drive me home in his car. He's got one of them big, fancy Range Rovers. Looks brand new.' He raised his eyebrows. 'And her mam's got a car – well, a van. You know, for her business. She's got the fruit shop up near the Market Square, "The Fruit Basket".'

Beryl picked up her mug of tea, her brow furrowed in thought. 'Oh, is *that* who her mam is? I don't go in there very often, but she's always been quite friendly. Spuds are cheaper in the Co-op, though. And what about her dad – didn't you say that he's a solicitor?'

'Aye. Frank Bryant, from Bryant & Harding. I think her dad normally does the court cases, and the other guy, Harding, deals with all the property sales, and stuff,' Ged explained. 'And then Julie's going to Tech to train as a hairdresser so that she can take over her auntie's salon once she's qualified. You know, Silver Scissors?'

'I remember her saying, when she came here for tea. Right old business-family, aren't they? But then again, just 'cos you've got a house full of fancy stuff don't mean to say you own it. For all we know, it could all be on the never-never,' Beryl commented. 'We might not be posh, but it's all bought and paid for wi' honest money.'

'True,' replied Ged. Although from what he'd seen and heard today, he deduced that Julie's family were rolling in money. He chose to change the subject. 'I'll probably see Julie at College when I start on day release for the electrician's apprenticeship.' Ged fidgeted with his mug of tea even though he had no intention of drinking it. He took a deep breath before going on, as he knew that he was about to enter sensitive territory. 'Dad...I, er...I was wondering if I, er...'

Jud looked at his son. 'Spit it out, lad...'

'I've been thinking, I still want to be an electrician, but perhaps going down the pit's not for me. Would it bother you if I didn't?' There. He'd said it.

Jud looked crestfallen. 'Is this about the pit not being *posh* enough now you've got this fancy-pants new girlfriend?'

'No! No...it's not that at all. I keep thinking about the Markham pit disaster. You lost Uncle Brian, your brother...It bothers me,' admitted Ged.

Jud topped up his mug of tea and lit a cigarette. 'All the new lads think that, Ged. It's only natural. It's a bloody big, dark hole in the ground. But Markham was six years ago, m'lad. Things have improved – safety, and all that.' He could see that Ged didn't look convinced. 'Let me tell you this,' he continued, 'you've more chance o' getting hit wi'a van than for lightning to strike twice. Where else will you get a coal allowance, a pension, good training and good money? It's as safe as any other job. Not the cleanest, I admit. But as careers go, it ain't too bad...' Jud put a rough but reassuring hand over his son's hand. Ged noticed that even though he was now sixteen and a young man, his hand was still dwarfed by the size of his dad's.

Ged sighed. 'Okay, I'll give it a try...'

'That's my boy...' Jud changed tactics and tried to lighten Ged's fears with a touch of humour. 'Mind you, I still remember the first time I went down in the cage. Nearly shit me pants...' and he bellowed with laughter.

CHAPTER 9

Proposal

1980

The evening sun was just beginning to set over the fields, creating a marmalade-orange glow over the piles of golden hay-bales. The surrounding landscape was framed by the dark and dappled silhouettes of trees and hedgerows, broken only by the lights of the nearby cottages. Ever the watchful sentinel, the geometric shape of the castle was backlit on the distant horizon, the spire of the parish church just visible, standing guard by its side. Ged and Julie walked into the field holding hands, the stubble of the freshly-cut corn spiking at their feet and ankles. They searched the field and found a suitable looking pile of hay-bales by which they could sit and lean against, and watch the sun go down on the day. It was their special, uninterrupted time together, their "putting the world to rights" time, as they called it. They'd discovered this place last summer, when they first started courting. It had offered them a place of privacy and solitude in which they could get to know each other better, away from the teasing of mates, or the prying eyes of nosy gossips.

The muted distant clanging of the church bells carried their melodic tones over the air towards them, the Campanology Club obviously having their Thursday evening practice. Ged nodded in the direction of the church.

'Do you believe in God?' he asked.

'Do I? No, not especially,' she replied. 'Do you believe in God?' She returned the question.

'Nope.' His answer was straight, direct.

'Why not?' she asked, slightly taken aback by his abruptness.

"Cause of all the wars and stuff. All the starving kids in Africa. All the bad things that happen – murders and rapes, and such like. I can't believe that any God would allow that. Seems bizarre to allow that to happen when we're all supposed to love each other in the name of "God",' he replied philosophically.

'Same here. Totally agree. And wasps – why did He make wasps?' she replied, waving her hand around to defend herself against a wasp that was showing an interest in her Lilt. 'Anyway, why do you ask? I never expected to hear you discussing the pragmatics of religion.'

'Prag-what?' He looked puzzled.

'Pragmatics – a discussion about the ins-and-outs of something,' she clarified.

'Like the pragmatics of sex – that's all ins-and-outs...' He laughed, wiggling his eyebrows. 'You and your big words. Anyway, the reason I wanted to know whether you believed in God or not was for when I ask you to marry me. Just wondered if it would have to be a church wedding...' His words hung in the air. Julie slowly swivelled her head in his direction.

'Say that again...' she whispered. She looked at him full on.

'I said that I wanted to know, because...'

Julie cut him off mid-sentence, and pulled him towards her, blocking his words with a deep kiss. She faced him, nose to nose,

'So, you're going to ask me to marry you one day?'

'Yes.'

'Why not now? Why not right now?' she murmured, her voice husky.

'I don't have a ring or anything...'

'That doesn't matter. Try it.' Her heart was thumping in her chest.

'Wait a mo', I've got an idea,' said Ged, as he ripped the metal ring-pull from the Lilt can. He then lifted her up and sat her on a hay-bale before going down on bended knee and gently taking her left hand in his, his right gripping the now-precious ring-pull.

'Julie Elizabeth Bryant...'

'Yes!'

'I haven't asked you yet...'

'Julie Elizabeth Bryant, would you do me the honours of becoming my wife one day?' He looked up at her, expectant. 'And now you're supposed to give me a reply...'

She looked at him, but the word stuck in her throat. She could hardly believe that this was really happening to her. It couldn't have been more perfect.

'Yes! Yes! Yes, Gerald Alan Steele. Yes, I'll marry you!' she confirmed breathlessly, as she launched herself off the hay-bale onto Ged, laughing and covering him in kisses.

'I'll take that as a "yes" then...'

They held hands as Ged walked Julie home from the fields to the village, relishing the security of each other's touch. Something felt different. They now had a secret.

'So, you promise you won't tell anyone – not even Helena?' Ged said in a low voice.

'And don't you say anything to Col,' Julie added.

'Nope, promise.' He kissed her left hand, narrowly missing his lips on the sharp metal of the ring-pull. 'Scout's Honour.'

'You're not a Scout. Anyway, when's our big day going to be?' she asked.

'Big? I didn't think you wanted the church and all the big white dress and stuff?' He looked at her, surprise written all over his face.

'I was speaking metaphorically ...'

'Meta-what?'

'Oh, don't start that again...' She laughed, and elbowed him playfully.

'Won't your mum and dad be disappointed if you don't have a church wedding? I mean, don't they do stuff for the church – with the WI and Rotary?' Ged asked.

'They do, but...sometimes I think they're just being hypocrites. Trying to look good in the community, and all that shit. I think they just believe in God when it suits them.' She rolled her eyes disapprovingly. 'What about your parents?'

'Nah. They gave up with all that religion stuff after me Uncle Brian got killed in the pit disaster. He was dad's twin brother.' Ged went quiet. 'It hit him hard...'

'Sorry to hear that. I didn't realise your dad was a twin. More twins in the family line, eh.' Julie tried to jolly him up. 'Anyway, there's no rush. We're both still only training – be another couple of years before we qualify.' She hugged him encouragingly. 'We'll know when the time feels right. Besides, we'll also need to find a house...'

Ged laughed, seizing the opportunity to tease. 'What? You mean you don't want to live with either of our parents? There's plenty of room at your place.'

Julie shot him a sharp glance. Ged grinned and held up his hands in mock defeat.

'Hey, just kidding. Of course we'll need our own place.' A rush of nervous adrenaline coursed through him, causing a wobble to appear in his voice. 'Wow, getting quite grown up all of a sudden, aren't we?'

Sensing his sudden apprehension, Julie took his hands and pulled him towards her.

'Like I said, no rush. But in the meantime, let's just try and save a shit-load of money, eh.'

Ged looked deeply into her dark-chocolate brown eyes. 'Sounds like a plan. Our secret?'

'Our secret.'

Mrs Julie Elizabeth Steele. Yes, she quite liked the sound of that...

CHAPTER 10

The Great Divide

1981

Icy cold globs of February sleet beat a perpetual rhythm on the kitchen window, sticking to the grime before sliding down under its own weight. Ged shuddered, grateful to be in the cosy warmth, as he wriggled his toes against the heat from the open fire. His mam was deep in concentration, reading glasses perched on the end of her nose, as she looked over the "Itinerary" for Ged and Julie's upcoming engagement next weekend. Years of threading needles and close work over the sewing machines had finally taken its toll on Beryl's eyesight, having now succumbed to the need for reading glasses. The party was to coincide with Julie's 18th birthday, as a joint celebration. Julie's mother, in her capacity as "hostess with the mostest", had taken it upon herself to organise the party. Not that Beryl minded – she guessed that Jean was better placed than she was to organise such a fancy party. Jean had already booked the local Assembly Rooms in Castle Ridge – perfect because it had a large hall with a stage and a bar area. She had organised someone from The Cricketers to come and do the bar, and the ladies from her local WI group had put together a suggested list of food for the buffet table. Jean had sent a neatly typed carbon-copy of the "Itinerary" to Beryl to see if she wanted to add any suggestions.

Beryl looked up from the sheet. 'There's a lot of foreign stuff on here,' she rasped. 'What's vol-au-vents aux champignons?' she asked, pronouncing all the consonants.

Ged looked puzzled by his mam's pronunciation. She tried again. Slowly.

'Oh, you mean vol-au-vents aux champignons,' he said, with a sense of a French accent. Beryl looked at him with hard eyes.

'They're little rounds of puff pastry filled with creamed mushrooms,' he explained with confidence, as though he'd eaten them all his life.

'Well, why the bloody 'ell can't she put that? And what's this – prof, profit-er-oles?' She endeavoured her best to say the foreign word.

'Profiteroles, Mam. They're posh little sweet pastry puffs, filled with cream and topped with chocolate.' He didn't bother trying to explain what choux-pastry was.

Her eyes narrowed as she looked at Ged. He'd changed sides. He'd learned to speak French since going out with Miss Fancy Pants. 'So, where's the sausage rolls? Where's the cheese and pineapple on sticks? And the potted meat sarnies?' Beryl looked exasperated as she waved the sheet of paper under Ged's nose. There was too much on the menu that she didn't understand.

'There's all kinds of open sandwiches, Mam – egg and cress, salmon and cucumber, and liver-paté with tarragon, and I'm pretty sure that Jean's organising "pigs in blankets". Plus platters of sliced fruits with selected cheeses.'

'Pigs in what?'

'Blankets, Mam. Blankets. They're sausage rolls...' Frustrated by his mam's culinary naïveté, Ged began grinding his teeth together. A year and a half of being exposed to Julie's mother's cuisine had extended his food knowledge way beyond the realms of cuisine a-la-Beryl – the local chippie, packet or tin.

'What about the fruit cake? What about the Black Forest Gateau?' she asked.

'Jean's friend, Annabel something – er…Singleton – is doing the engagement-birthday cake. And I'm sure there's a BFG on the list. Here, let me see.' Ged came and stood behind his mother to look over her shoulder at the list. He'd never really taken much notice of Beryl in "close-up" – his mam had always been his mam. But today, right now, he noticed the dark roots showing through her bleached blonde hair, the nicotine stained fingers, and the cloying smell of sweat and fried food. He made a mental note to ask Julie if she would do his mother's hair for the party. Have a bit of "girl-time" together. His mam would enjoy feeling pampered, and he was sure that Julie would appreciate helping her future mother-in-law to look half-way decent. 'Here, look. Here's the Black Forest Gateau.' He pointed to an item on the list. 'Gateau aux cerises noires.'

'Oh, for fu…' It was too much for Beryl.

'Mam!'

Beryl could feel her nerves beginning to get the better of her, the thought of hob-nobbing with what she called "the money brigade".

'I'm sorry, love, but French this, and French that. I don't think many folk from Castle Ridge did French at school. Tell Jean the menu's fine – just to put it in English.' Careful not to offend Ged, she carefully folded the "Itinerary" and placed it on the table before standing up to make a pot of tea. 'What about the entertainment?' she asked, reaching into the cupboard for the box of Tetley's.

'Some of the lads at work play in a club-band. I think you might know them – Eddie, Mick, Neil and Baz, from Shady Deal. I'm sure they've played at the Miners' Welfare before. Anyway, I've arranged for them to play a warm-up set for forty-five minutes. Then there's the buffet and a disco for a couple of hours – we've booked The Music Machine to do the disco.

The band'll come back on stage around quarter past ten until eleven-ish. We've hired the hall until midnight, so that'll give us enough time to get everybody out and get cleaned up afterwards.' He went to the fridge to get a bottle of milk.

'Well, that's good to hear. At least it's not going to be some bloody fancy-pants string quartet, or whatever it's called. At least we'll be able to have a dance.' The relief was clear in her voice.

'Aye, Mam, you'll still be able to strut your stuff on the dance floor. There is one thing though, Mam...' He looked at her, merriment dancing in his eyes.

'What now?'

'There won't be any bingo...'

'Argh! Away with you, yer cheeky bugger.' She laughed. 'Now you're just takin' the piss!'

*

The bus pulled up at the stop near Julie's house in order to let Ged off. He fingered the little faux-velvet box in his pocket and felt a rush of warmth run through him despite the grey February drizzle. Today was the day – Julie's 18th birthday – the day that they would be officially engaged. Today was the day that they could step out from the shadow of their long-secret betrothal. The day that Julie could trade in the Lilt-can ring-pull for a real diamond engagement ring. It was only a simple solitaire – all that Ged could really afford on his apprentice wages. Plus, they were still secretly saving for the deposit on their first house.

Julie's family had invited him over for a small family gathering at their house, just the four of them. He'd already asked Julie's dad for "permission" to marry his daughter – unbeknown to Frank and Jean that their daughter and her boyfriend had long since hatched this plot for their engagement. Everyone was in the kitchen when he arrived – he felt comfortable enough to be able to knock and walk in, usually accompanied with a shout of "only me". A line of beautifully wrapped gifts sat on the breakfast counter-top, the overhead fluorescent lighting catching the silver bows and glossy paper, causing them to sparkle. Motown music played lightly in the background, filtering through from the music centre in the dining room. The atmosphere felt happy, expectant.

Frank carried in an ice-bucket containing a chilled bottle of Moet & Chandon champagne, before lightly tapping a spoon on a champagne flute to call the birthday celebration to order.

Ged had to concede that his fiancée looked beautiful. Helena had done Julie's hair for the occasion, creating a swirl of loose, dark curls to frame her face, and her make-up and nails had been professionally done at a local salon. She positively glowed. He felt a lump of pride rise in his throat, and an even bigger lump starting to rise in his jeans.

Christ, I'm a lucky git...

After toasting Julie's good health and her birthday, Ged went down on bended knee to officially propose to Julie, his Lady Juliet. His hands still shook with nervous apprehension just in case she said "no" when it came to the real-deal. His heart resumed beating with her acceptance, and his hands stopped shaking long enough to slip the diamond ring onto her finger. He traded Julie's delicate hands for a hearty handshake of congratulations from Frank and a tearful but very fragrant hug from Jean.

After another refill of the champagne glasses, it was time to open the gifts on the counter. The first was a long, slim package from Julie's Aunty Babs. Julie carefully opened the elegantly wrapped gift to reveal a diamanté "J" shaped key-ring that sparkled and twinkled in the light. Julie was mesmerised by its delicate prettiness. Next, Julie took up a flat, square envelope. Her face crumpled in puzzlement. It was from Uncle Jack at the farm. He was renowned for giving strange gifts. She opened the package to reveal two white pieces of plastic, each emblazoned with a large red "L" – learner-driver plates.

'Well, maybe I'll need them one day!' She laughed. Her parents exchanged a knowing glance.

Jean pushed another envelope towards Julie. 'Here, my darling, this goes with it.' The gift tag said "From the family", which indicated that they'd pooled together for something quite sizeable. Julie opened it, finding a gift voucher for a local driving instructor.

While Julie was busy opening her gifts, her father snuck outside to the garage. He came back a moment later, hiding a small box behind his back. He coughed lightly to get her attention – she was clearly so excited with the "L" plates and the prospect of driving lessons that she hadn't noticed him missing. He brought out the little box from behind his back.

'This is from your mother and me. You might find it useful once you've passed your driving test. Happy 18th birthday, darling.' He handed the beautifully wrapped gift-box to Julie.

Her eyes were wide with surprise and anticipation as she took the little box. She shook it and looked at Ged, as if for some kind of explanation. He shrugged his shoulders in denial of any knowledge. The box rattled. With shaking hands, Julie tore off the ribbon and paper, and opened the gift box. A set of gleaming car keys sat in the bottom. Julie's mouth fell open in genuine surprise.

'A car?' she asked. 'Are they car keys?'

'Go and look out of the window. See if you like it,' suggested Frank.

Julie ran to the sitting room window to look outside. There on the front driveway was a gleaming red Mini with a white roof, topped with a big red bow. The car even had private plates, JEB 63.

Ged suddenly felt very inadequate. How would he ever be able to compare or compete with this level of gift giving? He was marrying into a whole different world. He sincerely hoped that he and Julie would be able to find some middle ground. They'd managed okay so far. Hadn't they? His trance-like feeling of inadequacy was very quickly swept away by Julie's shriek of shock and excitement. And much to his relief and delight, it was his hand that she grabbed first to run outside and take a look at her new car.

Yes, life was certainly going to be different as a member of this family.

*

The taxi containing Ged and his family pulled up outside the Assembly Rooms. Normally, Beryl would travel by the number 82 bus, but tonight – the night of her only son's engagement party – she travelled in style by taxi. Ged insisted. Beryl, by her own admission, felt like the "Queen of Sheeba" as she stepped out of the car. Julie and Helena had given Beryl some girl-time earlier in the day, having touched up her roots, then set and blow-dried her hair. They even did her nails and some simple make-up. Ged wanted her to feel special. And she did.

Ged's colliery friends were already setting up their band equipment on the stage and the disco was setting up by the side. A flurry of activity from the WI ladies, overseen, of course, by Jean, meant that the tables of food and decorations were all in their right places. The bar was set up and ready to go.

Jean looked at her diamond encrusted watch and tapped the face.

'Ten minutes, everyone. Doors open in ten minutes.' She turned around to see Ged and his family walk in, and warmly welcomed them, hugging Beryl like she was a long-lost sister. After shaking Jud's hand, she fussed over the twins and Brenda, then hugged Ged and gave him a peck on the cheek. Ged noticed that there were often two sides to Jean – one where she was as nice as pie to the "common" customers that came into her shop, and another where she was bitching about them behind closed doors. He had once overhead Jean when she was chatting with Frank in the sun lounge, unaware that Ged was in the kitchen, within earshot of their conversation. She was talking about some poor woman on his estate – a single mum with four kids, all by different fathers. Jean had taken pity on her and put

50

a few extra apples in the woman's bag for the kids. But then she turned the conversation around to complain about the woman, as she was a known benefits sponger. But in all fairness to Jean, she had organised a wonderful looking party room – shades of blue and white balloons and garlands adorned the walls, the two buffet tables were sensibly located at the far end of the room with plenty of room for people to walk around, the band and disco were ready, and there was a table near the door for engagement and birthday gifts. There were even little vases of blue and white flowers on each of the tables.

Ged looked up when he heard the door to the ladies' toilets squeak open then clatter closed. There she was. His Julie. His Lady Juliet. She looked ethereal, wearing a floaty handkerchief-style dress in shades of tie-dyed blue, and strappy denim sandals. He couldn't recall having seen her in a dress before. Her dress fluttered as she walked across the room, and she somehow managed to turn a cold, grey February evening into one that emanated the warmth of spring. They held each other tightly, drinking in the feel, smell and heartbeat of each other.

Julie took a step back and held Ged at arms' length to admire him in his suit and tie. 'Wow, you've scrubbed up nicely,' she complimented him, humour in her voice.

'You don't look too bad y'self – don't think I've ever seen you in a dress before. Nice legs...' He chuckled.

Ged nodded towards his family and led Julie towards them to say hello. 'Thanks for helping me mam to get ready. She looks lovely, don't you think?'

The band took to the stage to welcome everyone, then called Ged and Julie to the floor to congratulate them and lead off the dancing. Naturally, the first song was *Rockin' all over the World*, in honour of their first dance together at this very same venue two years earlier. Other people joined them on the dance floor, and soon the evening of music, drinking and eating got underway – an eclectic mix of them and us; of teens and middle-aged folk; of rough stones and polished diamonds.

And of one particularly memorable incident – Col's shoe flying off while dancing the can-can with a little too much enthusiasm. After arching through the air, the shoe hit Julie's mum square in the back just as she was taking a delicate forkful of *gateau aux cerises noires*, which in turn arched through the air and landed with a delicate *plop* in Beryl's *Babycham*.

CHAPTER 11

Monsters '83

'You have got to be kidding.' Ged excitedly crushed out his cigarette and threw the butt into the plant-pot at the side of the back door to their cottage. Finding his cigarette ends scattered around the garden had becomes Julie's pet hate since they'd moved into the cottage – it made the place look "tacky". An observation that he'd had to concede. And he'd also been requested to call them "cigarettes" instead of "fags". Fags sounded tacky, at least in Julie's mind. Another observation that he'd had to concede. They'd spotted the place up for sale last summer while spending one of their usual evenings in the cornfields which backed onto the row of old Derbyshire stone farm workers' cottages. They instinctively knew that it was to be theirs. Despite their outward appearance, with their ripped jeans, denim, leather, and long hair, the estate agent was pleasantly surprised by their fiscal astuteness when they secured an offer on the cottage, having already amassed quite a sizeable deposit. Number 2, Ridgeway Cottages became the new home for Mr Gerald Alan Steele and his fiancée, Miss Julie Elizabeth Bryant later that autumn. Being engaged somehow made their "living together" more socially acceptable, certainly for Julie's mother. And in the short time that they'd lived there they'd already made their mark – a cosy blend of country-cottage gingham meets hippie bamboo and joss-sticks, achieved by Julie's creative eye, Ged's new-found DIY skills, and hours scouring second-hand ads for quality bargains.

'Ju...Ju...you've got to see this...' He stuffed the *Kerrang!* magazine under his arm and bounded upstairs two at a time into the bathroom. Julie surfaced from under the frothy water to find Ged sat on the toilet lid grinning at her like a loon, while waving the magazine around.

'Look – it's the line-up for this year's Monsters of Rock festival at Donington. Meat Loaf's on!' Ged could hardly contain his excitement at the prospect of seeing his favourite band. 'And Whitesnake too. They're headlining!'

'You're kidding!' Julie became equally infected by Ged's enthusiasm, Whitesnake being her band of the moment. Water and foamy bubble bath slopped over the edge as Julie reached over to have a look at the full page advert. Her skin was rosy from the heat, and glistened with a layer of bubbles. Ged could just make out the rose-pink buds of her nipples peering tantalisingly through the sheath of foam, and had to suppress the urge to lick her body. 'Can we go?' she asked. 'Or more to the point, can we afford it?'

'Wouldn't miss it for the world, even if we have to live on beans on toast from now until August!' Ged exclaimed. 'Pity it isn't Meat Loaf headlining instead of that tosser Coverdale,' he teased.

Julie took the bait. 'Aw, come on – there's no comparison. Coverdale is tons sexier than Meat Loaf.'

'Ah, but it isn't about "sexy", it's about voice. If you want sexy, you've got this.' He laughed, flexing his arm muscles. 'Anyway, Meat Loaf is a waaayy better singer than Coverdale.'

Julie flung a handful of bubbles, which narrowly missed Ged's head before landing with a foamy splat on the tiles behind. 'Who else is on the line-up?' she asked.

Ged looked over the page. 'Er, ZZ Top, Twisted Sister, Dio and Diamond Head. And that twat Tommy Vance is doing the commentary.'

'ZZ Top!' She almost did a flip in the water. 'Amazing album, *Eliminator*. When is it, anyway?'

'Saturday 20th August. Which actually gives me an idea – do you think you could get a few days off from the salon that week?' Ged's mind began to race as he started formulating a plan.

'I don't see why not. It's the summer holidays, so likely to be quiet. I'll check with Helena. Why – what have you got in mind?' Julie was bursting with curiosity.

'To make it a road trip that memories are made of, my girl...' He began taking off his clothes, singing as he stripped. 'Now, shift over, my Lady Juliet and make some room for this sharp, undressed man to get in. Then Romeo-Gerald will tell you all about it...'

CHAPTER 12

No Fuss, No Frills

The air in the pub's hotel bedroom hung thick and heavy with the scent of patchouli oil, cheap sparkling wine and sex-pheromones, cooked together by the cloying heat of the August afternoon. Ged moved off the bed and strolled casually to the window in order to open the heavy brocade curtains and let in some fresh air and light. Disturbed by the movement of the air, dust motes danced like floating golden glitter, illuminated by the shaft of sunlight. He shielded his eyes against the sudden brightness.

'Nice view,' he commented, as he studied the quaintness of the village, with its stone and white stucco cottages, framed with the bright, fresh green of the grass and trees, and accentuated by the colourful flower beds and azure blue of the cloudless sky. Julie looked up at Ged, admiring his lean, naked body.

'I'm sure the locals must be thinking the very same thing.' She laughed.

Ged blushed modestly, suddenly aware of his naked display at the hotel window. He drew one of the curtains back across and came to investigate what Julie was writing. She was seated at a small, old-fashioned, dark wood writing table, writing postcards. He moved her hair to one side and nuzzled the back of her neck. The limp remnants of this morning's daisy-chain crown remained partially tangled in strands of her hair, evidence of their earlier passion. He slung his arms over her shoulders, caressing her naked body close to his. She could feel the warmth from his torso as he pressed against her. Ged picked up one of the postcards – this one was addressed to Helena. There were three others on the table, all identical; one was to Col and one each to their parents. The picture was of a local place called "The Smithy" and said "Greetings from Gretna Green" below the image. Julie had written the same simple message on each one – "We didn't want any fuss. Love from the new Mr & Mrs Steele." A drawing of two intertwined love-hearts with J & G adorned the bottom-left corner of each postcard.

'Hmm, I wonder what kind of reception we'll get when we come home?' Ged mused, as he passed the postcard back to Julie. She began sticking stamps on them.

'Well, it's too late for second thoughts now, *husband dearest*,' she replied, as she fingered her wedding ring. The sunlight illuminated the smoothness of the new gold, and enhanced the sparkle of her single-diamond engagement ring.

They had hit on the idea of eloping to Gretna Green when they decided to get tickets for the Donington Monsters of Rock festival. By combining the festival with a week's touring holiday, they could get married in secret and then have the rest of the holiday and festival as their honeymoon. And what better way to wrap up a honeymoon than watching Whitesnake and Meat Loaf? Marriage had always been on their agenda, but Julie was afraid that her mother would take over the arrangements, and want to make a big, frilly, fussy showcase event out of it, just so that she could show-off to her snobby friends. This was far removed from what Ged and Julie wanted, preferring the simple solitude of their own company and doing it their chosen way. Eloping seemed like the perfect solution. Julie shuddered involuntarily as she recalled the painful memory of their engagement party last February, which had been combined with her 18th birthday. The mishmash of drunken teen friends and the wide social-divide of their two families sharing the same venue was still imprinted on Julie's mind. That said, she still couldn't help but smile at the vision and memory of Col's shoe flying off as he danced the can-can, the shoe hitting her mother square in the back just as she was about to take a dainty forkful of Black Forest Gateau which then landed in Beryl's drink. Perhaps they could still have a small, family-only celebration once they returned, if that's what their parents wanted. Her only regret was that her father didn't get a chance to walk his only daughter down the aisle…

Julie's thoughts were interrupted as Ged picked up the almost-empty bottle of Asti Spumanti from the nightstand and drained the last of the fizzy liquid into two paper cups.

'Here's to us, Mrs Steele,' he said, raising a paper cup. 'Now hurry up, I've got another stiffy growing – we've just got time for a quickie before the Post Office closes,' he quipped, while brushing a handful of colourful paper confetti out of the bed.

CHAPTER 13

The Gift of Disappointment

1984

Julie held her hands gently over Ged's eyes as step-by-step she guided him into the kitchen. She removed them briskly, and shrilled in a sing-song voice, 'Surpri-ise, happy twenty-first birthday, Ged!'

His face lit up like a true birthday child as he took in the sight before him. A multi-coloured banner of triangular shapes, clearly homemade from a magazine, was strung across the ceiling. The triangles fluttered slightly as the air below was disturbed by movement. A cluster of coloured balloons was pinned to the top of the kitchen door frame, while another cluster was tied to the chair where he usually sat. A largish square parcel sat in the middle of the kitchen table, humorously wrapped in pages from an old 'Kerrang!' magazine. Ged took Julie in his arms and kissed her playfully on the nose. 'Aww, thanks, wifey, this is so, so...'

'Cheap?' she cut in. 'Sorry it's all homemade, but I thought it wise to save money, just in case the miners' strike goes ahead.' She looked at him, hoping for approval of her purposeful frugality.

A cloud of uncertainty and realisation passed through Ged's dark eyes. 'Aye, we go to the ballot today. Some birthday present, eh!' He sighed at the looming prospect of a strike, the stark reality of hard times ahead. 'But c'mon. Don't let that spoil my day.' Ged resumed his excited birthday-boy persona and picked up the box, giving it a gentle shake and pretend sniff. 'Cool wrapping paper,' he quipped, his eyes now sparkling with humour, replacing the previous moments of gloom. He sat at the table and began tearing off the paper, revealing a Polaroid instant camera. His mouth fell open, then broke into a wide grin.

'Do you like it?' Julie came and sat beside him.

'I love it, it's great, thanks!' Ged carefully opened the box, afraid of damaging the sensitive equipment inside. 'This must've cost a fortune...' He let his words hang, not wishing to offend Julie's generosity.

'Don't worry. I've been saving for a few months to get you something special, and to take you away for the weekend. It is your twenty-first, after all. But – knowing that you might have to go on strike, I only used half of the savings to buy you this, and I've put the rest to one side until we know what's happening. And my mum's invited all of us for tea, rather than going out for a meal. We pick up your mum and dad at half six.' Her eyes sought his approval at her newfound sensibility, setting her usual lavishness to one side.

'A wise idea, my Lady Juliet,' he said. Ged noticed a slight glow in Julie's cheeks – she still relished being called "Lady Juliet", a playful reference to their different social backgrounds. He carefully took the camera out of the box to examine it, his eyebrows raised in approval.

'It's one of those cameras that takes photos without darkroom processing, or having to take a roll of film to the chemist's. They develop within minutes, after giving them a shake to dry them. I thought you might like a new hobby,' Julie explained.

'Without processing? Instant?' His smile began to widen. 'So nobody sees the photos?'

'That's right. There's no need for a darkroom or anything. Only you see what you've taken...' Julie stopped short her technical explanation when she saw the pouty, calculating look on Ged's face and mischievous twinkle in his eyes.

'So, no-one sees the photos, eh? They're private…?' His voice was loaded with suggestion.

'Gerald Steele! I am not posing for bedroom photos!' The colour shot into Julie's cheeks as she involuntarily began covering her body with her hands.

'Aw, c'mon. No-one else will see them. I think it would be really nice to have a picture of you showing your ti…' But Julie cut him off before he finished the sentence.

'No, Ged. Definitely not. Christ, you always have to lower the tone of things.' Her tone was suddenly curt, angry.

'Oh, come on. I was only joking,' he retorted, defending his suggestion. 'Pweez…' He gave her puppy-eyes. 'Pweez, let's not fight on my birthday.' He fluttered his dark eyelashes, causing Julie's defences to weaken.

'Okay. Maybe *one* slightly provocative pose to keep in your wallet. But nothing porno or cheap,' she conceded. 'From then on it's just photos of flowers, holidays and concerts. Deal?'

'Deal,' agreed Ged. He came and gave her a loving hug of thanks for his gift, and to acknowledge the time and thought that she had put into the decorating.

'So, what's the plan for the day, then?' she asked, busying herself with making a pot of coffee and some toast for them.

'There's a ballot meeting later, to put strike action to the vote. Then another meeting tomorrow for the results.' He could feel his shoulders tensing at the prospect, so began helping Julie to make breakfast as a distraction.

Unconsciously, they both suddenly stopped what they were doing and held each other tightly, each lost in their own thoughts of what possibly lay ahead.

It was a moment that didn't need words to explain how they were feeling.

*

The Union meeting at the Miners' Welfare was packed to capacity. The tension in the air hung as heavy as the grey cigarette smoke. Ged looked around and took stock of how many father-son partnerships were in the room. This was when the full realisation of family bonds within the industry really struck home. Mr Wilson and Ben, Sam Carter and his twin boys, Jeff Coupe and his son David. And they were just the families that he knew. Others he recognised, and could now make facial connections. The strike was going to affect a lot of families.

He also realised that there would also be many divided families, torn apart by Union differences – some had balloted for the right to work, others for the right to strike.

The Chairman of their local branch of the NUM took to the stage and tapped the microphone, calling the men to order. Chairs scraped as the older generation sat, their younger counterparts choosing to stand, shoulder to shoulder. The air bristled with anticipation as the room quieted.

'As we all know, the industry received the shock news from the Chairman of the Coal Board, Mr Ian MacGregor, when he announced plans to close twenty pits. Pits that he declares to be uneconomical.' The crowd began to murmur. The union leader held up his hand to quiet the men. 'The proposed closures will mean the loss of twenty thousand jobs. Twenty thousand of our brothers will be on the scrap heap. Cortonwood, the first of these pits earmarked for closure, has already downed tools in protest.' A mixed wave of anger and support rippled through the men. The union leader again raised his hand for silence. He continued to hold his hand aloft, turning it into a clenched fist of aggression and defiance.

'As you know, the President of the NUM, Mr Scargill, has called for our members to ballot, to join with our brothers in support.' A united murmur of agreement filtered around the room. 'Our ballot, here at Castle Ridge, shows that our members wish to join the protest. As from midnight, we officially declare ourselves to be on strike, and down tools.'

Ged looked at his dad as a cheer of support went up around the room, and was surprised to see Jud displaying a tight-lipped nervousness.

'Best prepare y'self for a long, messy fight, son.' Jud put his head down, then reached into his pocket for his cigarettes. 'Here, enjoy one of these while we can still afford 'em,' he said, offering the open packet towards Ged. As Ged lit his cigarette, he noticed one of the younger lads crying, being consoled by an older man – the boy's father, he presumed.

'What's up w'young lad, d'ya reckon?' he asked Jud.

'Most likely an apprentice. It's hard for them – they risk losing their training and apprenticeship if they go on strike. But on the other hand, no-one wants to be a scab,' Jud explained.

Ged looked at his father, wide-eyed, grateful that he'd long since finished his apprenticeship, and qualified. 'Poor sod, damned if he does, and damned if he doesn't.' He shook his head.

'Aye,' nodded Jud, 'a strike can tear a family apart...'

After the meeting had drawn to a close, Ged said his goodbyes to his dad and caught the bus up into Castle Ridge market square. As the bus rattled its way up through the estate, Ged reflected on the union meeting. He noted how quickly the mood had changed once the ballot revealed a strike situation – an air of aggression had descended over the men and the meeting became charged, volatile. Men that he'd known for years, usually moderate by nature, had become swept along with the tension. News had come through to the meeting that the nearby Nottinghamshire miners had voted in favour of working. Picket-line skirmishes were likely to become the norm for the foreseeable future, particularly as Mr Scargill was threatening to send groups of "flying pickets" to try and stop any working men from entering. The rallying chant of "Miners united, will never be defeated" had already become the war-cry of the picket lines, as one by one, collieries up and down the country turned into battle grounds.

He hopped off the bus near Julie's salon and went to break the news. The days, weeks, maybe even months ahead, were likely to be tough. Ged was grateful that he'd recently had a delivery of coal from his consignment. They would have to try and eke it out. There was no guarantee that he would be able to get any extra from Col's coal haulage company, as his yard had already been commandeered for the power companies.

The salon was a bustling hive of activity when he entered. Julie was just finishing with a client. Her face took on a mask of worry when she looked up and saw Ged walk through the door. She quietly gave the lady her change and ran around the counter to him.

'How did the meeting go?' she asked, ushering him to one side so that they could talk more privately. 'I'll be with you in a minute, Mrs Jones,' she said, acknowledging her next customer.

'The men voted to strike. We officially start at midnight.' Ged found it hard to conceal his worry. 'There's talk of it going on for a few months – the power stations have apparently been stockpiling coal, just in case.'

'Which means what?' Julie asked, unsure of the implications.

Ged could sense her concern. 'It means that they can keep going for a while longer at least, without us. The country won't grind to a complete standstill straight away,' he explained.

'Is that good, or bad?'

'Bad, really. It means that we have less initial impact, so there's a risk that the strike could be a long one, until their stockpiles run out. Plus, we've heard that the Nottinghamshire miners have voted to continue working. They've got us by the balls.'

This was the first time in Julie's life that she'd been presented with the challenge of little or no money coming in. It was a daunting prospect. She could feel her usual cluster of wasps stinging around her stomach. 'I'd better get back to work,' she said, kissing him discreetly on the cheek.

'Aye, I guess one of us had better keep working.' He tried to make their reality sound lighter, in the hope of not setting the seeds of worry too deep for Julie.

She similarly tried to sound light in her reply. 'Well, if nothing else, you'll have more time for your new photography hobby. And for your allotment – we're gonna be needing those veg...'

CHAPTER 14

A Sign of the Times

'**S**cab, scab, scab, scab…' The chant of the picket line miners at Castle Ridge colliery rose in volume, its intensity echoing around the entrance to the coal yard, warriors and champions of the National Coal Board, defending all that they held dear.

Cold.

Wet.

Desperate.

Defiant.

Ged linked arms with his dad, fists held aloft, punching the air.

'Maggie, Maggie, Maggie, out, out, out…'

'What do we want?'

'Work.'

When do we want it?'

'Now!'

'Maggie, out, Maggie, out…'

The surge pushed from behind as the bus carrying the working miners eased slowly through the affray, causing Ged to stumble and fall towards the side of the bus. He felt his forehead connect with the metal grid protecting the bus windows, before being yanked backwards by Jud.

'UDM bastards,' he screamed, banging his fists on the side of the bus. 'Scabs!' He touched his forehead and looked at his fingertips. A smear of crimson confirmed that he'd been cut. He hammered on the side of the bus again, retribution for the injury it had caused.

The pressure of the crowd intensified behind Ged and his dad, enveloping the rear of bus as it entered the gates of the colliery. Ged began kicking the bus panels, each kick in rhythm with the police as they beat on their riot shields. They moved towards the throng of miners, intimidating, purposeful.

'Stoppit, y'daft twat, you're going to get yerself arrested.' Jud grabbed Ged's arms, pulling him away and into the crowd, as the battery of police shields pushed forcefully towards them, the police beating time with their truncheons. Missiles of rocks and clods of earth began flying through the air towards the bus and the police, causing shrapnel of stones to ricochet over the crowd. Each successful landing was celebrated with a cheer, and encouraged another round of menacing chants and missile launches.

'C'mon lad, this is going to get ugly.' Jud turned against the tide of men in an attempt to avoid injury and arrest. 'The front line is no place for us. We've done our bit for today.'

Julie walked by her parked-up Mini on the driveway and let herself in through the kitchen door. She preferred to come in through the kitchen door when it was wet outside, so as not to mess up the front hallway carpet – she still had some pride. The once cosy home felt as cold inside as it did outside, her breath visible in a wisp of white cloud. Julie shivered, the cloying dampness from the cold October drizzle having made its way through her denim jacket – time to dig out her old Afghan coat if she wasn't going to be using the car in order to save money. The heating elements of the little two bar electric fire grinned wide, inviting her to switch it on.

What are you grinning at!

Julie flicked the switch and waited for the red, glowing warmth of the bars to reach her hands as she stood in grateful supplication before it. The heat began to return to her fingertips. She unzipped her boots then shook the drizzle off her jacket before going through to the front hall to hang it up to dry. A pile of envelopes lay below the letterbox. Not good. Envelopes usually equated to bills.

Or reminders.

The two men, father and son, fell into step as they trudged their way up through the bleak, grey Coal Board estate, yellow lights from the house windows the only cheer cutting through the gloom. Ged turned the collar of his donkey jacket up to shield his neck from the steady drizzle that had started to fall. Naked tree branches rustled together in the late autumn breeze, while the rotting remains of their once glorious leaf colours lay mangled and slimy on the ground.

'How much longer d'ya reckon the strike's going to last?' Ged asked, looking towards Jud as though he might have all the answers.

'Set yourself in for a long, bleak winter, lad. Maggie and MacGregor are hard nuts. They won't back down in a hurry. They've got Scargill where they want him.'

Ged's shoulders sank at the prospect. 'We've got nowt left in the coal shed, nowt to burn. And we can't get any coal from Col's yard, as he's had to let it go to the power stations. Christ knows how we're gonna get through the winter.'

'Same here, lad. Somehow it don't feel right that our lasses are the only ones bringing the money in.' Jud looked downcast, humbled at no longer being the breadwinner.

'Aye. But do you know what's pissed me off the most? Some bastard's been and nicked the veg off me allotment. Carrots, cabbage, leeks, the bloody lot.' Ged kicked a stone off the pavement into the road.

Jud's brow furrowed as he tried to make sense of the injustice that his son felt. The allotment was Ged's pride and joy. 'Maybe they have a family to feed, lad. At least you can get veg from the in-laws.' A perplexed silence hung over them for a time, each man deep in his own thoughts.

'I know where there's some old timber…' mumbled Jud, knowing what he was about to suggest was wrong, out of character. Ged looked at him, waiting for him to continue. 'There's a pile of old railway sleepers at the back of the disused rail depot just off Quarrystone Lane. The one that's down in the copse, not far from Col's yard. We could nip there once it's gone dark…' Ged nodded a silent approval. 'Besides, if anybody sees us, we could always say that it was for Bonfire Night,' defended Jud.

Needs must. Miners united, and all that.

Now Ged understood why someone had nicked the veg from his allotment.

As Ged headed up the side of the cottage, he could make out the yellow glow from the kitchen light reflecting through the square pane of the door. He guessed that Julie and Helena must've closed the salon early if there wasn't much to do. Spending money on haircuts and perms seemed to be at the bottom of the agenda for the locals these days. He felt for the girls – they'd worked really hard to build up the salon business after Julie's aunty had retired and passed it on to her. Injected a bit of young blood and vibrant energy.

He began kicking off his work-boots as soon as he entered the kitchen. 'Ay-up love, I'm…'

Julie looked up from the glass-and-chrome kitchen table, tear-damp hair stuck to her face, mixed with streaks of black mascara.

'Look at it! Look at it…' she screamed between sobs, before screwing up the piece of paper in her hand. 'They want to come and cut off the electricity.' She swept the envelope and crumpled notice onto the tiled floor.

Ged looked puzzled. He bent down to pick up the paperwork and began to un-crumple the final demand. 'But I thought it had been paid. I thought we were up to date with everything.'

Julie looked at him pitifully. 'I forgot to pay it. Then I ignored the reminder because I'd spent the money on food and stuff.' Her voice became small. 'I'm so sorry...'

Ged scratched his stubble and ran his fingers through his damp hair, careful to avoid the cut on his forehead. 'Do we have any spare money anywhere to pay for it?'

Julie shook her head, unable to look Ged in the eye.

'Damn!' He banged his fist down hard on the kitchen table causing Julie to jump. 'For God's sake, woman, how could you have been so...so...?' He stopped short, unwilling to say what he thought. Julie remained fixed, head down. Her shoulders began to heave with pent-up sobs. Ged turned on his heel and stared out of the kitchen window, watching the beads of drizzle pool together, then trickle downwards as they burst under their own weight. He heard the scrape of a chair behind him, metal grinding on tile, then felt Julie's hand slip into his. He turned towards her then curled his arms tightly around her shoulders until her sobs subsided.

'I'll sell the Mini...'

Ged looked at her incredulously. 'No! No way, lady. That was an eighteenth birthday present from yer mam and dad. You can't sell it. I won't let you.'

'What then, eh? Ugh, I-hate-this-strike...' She began pounding her fists on his chest. 'I hate not having any money...'

'Welcome to the working class world, Julie. Welcome to my reality,' countered Ged, his tone turning gruff, defensive.

'What? No, I didn't mean...I didn't mean anything by it. But this is the first time in my life that I've had to really struggle. I'm sick of feeling like a bloody Oxfam case.' She went and sat back down. 'Look, this is my mess. I'll see if my dad can help – just this one time. And I'll pay him back. I promise.'

She looked at Ged, and could see straight away what he was thinking. She answered for him, 'Yes, I'm running to daddy. Okay, there, I said it.'

A wry smile played on the corner of Ged's lips. 'Well, I guess we're both going back to our roots on this one. You can go running back to your *daddy* for money. Meanwhile, I'm going out with my *daddy* later tonight, cos we know where there's a pile of wood for free.'

Julie looked shocked, panic written all over her face. 'But that's stealing!'

Ged rolled his eyes. 'No shit, Sherlock! And if we get caught, then maybe your daddy will help us out too. It's a win-win situation.' He strolled over to the power point where the electric fire was plugged in and turned it off, then held out his hand towards Julie. 'C'mon, my Lady Juliet. I know a place where we can keep warm for free.'

CHAPTER 15

U Turn

Julie's mum stood up and turned off the television, irritated by the BBC's local 'Look North' news roundup.

'Miners' strike this, and miners' strike that. I'm sick to death of hearing about Scargill and his flying pickets. All that rioting and fighting. You'd think that after being on strike since March that the miners would have given up by now. If you ask me, they should accept this new pay incentive from the NCB and get back to work,' she complained. 'All this dissent – it makes me nervous.'

Frank looked up from his newspaper.

'In case you hadn't noticed, Jean, your son-in-law and his father are one of those striking miners fighting for the right to work and keep the local colliery open,' he defended. 'Think of it this way…' he tried to continue.

'Oh, here we go, one of Frank Bryant's famous summing-up speeches…' she retorted.

'Think of it this way,' he continued, undeterred, 'if the local colliery closes, where will the local workforce go? I'll tell you where – the dole queue. At the expense of our taxes to fund their unemployment benefit. There *is* nothing else for them around here, Jean. And here's another thing – who will have the money then to buy your fruit and veg, or my legal services, or get a haircut at our daughter's salon? No-one. Think about the knock-on effect. I know I do.'

'Well, I'm on the side of Mrs Thatcher – if a business is uneconomical, then surely it needs to close? I would close my business if it was losing money.' Jean looked at Frank, unconvinced by his reasoning.

'No, you wouldn't close it. You would fight for it. You would look for ways of keeping it going, cutting costs, before throwing in the towel. That's just what these men are fighting for. And that's just what we need to do.' He stood up and took out his handkerchief to clean his glasses.

Jean smiled. It was his usual habit once he got up on his soapbox about something.

'I think we should do something to help them,' he continued. 'It's December, and it's bloody cold. Christmas is just around the corner.' He pushed his newly cleaned glasses back on and paused for effect. 'Let's face it, Jean, their situation is pretty bleak. It wasn't that long ago that there was a robbery on the local building society agency, remember. Didn't the police put that down to being a desperate miner? A sign of the times?'

Jean nodded. Her mind recalled the nervousness which reverberated throughout the business community – who would be next?

'I think we should enlist the help of the community – rally everyone together. Try and help the miners.' He looked at Jean, his eyebrows raised, expectant.

'Ah, like everyone rallied around after the '73 pit disaster? People are still talking about how Mr Jackson came down to the pit head with hot coffee and soup from the café, for the rescue teams and waiting families. It prompted the whole community to join in and help.'

'Exactly! But you remembered Mr Jackson's name – his café is still a thriving business. And it's been what, ten, maybe eleven years since the tragedy,' replied Frank.

'Okay, go on...' she urged.

'We could do the same. Food parcels. Maybe you and your brother could donate some fruit and veg – potatoes, sprouts, tangerines, that sort of thing. I could have a word with the lads at the Rotary Club – the manager of the Co-op is a member, maybe he could donate some tins of ham. Arthur Jones might be able to supply some chickens or sausages from his farm shop.'

Jean took up the thread. 'I could speak to the ladies at the next WI meeting – maybe we could bake some cakes and mince pies to donate? Oh, Francis, yes, I can see what you mean now. It's a wonderful idea.'

'Francis, my Sunday name! Must be doing something right. But you reap what you sow, my dear. You of all people should know that, coming from the Halliwell veg farming dynasty.' Frank laughed at his own analogy. 'We'll need to speak to our Julie and Ged of course. Get them to liaise with Ged's father. He'll know who the neediest families are.'

'Oh, Frank, I've had another idea. If we get them to organise giving out the food parcels at their Miners' Welfare, we could perhaps organise a little Christmas party for the miners' children.' She clapped her hands together at her own suggestion.

Frank was also beginning to run away with the concept. 'I could borrow the Santa outfit from the Rotary. We could make sure that word got to the local press, get some positive coverage.' He tapped the side of his nose and gave a knowing wink.

'Well, I must concede, Frank, you're a genius at making sense out of madness,' Jean said, reaching for the box of After Eight mints on the coffee table.

'That's the trick, you see – you can still support dear Maggie, the locals don't need to know that. But by supporting the locals, you're supporting the future of your own business. People will always need potatoes, and judging by the rioting and arrests on the picket lines, people will always need a solicitor. And that, my dear, is why I win all my court cases. Sherry?' He stood up, and walked over to the sideboard.

'Oh, please. A large one.'

'Careful, dear, we don't want your halo to slip...'

*

Jud Steele strode purposefully across the Welfare, his hand outstretched.

'I honestly can't thank you enough, Frank, Jean, for what you've both brought to the community today.' He shook Frank's hand, illuminating his genuine feeling of gratefulness. Frank noticed how rough Jud's hand felt in his own soft hand. 'To see all these smiling faces. It'll make a big difference to them, help boost their morale,' said Jud.

Frank pulled off his Santa beard, and wiped the sweat from his face.

'Well, your fight is our fight, George, er Jud.' Frank always found it difficult to call him 'Jud'. 'So happy that we could help.' He looked around the room. Yes, the community had certainly pulled together and been generous with their donations: toys and sweets for the kids, fruit, veg, meat, pastries; even party crackers and lemonade. Julie and Helena had volunteered their services for the day and offered a free shampoo and set for the miners' wives, and also got one of the other local salons to join in, so that the ladies could have a day of feeling pampered. *The Derbyshire Times* and local *Castle Ridge Weekly* had been invited to cover the story and take photographs. It made heart-warming news at a time when people were feeling their most desperate.

And of course, Frank Bryant, of Bryant & Harding, Solicitors, member of the Castle Ridge and District Rotary Club; Jean Bryant of The Fruit Basket, together with the ladies of the Shirecliffe WI group; and Julie Steele and Helena Blakeley of Silver Scissors all received a special mention for their tireless efforts in rallying the local community together in a united show of support.

CHAPTER 16

Sick

1985

Julie flushed the remnants of last night's chicken stir-fry down the toilet and shakily moved over to the bathroom sink to wash her hands and rinse away the sour taste of puke from her mouth. She looked in the mirror and had to concede that she looked like shit. She stuck out her tongue and inspected it in the mirror, not sure what she should be looking for. It was lumpy and sore around the edges. Julie poured herself a glass of water and took a couple of paracetamols from the medicine cabinet before heading back to bed. Her head was throbbing and every bone and joint in her body ached. Damn, she hated being sick.

As Julie hauled herself back into the warmth and comfort of her bed, she was grateful that it was Monday and therefore not a salon day. Going to the wholesalers would just have to wait. Ged had long since gone to take a stint on the picket line. So how come he wasn't sick? He'd eaten the same as her. The chicken hadn't tasted "off". Strange. Then again, it was the beginning of February – the flu season was still in full swing, and the salon had had its fair share of coughing and sneezing old biddies recently, all unwilling to give up their hair appointments. *Selfish bastards*, she thought to herself.

She plumped up the pillows and settled into their softness, allowing sleep to claim her until her next bout of throwing up.

Although Julie's Mini was on the driveway when Ged arrived home from his shift on picket duty, the windows of the cottage were in darkness. The curtains were still drawn downstairs and there was no sign of life within – no used coffee mugs, no music playing, nothing. Everything was as he'd left it at six that morning. Puzzled, and admittedly a little nervous, he kicked off his boots and bounded up the stairs towards their bedroom, unsure of what he wanted or hoped to find.

'Julie? Julie, are you home?' he whispered. For some strange reason, it seemed wrong to shout, wrong to break the silence. Cocking his head to one side, he strained his ears for any response or sign of life. Nothing. He noticed that his hand was shaking as he reached for the bedroom door handle and cautiously pushed the door open. In the dim light, he could just make out the lumpy shape of someone in bed.

'Julie, love. I'm home.' He approached the bed, his hand gently touching Julie's cheek. She was burning hot. He gently shook her, rousing her from her sleep. Her eyes flickered open, vacant. Realising that her mouth was dry, he passed her a glass of water from the bedside cabinet. It took her a few minutes to re-orientate herself before she could speak and tell Ged how her day had been. It had not been good.

After three days of no change, Ged felt at a loss with Julie's situation – she was still unable to keep down any food, and every bone, every joint ached and caused her discomfort when she tried to move. Convinced that this was more than the flu or food poisoning, he arranged for one of the doctors from their local surgery to make a house-call.

A sigh of relief escaped from Ged when he saw the doctor's Saab pull up in front of the cottage. He noticed that it wasn't their usual GP, but that aside, he could tell by her shock of curly red hair that she must somehow be related to the old man. Now fully qualified, the young Dr Wilson Jr had just joined her father at the local practice. Ged hoped that she hadn't inherited her father's gruff bedside manner – he could be a curt, grumpy old bugger at times. Her handshake was firm and reassuring when she introduced herself to Ged, and her voice and tone suggested she was the opposite in character to her father. He also noticed her tiny "Ban the Bomb" earrings and caught a faint whiff of patchouli oil as she passed him to go upstairs to see Julie. Ged instantly warmed to her and decided that she was on their side.

After asking a battery of questions and thoroughly checking over Julie, Dr Wilson gave her opinion and diagnosis. This was not the news or the diagnosis that either Ged or Julie had been expecting – Julie was in complete shock. Ged smiled to himself as he looked at the junior Dr Wilson's earrings – despite her support of banning the bomb, she had just dropped a mega-ton version on the Steele household.

Ged opened the front door to let Dr Wilson out.

'Thanks for coming, Doc. At least now we know what it is, what we're dealing with.' He offered his hand towards her, in a shake of gratitude.

'Just make sure she gets plenty of bed rest and fluids. Hopefully she'll be over the worst of the sickness in a few days, and should be able to get up and about. That said, she might still feel nauseous for the next few weeks. Have her make an appointment to come and see me at the surgery as soon as she's well enough.' She smiled reassuringly at Ged before turning away and going out to her car. He watched her walk down the driveway, his mind already deep in thought.

Ged headed into the kitchen and started warming a can of Heinz Chicken Soup, remembering that his mam always said that it was the best medicine. It had gotten him through many an illness as a young'un. Although to be fair, Julie wasn't really ill, not as such. He poured a glass of Lucozade – another one of his mam's healing classics, and put it onto a tray ready to take upstairs. He decided against making a slice of toast, opting to keep things light and liquid. Wow, the doctor's news was certainly going to be a life-changer for them. He shook his head in disbelief, his smile broad. Not only had he bagged the prettiest lass in the area, but now he was going to be a dad.

Balancing the tray carefully, Ged made his way upstairs, endeavouring not to spill the soup and Lucozade. He imagined himself gently carrying a tiny newborn in his arms. As he pushed open the bedroom door, he caught the sound of Julie snuffling as she wiped her eyes and nose with a tissue. Her face looked gaunt, her eyes dark and hollow, in the white-yellow glow from the bedside lamp.

'Here's some soup and a drink for you. Got to try and get some strength back into you.' Ged lay the tray on the bedside table as he sat down on the bed bedside her and took her hand. It felt paper dry. He lifted her hand towards his lips ready to kiss it gently, but she snatched it away, leaving his hand empty.

'How-the-fuck….?' Julie's words hung in the air, their sharpness taking Ged slightly aback. He realised that he was opening and closing his mouth goldfish style, unable to find the right words to say. Her glare stung, causing his stomach to lurch.

'How the fuck can I be pregnant?' she hissed.

'I…I thought you'd be happy. Aren't you happy? We're going to have a baby…' Ged countered.

'Happy? I've just been told I'm pregnant. The whole point of being on the pill is so that you don't get pregnant…' Her voice began to rise and croak. 'I'm not ready for this. *We're* not ready for this. You're on strike, in case you'd forgotten!' Hot tears sprang from her eyes. Ged leaned forward in an attempt to gently wipe them away with his thumb, only to find his hand slapped. The slap stung both his hand and his heart. Admittedly, the timing was a bit off, but still…

He took a deep breath, his mind frantically searching for the right words to say, desperate to avoid any more rebuffs from Julie.

'The only thing I can think of, is that you threw up quite a bit around Christmas and New Year, remember? You did have quite a lot to drink at your parents on Christmas Day, and at Col's New Year party.' His eyes sought hers, hoping for some notion of acceptance. 'Isn't that supposed to lessen the effect of the pill? And, er, you know, we celebrated Christmas and New Year with a few rounds in the bedroom, if you get my drift.' His mind wandered back to Christmas morning, having gift-wrapped his dick with a big, red bow, as well as seeing in the New Year with a sneaky celebratory shag in Col's bathroom before Julie threw up. 'It all adds up…'

'How can we have been so careless…?'

'Careless? It's what married people do, Julie. It just happens. It's not like you're on your own in this, you know. It's my baby too…' In a bid to break the tension, he reached over for the tray of soup, 'Here, have your soup before it gets cold. You've got to eat something…'

'Don't patronise me – I don't want any fucking soup.' Her words came out harsh, vehement. She lurched forward, deliberately unbalancing the tray out of his hands, causing a liquid arc of soup and Lucozade to splatter across Ged and the carpet. He recoiled in shock as the warm and cold liquids soaked his tee-shirt and torso.

'But…'

'Go!' she screamed. 'Get out…leave me alone…'

Huddled under his NCB donkey-jacket, Ged sat on the back doorstep, mug of tea in one hand and roll-up cigarette in the other, relishing the calming effects of the evening sounds. A strong breeze shook the winter-brittle branches of the silver birch trees at the bottom corner of the garden, causing them to rattle and scrape together. The blue-blackness of the night sky was punctuated by the stars as they switched on, one by one. He watched the orange-red glow of his cigarette as he inhaled deeply, expelling the white smoke into the chilly night air. Once Julie had finally calmed from her outburst and they had managed to have some kind of reasonable dialogue, they had decided to keep their baby-news secret for a while longer – at least until the first check-up had confirmed everything was okay. Her sickness had been diagnosed as an extreme form of morning sickness, hyper-something or other, and could last for weeks. The aches and pains could be attributed to her body getting used to the pregnancy hormones. In the meantime, they would cover their tracks by saying that Julie had a particularly virulent strain of the flu as an excuse for not going out. This was not how he'd envisaged receiving the news of his wife's pregnancy. Then again, he could tell by Julie's reaction that this had not been the way she'd imagined it either. Although, in fairness to Julie, she was probably just worried, what with him being on strike and money being tight. He really wanted to feel happy, but had to admit that his ego felt a little deflated.

Ged stretched out his legs and crossed one over the other in a bid to get comfy on the cold step. But that was one hell of an outburst that she'd had – her sudden rage had rattled him. Blaming him, like it was his fault. Didn't it take two to make a baby? Their love-making was always urgent, passionate. She wanted him as much as he wanted her. Realising that he was shivering, he tipped the last of his now-cold tea into a nearby plant pot and used the moisture to extinguish his cigarette, flicking the tab away into the night, not caring where it landed. He looked heavenward in the hope that his Granny Steele was looking down on him – and he knew exactly what she would have said…

Shit, bugger, damn and blast it!

CHAPTER 17

22 + 2

The dry heat and stark fluorescent lighting from the doctor's surgery hit Julie as soon as she walked into the entrance vestibule, a stark contrast from the damp, foggy chill of the February day beyond the door. She squinted her eyes in an effort to adjust to the artificial brightness. Suddenly hit by a wave of nervous nausea, Julie rummaged in the pocket of her black leather trench coat for a Polo mint. As she undid the buttons, she noticed that they were already stretched tight across her belly. She sighed. Julie shook off the droplets before hanging it on the coat rack. After checking in at reception, she found a place to sit near an elderly lady, a healthier choice than sitting next to the young mum who was nursing a couple of coughing and sneezing snotty nosed kids.

Oh dear God, is that what I've got to look forward to?

She exchanged a polite nod with the elderly lady as she sat down. Julie found herself unsure of what to do with her hands. If she cradled her hands over her tummy, that would signal acceptance of her condition, while putting her hands on her lap would signal denial. In reality, she wanted to punch it and make it go away…

Noticing a pile of magazines on the coffee table, she chose to take something to read to occupy her hands. Her sweater felt cold and clammy against her back as she settled back into the chair. The intercom crackled into life – saved by the intercom.

'Julie Steele to Surgery 4. Julie Steele to Surgery 4. Dr Wilson Jr will see you now.'

Julie nodded a polite acknowledgement towards the old lady before heading across the waiting room to see the doctor, her footsteps slow and reluctant. What was she so afraid of? Wasn't having a baby the most natural thing in the world?

Dr Wilson Jr looked up when Julie entered the room, her smile broad and friendly. She welcomed Julie with a handshake, and offered her a seat by the desk. Julie looked around the room. It was an odd blend of solid wooden desk and leather chair, presumably left over by the newly retired Dr Welch, mixed with what Julie could only describe as 'hippie-looking' trinkets and rugs. There was even an oil-burner on her desk, emanating a warming but sickly fragrance of orange and cinnamon.

'Well, you're certainly looking a lot better than the last time I saw you, Mrs Steele. And happy birthday, by the way.' She smiled at Julie.

Julie had almost forgotten that it was her birthday today. If the truth be known, she wasn't really in the mood for celebrating. She returned the doctor's smile in an attempt to lift her mood. Dr Wilson went through a list of questions with Julie in order to determine the approximate date of conception and due birth date. After checking Julie's temperature and blood pressure, Dr Wilson asked Julie to undress and lie on the medical bench so that she could carry out an examination. As she lay on the bench, Julie noticed that her stomach was no longer flat – it was already beginning to swell and curve with a distinctive lower-belly baby-bump. She discreetly wiped away a tear. Dr Wilson began her examination, her hands warm and smooth as they probed Julie's abdomen. Her brow furrowed intently as she listened with the stethoscope. Puzzled, she examined Julie's belly again, while listening closely.

'Well, judging by what I can feel, and our calculations, I think you're at least eight weeks along. That would give you an approximate due date around the first week of September. There's one more thing, Julie...'

Startled by Dr Wilson's last comment, Julie looked up, her eyes wide, nervous. The doctor smiled, and put her stethoscope to Julie's belly again, as if for confirmation.

'I'm pretty sure that I can hear two little heartbeats. Would you like to listen?'

Julie levered herself up onto her side and retched.

The glass pane was cool against the side of Julie's face and forehead as she leaned against the window in the spare room – the room that would become the nursery. *Twins.* She stared vacantly, unseeing, at the dark fields beyond. They were dressed in their winter grey and brown, faintly striped with old corn stubble from the pre-winter ploughing, ironically helping to regenerate the earth with new life. The fields where she and Ged had spent many evenings together, as teens, as young lovers, as an engaged couple, before spotting this little cottage up for sale. The sound of the telephone jolted Julie from her blank reverie. She decided not to answer it. The caller remained persistent, waiting for their call to be answered.

'Fuck!' She ran downstairs and grabbed the receiver, breathless, her voice snappy when she answered.

'Well, happy birthday!' Helena's voice trilled with her greeting, ignoring her best friend's grumpiness. 'How are you? Feeling any better?'

Julie was caught off-guard. 'Erm, okay, I guess.' Her mind raced for a plausible answer. 'Still feeling a bit icky. I, er, went to the doctor's today for a check-up, and she's given me a couple more days off work,' she lied. 'Just as well it's Monday, not a salon day, eh?' She felt a stab of guilt in leaving Helena to hold the fort with their hairdressing business while she'd been languishing in bed, sick. As if their business hadn't suffered enough during the strike.

'That's a shame to hear. I was hoping to come round and bring you something...'

Julie cut her off with a sharp interjection. 'No! I, I mean, no. It's very thoughtful of you, but, erm, I'd rather not pass this sickness on to you. It wouldn't do for us both to be sick, eh?' Julie drummed her fingers, willing Helena to disconnect the call. 'Look, I'll call you later in the week. I should hopefully be back at work by Thursday...' The silence felt un-naturally long between them.

'Okay,' replied Helena. 'But call me if you need anything. Hope you soon feel better, yeah.'

The line went dead. Julie replaced the receiver into the telephone cradle. The full realisation of it being her birthday hit her – no doubt she would soon have a telephone call and visit from her parents. She looked at the single birthday card on the rustic brick mantelpiece – a glittery red rose with gold lettering, saying 'To a wonderful daughter-in-law.' It had arrived in the post this morning from Ged's parents. They still didn't have a telephone or a car, so Beryl always made sure that cards arrived on time.

Julie was sat at the kitchen table drinking a stomach-calming mug of peppermint tea when Ged came home after his stint on the picket line. Ever the thoughtful, sentimental one, he had bought the largest card he could afford, as well as a bunch of freesias and a little box of sweetmeat.

'How's my birthday girl?' He piled all his gifts onto the kitchen table before enveloping her in his arms and smothering her in kisses. Julie tried to wriggle free but realising that Ged was taking no notice, she softened into his arms, allowing him to express his salutations. He finally released her, and cheerfully began making himself a mug of coffee while Julie opened her card. Typical of Ged to buy a soppy card – one with a cute teddy holding a big, red heart, and the words "To My Darling Wife" emblazoned across it.

'Aww, cute! Thanks, Ged.' She stood the card on the table then opened the little box of sweetmeat – her favourite, Rose and Lemon Turkish

Delight. She only hoped that she would be able to keep them down. 'You're so thoughtful...thanks.' She reached out towards him, taking his hand. He came and sat with her, bringing his mug of coffee with him.

'The flowers are beautiful. They must have cost you a fortune!' Julie picked them up and inhaled their fragrant perfume. Ged was about to say that they had a good deal on at the Co-op, but thought better of it.

'Ah, nothing's too much for my girl. Here, let me take them and put them in water.' He went over to the sink to find a vase, and started to arrange the little bouquet.

'I got a card from your family today, and Helena called to wish me well. I told her that I was still feeling icky, but should hopefully be back at work by Thursday. And mum called to say that she and dad will pop round later,' she explained.

Ged turned towards her, his flower arranging task complete, but remained near the sink while they chatted.

'Hey, how did the appointment go at the doctor's this morning?' Ged smiled, remembering that it was Julie's first official pregnancy check-up today. 'Did the doctor give you a date?' He noticed a visible change in Julie's demeanour – her smile vanished and a cloud seemed to fall over her.

'It's twins. She thinks that it's twins...' came the cold, sharp, matter-of-fact reply.

Ged took an open-mouthed moment to absorb the news. 'Twins...Wow! I mean...wow...twins!' He could barely speak with any sense. His brow furrowed. 'You don't seem very happy...' A long moment passed. He could feel his heart-rate starting to quicken as he searched her face, her eyes, for some form of joy or acceptance. His answer came in the form of his coffee mug, still full with steaming coffee, hitting the wall and shattering behind him in an explosion of hot, dark liquid and shards of ceramic. He instinctively dodged to one side, his senses keenly alerting him to the flying projectile before it hit the wall. She lunged for him, fists pounding at his chest, at his face. He managed to lift his arms up to defend his face from the blows before stepping to one side. She stopped her tirade, her breath coming in short, heaving jags. Ged stood stock still, unsure, unbelieving – the atmosphere between them fully charged. Julie turned her back to Ged.

'Yes, it's twins. Due at the beginning of September.' She looked up at the clock as she walked out of the kitchen. 'My parents will be here soon. You'd better get this mess cleaned up, then go and get changed.'

No apology. Nothing.

Distracted and deep in confused thought, Ged had just finished snapping together the poppers of his denim shirt when he heard the doorbell ring and his in-laws arrive. He could hear muffled, excited greetings being exchanged. He quickly surveyed his image in the wardrobe mirror – his eyes looked hollow and sunken.

Let's get this show on the road...

Julie was already squealing with delight at the silver charm bracelet her mother was just fastening around her slender wrist. A delicate charm of two hearts melded together, with the letters J and G engraved on them, was already on the bracelet. She came and slung her arm around Ged's waist, as she proffered the bejewelled wrist for him to look at. Her eyes sparkled, no trace of their former malice evident.

'Look, Ged, isn't it beautiful?'

He cautiously kissed her on the nose before greeting his in-laws and sitting on the sofa. Julie came and sat on his knee, her demeanour relaxed. Ged could finally feel his own tense body relaxing at her soft warmth and clean scent.

'And, of course, we can't have a birthday celebration without champagne,' declared Frank Bryant, producing a chilled bottle of Moet & Chandon from behind his back. Frank's extravagance always made Ged feel slightly uncomfortable and inadequate, illuminating the differences between their two families – an area where they would always run parallel, never congruent. Ged's family showed affection. Julie's family showed money.

Julie burst into a fit of giggles, and took Ged's hand in hers. Her voice became coy, as she looked at Ged and then to her parents.

'W-eeell, erm, I...WE...have some news...' Her eyes lit up. 'I'll have to give the champagne a miss – for a while at least.'

Her parents exchanged puzzled glances.

'We're having a baby. Well, twins, actually. Isn't it wonderful? You're going to be grandparents!'

Ged felt like he'd just been hit over the head by a cricket bat.

Where the fuck did this change of heart come from...?

CHAPTER 18

Reality Check

Two porcelain-white, bloated lower legs glared up at Julie as she sat on the edge of the toilet seat to remove her surgical stockings, the indented lines and ridges from the elastic still clearly visible. *Christ, they look like a couple of over-inflated Zeppelin air balloons.* Involuntary tears began to well in the corners of her eyes. Standing for hours on end in the salon was taking its toll; her hands, legs and feet were puffed up to the point of discomfort. She had already removed her wedding ring and put it onto her pinkie-finger for fear of it cutting off the circulation. It was evidently coming time to talk to Helena about their partnership at the salon. *Damn!* She and Ged were just starting to get back on an even keel after the miners' strike was called off, and were back to two wages coming in. She looked at her split and peeling fingernails while she considered her options. Wasn't she supposed to be "blooming" now that she was in the second trimester? All the so-called experts kept telling her so.

Julie made her way to their bedroom to have a little lie-down. Ged was on afters, so wouldn't be home until after ten. At least she didn't have to worry about getting any tea ready. A pile of books sat on the night stand – all of them about pregnancy and motherhood, and all of them full of shit. *A-Z of Pregnancy; All You Need to Know About Motherhood; Pregnancy,*

Birth and Parenting. She had read every page, absorbed every word. None of their advice seemed to fit her reality. One joker said that at this stage of pregnancy, hair was usually thick, strong and shiny.

No.

No, it wasn't.

It was coming out in handfuls, blocking up the plug-holes.

It was lying in a matted ball in the waste-bin.

Such was the shock at losing so much hair that she had even recently launched her hairbrush at Ged. Poor sod, the brush had hit him smack in the face.

Julie plumped up her pillow and allowed the tears to flow, to wet the hair that she was losing. The way she saw it, her only option was to go part-time until she could find someone with whom she could lease out her "chair", thus enabling her to take full-time maternity leave. At least she would still have some money coming in, and Helena would have someone to help her out at the salon. It was a win-win solution. She would call Helena later.

The last of the golden rays from the evening sun slid around the side of the house, casting her bedroom into shade. Julie preferred the mornings in their bedroom, the sunrise welcomed them awake with its fingers of light. Their bedroom was painted a soft lilac, with accents of lighter and darker shades in the bedding and cushions. She turned her thoughts to the colour scheme for the twins' nursery. It had to be called a "nursery", not bedroom. That was the "in" word these days, according to the furnishing-and-decor magazines. She picked up one of the magazines to see if it offered any inspiration. The sun would set on the nursery, on the west side – an opportunity for a warm and cosy colour scheme. Page after page of "perfect" looking nurseries passed before her eyes, each one lavish, each one expensive looking. She sighed. There were times when she hated having expensive tastes on a limited budget! Though one design did catch her eye – a little cottage style room, in shades of soft yellow and white, with gingham curtains, and a white crib. Perfect. That was the one.

Her mind finally settled.

She allowed sleep to creep in and claim her.

CHAPTER 19

Life Changes…

The distinctive warble of the Trimfone jolted Ged bolt awake, causing him to almost roll off the sofa. He rubbed his eyes as he answered. It was the hospital – they'd had to rush Julie down to theatre for an emergency caesarean, unable to hold off delivery any longer. He'd only been sent home a few hours earlier, reassured that Julie was settled and sleeping, and that he should also get some rest. He looked at the clock over the stone fireplace – 2.45 am. He'd obviously fallen straight to sleep on the sofa the moment he'd sat down. He geared himself into action, first grabbing the Polaroid camera and a spare pack of photo cartridges and putting them by the door. Being ever the soppy romantic, he'd taken two photographs of Julie every month, watching the bump of their babies grow. The photos had been carefully dated and put into two albums; one for each of the twins, to give them on their 18th birthday – Ged had it all planned out. However, today he would be using it to take photographs of the new arrivals to show the grandparents-in-waiting. He planned on calling Julie's parents with the baby-news once the hour was decent, but his own parents still didn't have a telephone. Then again, that was the instant beauty of a Polaroid camera – he would surprise them later with photos of their new grandchildren.

Ged bounded upstairs to the room that Julie had prepared for the twins. Julie called it "the nursery", some fancy name for a baby's bedroom. He turned on the light and looked around the room – he had to concede that Julie had done an amazing job in putting together *the nursery* despite not feeling well. He had offered to help, but she insisted this was her project. She had painted the walls a soft yellow, the woodwork white. Julie's parents had bought two white cribs for the twins, and his mam had made the yellow and white bedding sets with matching yellow and white gingham checked curtains. A little mat with a teddy motif lay on the floor between the two cribs, and an elegant cane peacock chair graced the corner. A set of white drawers was already stuffed full of clothes that Julie couldn't resist buying for the babies. Ged grabbed the bag that she had put together for the big day – two sets of yellow and white baby clothes for coming home in, nappies, spare clothes for Julie, big knickers and big sanitary pads, magazines, her Walkman and a few cassettes, chocolate; she'd thought of everything. In a flush of sentimentality, Ged stopped to ponder all their achievements over these past six years together, and here they were on the threshold of becoming parents. He allowed himself a small rush of pride – all things considered, he hadn't done too badly for an 'Estate lad'.

There was very little traffic on the road as Ged drove Julie's Mini down to the hospital. Knowing that he had a long night ahead, he wound down the window in a bid to revive himself, relishing the warmth of the August night air on his face. He pressed the 'play' button on the car's cassette player, and wasn't surprised to hear Bon Jovi's *7800° Fahrenheit* kick in. Julie had gone nuts for this new band, although Ged rather suspected it was because she fancied the lead singer.

The car park at the Royal's Maternity Wing was virtually deserted. Too tired to walk far, Ged chose a parking spot close to the entrance. He grabbed all he needed to take in and headed to the ward where Julie was being cared for. As he made his way along the grey corridors, his mind simultaneously strolled down its own corridors of reflection – Julie had had an awful pregnancy, nothing had gone right from the outset. First she'd been plagued by many months of dreadful morning sickness, then anaemia. But things got progressively worse, particularly once her hair started falling out. Her crowning glory became her worst nightmare as it thinned day by day. Ged had often found her in floods of tears, her hairbrush full of long, dark hair. She'd even launched the hairbrush at him on a number of occasions, once giving him a black-eye as it hit him square in the face. But he knew that it was just her hormonal frustration begging for mercy. By the middle of her pregnancy, her hands and face had begun to swell, and she was constantly dizzy, plagued by headaches and high blood pressure. And all he could do was stand by and watch his wife crumble before his eyes, see-sawing between pushing away any offers of help then complaining because "nobody cared".

He felt useless.

He felt confused.

He felt guilty.

Having diagnosed pre-eclampsia, her doctor had mercifully taken charge and had Julie admitted to hospital for complete bed rest. And now the hospital doctors had elected to deliver the babies early – at least five weeks early. It would soon be over, and they could welcome their twins into the world.

The closer Ged got to the ward, the tighter the knot in his stomach became. Having called him earlier, the ward-sister was already primed and waiting. She helped him to gown up, then led him towards the delivery rooms. Her voice was soothing and reassuring as she explained the procedure and what to expect. His wife was already in Delivery 5, being prepped with the epidural.

He recognised the hysterical cries as they neared the delivery room – Julie's. He quickened his pace.

'Ah, Mr Steele.' The midwife looked up from massaging Julie's shoulders, relieved to see him. 'Look, Julie, your husband is here,' said the midwife in an effort to soothe and calm Julie. The medical team were busy flitting around, hooking up monitors, checking equipment and putting the screen in front of Julie's bloated belly so that she wouldn't see the incision when it was made. Ged quickly took Julie's hand, careful not to pull out the cannula, and covered her face with reassuring kisses, murmuring sweet-nothings to conceal his own nervousness,

'I'm here, babe, I'm here. You didn't think I would miss the main event, eh?' Julie gripped his hand. 'I'm scared...'

He looked deeply into her eyes as he spoke. 'Yeah, me too. But this is it, eh. Two becomes four.'

'We're ready to make the incision now, Mrs Steele. You might feel some tugging as we deliver the babies,' said the obstetrician.

The midwife felt Julie's shoulders tense beneath her fingers. 'There, there, dear. It will all soon be over, and you'll have your beautiful babies.'

It was no good – Julie began to shake.

The midwife endeavoured to engage her in a distracting conversation, 'Have you thought about any baby-names? You're going to need some soon.'

That seemed to help take Julie's mind from the delivery, and she was quick to take up the thread. 'Mostly just girls' names,' she replied. 'Classics, such as Rachael and Elizabeth. Perhaps Victoria. I think we need to meet the babies and see what their personalities are like.'

'What about boy-names?' the midwife continued.

'Strange as it may sound, but we haven't thought of any really,' Julie clarified.

Ged laughed, and entered the conversation,

'A house full of girls? No way! Just so long as their initials don't spell something funny, like my initials do. Been the bane of my life, it has.'

The midwife looked at him quizzically. 'Okay, explain...' she said.

'My initials are G-A-S – GAS. For Gerald Alan Steele. I've lived all my life being the butt of fart-jokes. Right from being at school. It gets tiring.'

'I can only imagine,' agreed the midwife, rolling her eyes.

The spluttered cries from a newborn baby interrupted the conversation, as the obstetrician delivered the first twin. He gently held the baby aloft so that Julie and Ged could see their first-born – tiny, wrinkled, slimed with blood and wax, and with a shock of black hair. 'Looks like you'd better think of a boy's name. Congratulations to you both, you have a little boy!'

The baby announced his arrival to the world with a loud, choking cry. The nurse gently took the baby boy and wrapped him in a swaddling blanket while the obstetrician clamped and cut the cord. Ged and Julie couldn't wait to meet their baby son, their first-born.

'Wow, he's got good lungs,' said Ged. 'Think this one's going to grow up to be a singer!'

'Then he shall be given a singer's name,' said Julie. 'How about Jon, without an 'h'? You know, after the singer from Bon Jovi...'

Ged grinned at Julie, then looked at their newborn, who was still exercising his lungs at full capacity. 'Jon without an 'h' it is, then. Welcome to the Steele family, Jon,' and he gave his new son the softest of kisses. He kissed Julie too, and whispered a tender 'I love you'.

'Shall we see what comes next?' asked the obstetrician. One of the assisting nurses took Jon without an 'h' to be weighed and checked over. This set Julie into a panic – she could feel her pulse starting to race, matched by the bips on the monitor. Ged sensed his wife's unease, and cradled her while the obstetrician began delivering baby number two. He also sensed the obstetrician's unease as he began speaking in hushed tones to the nurse assisting the delivery. Julie was starting to haemorrhage – they needed to get the second twin delivered quickly so that they could attend to Julie and stem the blood loss. Although Ged did his best to conceal the sense of urgency now filling the room, Julie picked up on the vibes and began to panic. Baby number two made no sounds and was more docile at delivery. The nurse immediately took the baby over to her assessment area to administer suction and massage. Tension-laden moments passed before they heard the second spluttered cry.

'Congratulations, you have another little boy. Like two peas in a pod, they are,' said the nurse. As she swaddled the second twin and passed him to the midwife, his tiny flailing arms knocked her pen off the counter-top. 'Well, it seems like this little one is going to be a writer,' she chuckled.

'Well, if he's going to be a writer, then his name needs to be William,' announced Ged. 'All the best writers are called William.' He looked at Julie, hoping that she approved of his choice. She nodded, and smiled wanly. Her dark eyes were glazed, leaden with exhaustion.

With her voice barely audible, Julie murmured, 'William is a beautiful name for a beautiful boy.'

Before being taken and put into their incubators, there was just time for a quick cuddle with the twins while the nurse took photographs of them with Ged and Julie.

And then Julie screamed – a deep, guttural, tension-releasing scream, before passing out.

CHAPTER 20

New Roles

The hustle and bustle of the hospital's morning routines had already started when Julie came to. She lay still for a moment, assessing the noises around her before slowly opening her eyes, adjusting them to the light. She realised that she was back on the maternity ward. The other three beds were in use; one next to her, and two opposite. The sheets on the bed next to her were crumpled, the bed and clear plastic cot empty. Gone to nurse the baby, maybe? The two beds opposite were occupied by sleeping mums, and sleeping babies in cots beside them. She could hear a breakfast trolley rattling somewhere close by. Ged was snoozing in an armchair by her side – he looked crooked and uncomfortable. Her body felt sore – very sore. And her boobs felt like over-ripe watermelons on the point of exploding. She desperately needed a drink of water. Julie suddenly realised that the twins were nowhere to be seen. Panic began to rise, making her breath come in sharp jags.

'Ged. Ged,' she growled under her breath, trying not to disturb the sleeping occupants. 'Ged…' She managed to suppress a rising scream.

He opened one eye, and smiled. 'Hey, mamma, that was some night.' He stretched and stood up to kiss her.

'Never mind that. Where are our babies? What's happened to them?' she hissed. Ged sensed the panic in her voice.

'They're okay. They're in incubators because they were born early. They're tiny so the obstetrician wanted to give them a bit of a boost.' He tried his best to sound reassuring. He poured her a glass of water and sat on the edge of her bed while she drank it down. She was desperately thirsty, and desperate to know what was going on. Ged poured her another glass, then filled her in with the blanks after she had passed out.

'I passed out? I don't remember...'

'Yep, you gave us quite a scare. Screamed the house down, then passed out.' Ged smoothed her hair away from her eyes and face, then tilted her chin upwards to kiss her. 'But it's all over now. We have our beautiful baby boys...'

'Jon without an 'h', and William?' she checked.

Ged smiled and chuckled. 'Yes, Jon without an 'h', and William. The singer and the writer.' He paused a moment before continuing, 'I was wondering about giving them both a second name. After all, we both have middle names.'

'Anything in mind?' Julie asked, feeling a little calmer.

'Hmm, well in honour of our first dance together, when we first met, I was wondering about adding some Quo names.'

'You mean like Rossi and Parfitt?' Julie cocked her head on one side, puzzled.

'No, silly. After their first names – Francis and Rick, well, Richard. So it would be Jon Francis, and William Richard Steele. What do you think?'

'I love it! Names with meanings behind them,' she exclaimed. 'Did you know that Francis is also my dad's real name? But everyone calls him Frank.' She beamed. 'So, when can we see Jon Francis and William Richard?'

'I'll go and speak to the midwife in a moment. She told me to let her know once you were awake so that she could check you over and bring you some pain relief.' He smiled, and took Julie's hand to reassure her.

Julie settled back into the deep, elevated pillows. Her belly hurt, and she felt wet and uncomfortable from the blood loss. She noticed a vase of yellow and white roses on her nightstand. The same colours as in the twins' nursery. 'Who brought the beautiful roses?' she asked.

'Moi. Do you like them? I got them from the hospital shop while you were sleeping. I chose white for purity, and yellow for sunshine. In honour of the twins.'

'God, you're such a poetic romantic, Ged Steele,' she said, gently squeezing his fingers.

'I know.' He grinned. 'A hopeless poetic romantic. Anyway, I'd better go and let the midwife know that you're awake.' He suddenly stopped dead in his tracks, 'Shit, I'd better call your mum and dad to let them know that they're grandparents! And I'll call me mam at the factory and get her to come to the phone so that I can tell her too. I won't be long.' And with a lightness that he hadn't felt in ages, Ged went off to find the midwife and a payphone.

The doors to the ward opened a short while later. It was Ged returning, accompanied by a midwife pushing a wheelchair.

'Both sets of grandparents are over the moon, and they'll be along this evening at visiting time. Everyone sends their love and congratulations,' said Ged, in a beaming, 'proud new father' way.

Julie nodded and smiled her affirmation. She noticed that it was a different midwife to last night; younger. Maybe they'd changed shifts. Hopefully this one wasn't as brusque as the older 'no-nonsense' midwife. Julie felt small, fragile. She needed some TLC, not brusqueness today.

'Well then, Mrs Steele, Julie, shall we go and get you cleaned up then find these babies of yours? I'll give you some pain relief as well.' The midwife had a lovely, soft Irish lilt. Julie felt instantly at ease, as they helped her out of bed and into the wheelchair.

After tending to Julie's needs, the midwife wheeled her through to meet up with Ged in the nursery area. The twins looked so tiny, so fragile, in their incubators. They twitched in their sleep. Jon had mercifully stopped crying – Julie recalled him being very vocal at birth.

'Can we hold them?' she asked.

'Not at the moment,' replied the midwife. 'The paediatrician wants their lungs to get stronger before they're lifted out. But you can put your hand through this opening to stroke them. You need to wash your hands first, though.' She manoeuvred Julie over to the sink, and Ged joined her in hand washing.

Nervously, with feather-soft touches, they stroked each of the twins, and held their tiny hands, the blue veins visible through their delicate skin.

'They're so tiny,' Ged whispered, in awe of his newborn sons. 'Like they'll break.'

The mere touch of the twins caused Julie's boobs to start leaking. Embarrassed, she tried to hide what was happening. The midwife gently reassured her that it was normal, and persuaded her to go and use the breast-pump to express the milk so that it could be given to the twins through tiny tubes. 'C'mon, I'll show you how. It's one of the best things you can do for them,' encouraged the midwife.

When the young midwife returned Julie to the ward, Julie looked red and flustered, her lips clenched tightly together. Ged geared himself for trouble.

'I am never, EVER doing that again,' she growled at Ged through clenched teeth, her tone firm. 'I felt like a cow on a milking machine. I've never been so embarrassed in all my life.'

'But what about the milk for the babies? You heard what the midwife said, it's one of...'

Julie intercepted Ged mid-sentence. 'Perhaps you didn't hear me the first time. I am never, EVER, doing that again.'

The mum in the bed opposite looked up at Julie's raised tone. Ged felt helpless – the heavy feeling of defeat had already returned. 'They're my babies too you know…I just want what's best for them…' His voice was low, soft. He looked at her, his eyes gently pleading.

'Then you bloody well go and express milk,' she sneered. 'Oh, and by the way,' she continued, 'while we're on the subject of "never-ever", I'm NEVER, ever, EVER going through having a baby again. NEVER.'

Her decisions, it seemed, were final.

End of discussion.

Ged left the hospital just after lunch armed with a list of "to do" jobs: call Col with the news, take a photo to Helena at the salon, stop by at the knicker-factory to see his mam and give her a photo, also arrange to pick them up for visiting, notify his shift manager that he would still need another night off, notify the Registrar of the babies' births and names. The list seemed endless. This was only Day One of parenthood and his head was already spinning. Ged conceded that his wife had every right to be grumpy after what she'd been through these past eight months, and last night. He eased the Mini out of the car park – he couldn't wait to get home and peel off his clothes and take a shower to eliminate the cloying hospital smell. He wound down the driver's side window to let in some fresh air as he entered the flow of traffic. *I'm a dad…*

After doing his list of chores, Ged stopped off at the chippie to grab something to eat – it was almost four o'clock by the time he finally arrived home. He kicked off his trainers in the hallway, recoiling as the smell from his feet hit him. The house already felt different – it felt ready to be filled by energetic little ones running around with aeroplanes. Ged realised that he was jumping ahead… *coffee, smoke and a shower, in that order…*

Before going for a shower, he stopped by their bedroom to get some fresh clothes. The bed looked tempting, and he had to fight hard to resist the overwhelming urge to lay down for a snooze, not trusting himself to wake up for visiting time. That would be fatal territory to wander into given Julie's present mood. However, he did notice two little icons from their courting days sat on the dresser, and that gave him an idea. He just needed to find Julie's sewing box.

When the two families arrived for evening visiting, they discovered that Julie's bed was empty. Ged noticed the older midwife from last night striding towards the group. *Oh no, what's up...?*

'Ah, these must be the new grandparents, congratulations.' Any brusque manner from last night had dissolved. Ged guessed that she must have been tired – after all, Julie can test anyone's patience...

'Where's Julie?' Ged asked, concern wavering his voice. The midwife took him by the elbow so that she could have a word with him on one side.

'She's expressing milk,' she explained, and winked at Ged.

'What? But...how? I mean, she...' Ged was completely baffled after Julie's determined outburst this morning.

'The poor girl was in so much discomfort when I came on shift. I encouraged her to give it one more go, and I sat with her. I showed her how to do it one boob at a time, and put a towel over each shoulder so that she could screen what she was doing. Be a bit more discreet, like. So that's where she is at the moment.' The midwife took Ged's wide-eyed look of relief as approval. 'Right then, shall we take the new grandparents to wash their hands and meet the twins? Look at 'em bouncing around like eager little puppies!'

CHAPTER 21

Homecoming

To Jon Francis Steele & William Richard Steele

Two hearts,
Now four.
Bound for Eternity.

Life is full of many roads,
Many directions, many journeys.
Some are well travelled, safe.
But never be afraid to change direction,
To explore the other side. To start a new journey.
You never know where it might lead.

But there's always one road,
The road to our door.
A road always open.
Of that, you can be sure.

G.A. Steele, August 1985.

'Do you think they'll like it?' asked Ged, as he folded the piece of paper and stuffed it into his back pocket.

Julie looked over at the sleeping twins sharing a crib, lying end to end, and wiped away a sentimental tear.

'They'll love it. I love it. Such beautiful words, Ged. You're such a penman.'

'I just wanted to write a few words, like. Let 'em know how much they mean to us. I thought I might go into town and get one of those printing companies to make it fancy, so we could frame it and hang it on the wall in here.' He joined Julie by the crib and put his arms around her shoulders. 'I got something else as well. Wait here.'

Ged returned a moment later with two familiar soft toys.

'Remember these?'

'Oh my God, they're our old teddies. How sweet, they have yellow and white neck bows!' she exclaimed, trying to keep her voice low so as not to disturb the sleeping twins.

'I had this idea to give them our first teddies as their first teddies,' he explained. 'But I've jazzed 'em up a bit, with bows to match their bedroom. Me mam taught me how to sew...' He held his head down, shy about being able to sew. 'So, your teddy, the one I won for you at the Summer Fayre, remember, can be for our first-born, for Jon. And then Jeff the Giraffe, the one you got for me, can be for Will.'

Julie took the teddies from him and brushed his cheek with a kiss, before gently placing them in the crib with the twins. Ged felt a glow of achievement, like he was getting off to a good start as a dad; like they were getting off to a good start as parents. He turned to take her in his arms, to savour the moment, but she'd already begun to slip away towards the door.

'Isn't it time for you to get ready for the night-shift?' she asked.

The magical moment had gone...

Julie sat for a moment and relished the quietness. She felt relieved that Ged was on the night shift on her first night home from the hospital – that way she wouldn't have to sleep with him, for a few nights, at least. She still felt fat and bloated. She didn't feel sexy. And she also felt very apprehensive. It was her first night home with the twins after the security of being in the hospital for the past ten days. The hospital had recommended that someone be with her to help for the first few nights, so her mum was going to call round on her way home from WI and stay tonight, and tomorrow night. Then Ged's mam would stay for a couple of nights after that. As much as she didn't always see eye to eye with her mother, Julie felt relieved that she was coming. Knowing her mother's penchant for tidiness, Julie quickly glanced around the kitchen. She was pleasantly surprised by how clean Ged had kept the house these past ten days, having expected to come home to a sink full of dirty dishes. But she also guessed that Ged's posse of female fans – her mother, his mam, and Col's mum – had taken it in turns to feed him. And judging by the huge pile of knitted bootees, matinee jackets and hats sat on the worktop, together with the half eaten apple and blackberry pie in the refrigerator, old Mrs Jessop from next door had also been for a visit. She smiled. *Ged was such a charmer.*

'Anyway, it's just a question of getting them into a routine. That's what the handbook recommends,' said Julie to her mother, while they were chatting over a cup of Horlicks. 'It also advises sleeping while the babies sleep, so I think that's what I'll do.' She yawned, and kissed her mum on the cheek. Julie noticed that her mother smelled of Chanel No. 5 – *of course, she's been to WI, so must impress!* 'I'm off up to bed. Night, night, Mum.' She paused momentarily. 'And thanks again for coming over.'

'Sensible advice, my dear,' replied Jean. 'But just remember – the babies haven't read the handbook. They'll do their own sweet thing…I'll come up and help you when they wake. I'll stay here on the sofa to give you some space. Good night, my dear.'

Julie didn't feel like she'd been asleep more than five minutes when she heard Jon begin to cry. She knew it was him, the loud one. Which, of course, disturbed William. He then began to grizzle. Julie got out of bed and went to them. Her stitches were itching, and she felt damp and sticky from the post-partum bleeding. *Ugh, I hate these big pads! Which one should I pick up first?* She was going to try and continue with breastfeeding, having managed to establish it at the hospital. As Jon was the first to start crying, she took him first, but couldn't get him to latch on properly. And it hurt. *Relax, relax, take a deep breath – you can do this...* Mercifully, Jean appeared by her side and took William to change him and stop him from grizzling while Julie fed Jon. Once Jon was satiated, they swapped babies, so that she could feed William while her mum changed Jon. Although only ten days old, and identical twins, she could already see their characters emerging. Jon seemed fractious and demanding, whereas William seemed gentler and more accepting.

Julie finally collapsed into an exhausted heap on her bed, the twins now fed, changed and sleeping. She looked at the clock – quarter to one. She crawled under the covers and awaited the next round of feeding and changing. As much as Julie didn't want her mother or mother-in-law taking over, she felt grateful for their offers of help – especially from Ged's mam, with her having experience of twins. Maybe for a couple of nights, until Ged had finished his round of nightshift, then she could do it by herself? Julie realised that she had to be careful of not burning her bridges too soon. This motherhood lark was certainly a lot more challenging than the magazines and parenting manuals painted it.

The next few days felt like an endless circus of midwife house-calls, visitors, feeding, changing, and crying. Julie noticed that Ged seemed almost relieved to be going to work. And Ged could tell that Julie was becoming irritated by the steady stream of visitors and well-wishers, when all she wanted was to be left in peace.

Reality was rearing its ugly head, yet again.

CHAPTER 22

Down and Out

April 1986

*C*lock on.
   Down.
   Down.
   Deeper.
   Down.
   Clock off.
   Go to the pub.

I hated the sound of the pit-cage as it rattled around me when we descended into the darkness of the earth. I had to close my eyes and select something from the juke-box in my mind, then focus on the images before me – a familiar guitar riff, wide-leg stance, head down, long hair shielding their guitars, as Status Quo powered their way into one of their anthems. It provided me with a momentary distraction from my fears.

   Down.
   Down.
   Deeper.
   Down.

I could never relax until we got to the bottom. The memory of losing my Uncle Brian in the '73 pit disaster always cast a shadow over this part of my working day. Me dad always told me to stop worrying. I was more likely to get hit by a van than for lightning to strike twice, he used to say. He said that I should be grateful I'd got a job down t'pit. It had a good pension and a coal allowance – it was all that any family man needed. Besides, it was one of those father-son things that was expected in the local community. If your dad was a miner, then it would follow that you would be a miner. It made the job of the school Careers Teacher a whole lot easier.

Clock on.

Down.

Down.

Deeper.

Down.

Clock off.

Go to the pub.

Night shift was best, though. There was something about night shift that was a bit more relaxed. Sometimes too relaxed. A welcome snooze, if I could manage to sneak off, and one of the other lads would cover my back. It sometimes felt like it was the only place that I could get a snooze in peace. Then the shift-foreman caught me. I tried to explain to him why I was so tired. But he's a hard-nosed sod. Add that to the verbal warning and the written warning for misconduct that already hung over my head...warnings that I've never told Julie about. Well, she's got enough on her plate with the little 'uns and stuff. I broke safety rules. If was too tired for work, then I shouldn't have turned in, he said. So, that's the end of my career (career!), pit pension and coal allowance.

Clock on.

Down.

Down.

Deeper.

Down.

CLOCK OFF. Thank you for your invaluable contribution to the National Coal Board, Mr Steele. Here's your P45. Begone. Never darken our doors again.

The pale, early April sun was creeping its way over the horizon as Ged walked up the side of the cottage towards the kitchen, his pace slow and heavy. He could just make out the muted silhouette of Julie pacing with one of the twins, and their stereo grizzling was clearly audible through the stone wall. Now was not the time to break the news of his new-found unemployment.

'Well, well, well, what's all this noise, young man? I've been to quieter Motörhead concerts,' he quipped, as he walked through the door. His gaze was met with the red-rimmed, tear-filled pleading eyes of his wife. 'Here, let me take him,' he said, as he gently lifted the sobbing Jon from her arms.

Julie's lips quivered as she nodded a silent, grateful thanks. Pent-up tears escaped and slowly slid down her cheeks. Ged kissed away her tears and gently nuzzled her nose.

'You go and get some sleep. I'll come and join you once the boys are settled.'

She had no energy left to protest, her footsteps leaden as she headed for the stairs.

Ged sat at the kitchen table and began quietly singing *Stairway to Heaven* as a lullaby to Jon while he cuddled and rocked him to sleep. Not wanting to be left out, Will began to grizzle again. Ged made a mental calculation of how many more months of teething pain lay ahead. It was a bleak thought.

After an exhausting hour of tears, bottle feeding and nappy changes, the twins finally settled. Ged wearily made his way upstairs with them, one at a time, and laid them in their cribs, before creeping out and heading to the bathroom to clean his teeth and get ready for bed.

Ged looked at his reflection in the mirror – dark rings sat below his eyes and his skin looked dirty and haggard. His eyeballs looked like a couple of red snooker balls. He soaked a washcloth in hot water and held it to his face, allowing the warmth to penetrate and relax, gratefully soaking up the heat. When was the last time that they had gotten a good night's sleep? He honestly couldn't remember.

He crept in beside the now sleeping Julie, careful to avoid catching her legs with his icy cold feet. Ged closed his eyes, but despite being desperately tired, sleep remained teasingly out of reach. His subconscious decided to have an internal conversation, back and forth, allowing him no space to interrupt – to tell it to *shut-the-fuck-up* because he *needed* to sleep. Ged entered that mind-numbing, catatonic state of being mentally awake with eyelids closed.

Resistance was futile. He let his mind get on with it.

Suddenly aware that it was daylight, Ged awoke with a start. As he allowed his senses to return, he noticed that it was almost two-thirty in the afternoon. He slowly levied himself out of bed and began to get dressed. Acutely aware that he still had to break the news of his unemployment to Julie, dark clouds of realisation crossed his mind – it was unlikely to be met with joy. A knot began to form in his stomach at the prospect.

The twins were asleep in their bouncy chairs, and Julie was busy rolling out pastry when Ged entered the kitchen. Her eyes looked a lot fresher than they did earlier, all traces of redness gone. He kissed her hair then busied himself with making some coffee.

'Mum dropped off some Bramleys, so I thought I'd make some little apple pies for you to take in your pack-up tonight.' Julie smiled at him, a picture of domesticity.

Ged noticed that his hands were shaking as he spooned the coffee granules into his mug. He hung his head, hiding his eyes behind his hair, then cleared his throat.

'I, er, I...I won't be going to work tonight.' His heart hammered in his chest. 'I, erm, I've been given the sack...'

Silence.

111

No response.

As Julie absorbed the information, her fingers began flexing and closing around the wooden rolling pin.

'Say something...' he added.

Ged suddenly felt the small bones in his left hand give way as the wooden rolling pin came crashing down on his knuckles. Stunned, he remained stock still. The second wave of pain forced him to move his hand out of the way and take up a defensive position.

Julie's eyes were wild, manic. 'Get out. Get the fuck out and don't come back,' she screamed. Her chest heaved in and out as she lifted the rolling pin again, ready to swipe at Ged. Will and Jon began to cry at the commotion. 'Go!'

Defeated, knuckles throbbing, Ged turned on his heels and made a dash for the kitchen door, just as the rolling pin glanced off his forehead, and clattered wood-on-wood against the frame before hitting the floor.

Ged hurriedly grabbed his denim jacket from the coat hooks in the hallway, denying himself the luxury of allowing tears to escape. His Polaroid camera was hanging next to the jacket, so he unconsciously took this as well. There was only one place that he could go – the sanctuary of his shed and allotment.

Once in the privacy of his shed, warm, salty tears were finally released. Ged sat in his old deck chair and looked at his hand. His knuckles were marbled red with shades of blue, and already beginning to swell. Gingerly, he tried to flex and move his fingers. Pain like he'd never before experienced shot up his arm and down his fingers. A wave of panic washed over him – if he went to the doctors or casualty, they were bound to ask questions. Weren't they? And he certainly couldn't go to his mam's – she would no doubt want to kill Julie if she knew the truth. If he did tell someone, would they alert Social Services? Ged's head throbbed as this plethora of scenarios ran around his mind. His answer – his *only* answer – was to do nothing. It would be his cross to bear.

He reached for the First Aid kit so that he could strap up his hand and fingers. As he unwrapped the roll of elastic bandage and cut some tape, his mind wandered. He realised that this wasn't the first time that Julie had laid into him.

His Lady Juliet had a dark side...

Without thinking, and without even realising why, Ged found himself taking a Polaroid of the injured hand and the bump on his forehead. He stared at the images as they emerged. Was this normal 'wifely' behaviour? He'd never noticed his mam lay into his dad like that. Sure, they occasionally exchanged a few angry words – but violence? Ged found himself making rational excuses for Julie's behaviour – she'd had a pretty rough year or so. Her pregnancy hadn't exactly been a walk in the park. And the twins could be difficult at times. Plus money was tight...

And about to get tighter.

Ged reached for his box of seed packets and took out his gardening diary – a meticulous collection of what had been planted, where, and which season. He remembered learning about the benefits of crop rotation in history lessons at school. He slid the pen from its little holster and used it to write the date of his injuries on the little white section at the bottom of each Polaroid, then hid them among the seed packets. Taking the photos somehow felt cleansing. Feeling suddenly compelled to offload his emotions, he flipped over the gardening diary to the clean pages at the back and began writing, recalling any other instances of her cathartic behaviour, be it calculated or reactionary. Ged looked at the page and read over his notes. A tear escaped. But the tear was for Julie – he felt like he was her betrayer. Betraying her by committing her secrets to paper. He snapped the diary closed and put it with the photos in the seed box, before returning the box to the shelf.

His stomach gnawed at him. Putting his primal instinct for fear to one side, he reluctantly allowed his primal instinct for nourishment to take over.

He headed home.

Ged recognised his parents' coats and shoes in the hallway before hearing their voices coming from the sitting room. He hesitated at the door before going into the lion's den. Word of his dismissal had obviously been beating along the colliery jungle-drums and had reached Jud.

'You daft twat – what the bloody 'ell w'you thinking?' bellowed Jud before his son had barely entered the room. Jud strode towards him. Ged flinched, half expecting his dad to give him a clip around the ear like he used to when he was little, and was relieved to only be shaken by the shoulders. 'You've got a young family. And now you've gone and got the sack.' Jud's face was inches from his son's. 'You've…' He noticed the bump, then noticed Ged's bandaged hand. He looked quizzically at his son.

Without even batting an eye, or betraying Julie, Ged said, 'Oh, this. Just been to the allotment and the shed door slammed shut on my hand. Then I stumbled over and stood on the rake, which whacked me on the head.' Ged mimicked the actions, his movements exaggerated. 'Like summat from a Laurel and Hardy film, it was.' He tried to laugh it off, hoping Jud would see the funny side and stop prying. The deflection worked, providing a much needed release of tension so that the family could figure out a plan to help. As reckless as Ged had been, his parents, being the parents of twins themselves, could relate to the debilitating tiredness that accompanied stereo-parenting.

Once Ged's parents had gone, and the twins were bathed and settled, Ged and Julie, having reached a truce, crawled into bed.

'Look at us – we're like a pair of old farts sat here in bed with a mug of Horlicks,' quipped Julie, nudging Ged coyly, playfully.

Unsure of Julie's change in mood, Ged's brow furrowed as he spoke. 'I'm really sorry about all this mess, Ju. Sorry that I've lost my job. I'll find something soon, I promise.'

Julie put her mug of Horlicks to one side and took Ged's hands in hers, careful to avoid any pressure on the injured knuckles. She moved her hands to his face and touched his lips with her fingertips, then moved towards him to kiss him deeply, passionately. Ged felt something being rekindled between them. Julie hadn't made a move towards him since the twins were born, eight months ago. Even before that – the rejection started during her tortuous pregnancy. Any attempts that he'd made to make love to Julie had been pushed away, or refused, or screamed at. Ged could barely remember the last time that they'd shared any intimacy.

He put his mug of Horlicks to one side and allowed Julie's hands and kisses to travel down his body, relishing the touch and feel of her lips, of her fingers, as they explored and caressed.

Apology accepted.

CHAPTER 23

Windfall

May 1986

The Sunday newspaper lay open at the sports section, amid the myriad of kitchen table detritus. Ged's dad shook the toast crumbs from the page as he looked back and forth from the football results to the cross-ridden strip of paper in his hand – a deep crease of concentration furrowed his brow. He sat for a moment, not quite believing. He counted again. Sure enough, the evidence was there in black and white.

'Beryl,' he bellowed. No reply. He bellowed again.

'What the bloody 'ell you shouting at?' she half-shouted in reply as she poked her head around the bedroom door. 'You'll wake the dead. What's up?'

'Quick, quick, come here,' replied Jud, his tone urgent.

She put on her fluffy slippers and quilted dressing gown, and clomped down the stairs to find Jud sat at the kitchen table. His hands were visibly shaking.

Concern piqued in Beryl's voice. 'Oh my God, love, what's up? You're as white as a sheet…'

'Check these numbers, will ya,' he urged, pointing to the newspaper in front of him.

Realising that the urgency wasn't medical, Beryl took the liberty of lighting a cigarette before sitting down beside Jud, her chair scraping on the linoleum floor. She grabbed the newspaper.

Jud drummed his fingers nervously while his wife looked back and forth from newspaper to strip of paper, drawing deeply on her cigarette as she concentrated on counting the crosses on Jud's football coupon. She looked at Jud. No words would come.

'It's...you know, it's...right, in't it?' Jud stumbled for the right words, fearful that he'd made a mistake – fearful that this moment would be snatched from them.

'Yes, love. It's right...' her voice trailed off. Shakily, she stubbed out her cigarette in the overfull ashtray and looked deeply into Jud's coal-dust rimmed eyes as if searching the recesses of his soul. She gently took his calloused hands in hers and pulled him towards her, her eyes brimming over.

'For God's sake, put that ticket somewhere safe...' she said, in the quietest voice she'd ever used.

*

Frank Bryant poured hot water into the cafetière, steam billowing up into his face. He removed his glasses and cleaned them with his neatly pressed white handkerchief before adjusting them back on nose. He turned to his daughter, smiling broadly.

'So, they've won how much?' he asked Julie again, not quite believing his ears.

'Almost one hundred and seventy thousand,' she confirmed. 'Isn't it great!'

'Well, good for them – yes, it's wonderful news. Tell them from me if they need any investment advice I can point them towards the right people.' Frank turned his attention to plunging the cafetière and pouring three cups of morning coffee.

'I will. But seriously, Dad, they're trying to keep it quiet. It's been a really tough week while they got it all confirmed and stuff.' She filled up the biscuit barrel with an assortment of chocolate biscuits and creams. 'Anyway,' she continued, 'they want to give some of it to Ged, Brenda, Lynette and Sharon, so that means Ged and I will be able to pay off the mortgage on the cottage. It couldn't come at a better time for us, with me not being back at the salon yet and Ged still out of work.' They walked together from the kitchen which opened out into the sun-lounge, to join Julie's mum. Frank placed the tray of cups and side plates onto the coffee table, while Julie brought the biscuit barrel.

'Any news on the job front? For Ged, I mean,' Frank asked, concerned that his son-in-law was still unemployed. 'It's been what, a month now?'

'He's trying really hard, Dad, but employers seem wary of taking him on. That said, he has an interview next Tuesday – Assistant Caretaker at Castle Ridge Infants & Primary. The pay's quite low, but it's better than nothing. If he gets it, he'll start in August, in preparation for the new school year.'

'Well, if he needs a reference, just let me know,' said Frank, trying to sound supportive.

Julie's mum busied herself with rocking the twins in the pram, feigning disinterest, but curious nonetheless,

'So, what other plans do Ged's parents have? I mean, well, they're not really designed to deal with so much money, are they, their sort?' she asked.

Julie could feel her hackles rising. 'What do you mean, "their sort"?' she asked, through gritted teeth.

'You know full well what I mean, young lady – you can't make a silk purse out of a sow's ear...' Jean defended, picking up her coffee cup.

'Well, if you must know, they're going to take early retirement at the seaside. They plan on buying a little bungalow in Skeggy. They've always enjoyed going there. The fresh air will be good for Jud's lungs,' retorted Julie, suddenly protective of her in-laws. 'They're going to start looking during the summer holidays, once the girls have finished school. Even their Brenda's going to move with them.'

'I always thought the "nouveau riche" went to Spain, not *Skegness*,' Jean added snidely, correcting her daughter's colloquialism.

'Oh, for God's sake, Mother, get down off your snobby high-horse, will you!' Julie could feel her pulse racing wildly – why couldn't her mother just be happy for them?

Frank knew it was time to intervene before it turned into a full-on mother-daughter cat fight,

'Well, I think it's wonderful news, Julie. You must convey our congratulations to them. And it's great for you and Ged too – it'll give your little family such a much needed boost.'

'Thanks, Dad,' said Julie, trying to calm down. She changed her tone towards her mother, softening her voice. 'Be happy for them, Mum. Let them enjoy their good fortune. Besides, these little guys get to benefit from that luck, and that can only be good, right?' She looked at her mum eye to eye, and then to the pram.

'Yes, you're right. I'm sorry, dear...' Jean lowered her eyes towards the sleeping twins, innocent players in the game of life. She paused before continuing, to ensure that her voice had a tone of genuine warmth rather than one of cool jealousy. 'Send them my heartiest congratulations too. You're right – they deserve this bit of good fortune.'

CHAPTER 24

Date Night

July 1986

The hum and chatter of the Friday evening pub crowds was already beginning to grow when Ged and Julie exited the ABC cinema. Julie immediately shaded her eyes with her hands as she made the transition into the last dregs of sunlight.

'Fancy a pint in the Wagon before getting somethin' to eat?' Ged asked, eager to make the most of the evening.

'Nah, I'm starving,' Julie replied. 'Popcorn isn't that filling. Let's eat.'

'So, what does my Lady Juliet desire? Chinese or Indian?'

'Hmm, Indian...I haven't had a good curry in ages,' she replied.

'Okay, curry it is. There's a good place on Chatsworth Road, let's go there.'

Ged led her by the hand as they crossed over the pelican crossing to head into the centre of town. He relished the feel of her soft hand in his, re-awakening his slumbering, suppressed passion.

'So, what did you think of *Aliens*? I noticed that it made you jump in places,' he teased.

Julie punched him playfully in the ribs.

'Well, it was a scary film,' she exclaimed, defending her jumpiness. 'That said, the action was absolutely amazing. Those aliens are really good actors,' she joked.

'Sigourney Weaver was pretty cool too...deserves an Oscar. She's a brilliant actress. The lengths she went to, to save that kid, Newt. Not even her own kid,' Ged noted.

'Guess that's just the lengths you go to, especially when kids are involved. How far would you go to save the twins?' she asked, suddenly becoming philosophically maternal.

'Aye, true. I'd walk over hot coals for 'em...' He burst out laughing, realising his coal-mining faux-pas.

'Remember when you took me on a date to see Alien, when we were first courting?'

Ged laughed as he cast his mind back.

'How can I forget! At least you didn't break my fingers this time.' He wriggled the fingers on his left hand. 'Remember – you grabbed them in shock when the alien burst out of John Hurt's chest?'

'Oh yes, then you screamed and everyone shouted "shh". Some even threw their popcorn at you!' She shook her head as she laughed at the long-forgotten memory, her dark hair catching the breeze.

'Well, if I remember rightly, my fingers were bandaged up at the time, after I'd cut them badly on the machinery at work. That's why I screamed – it hurt!' Ged joined in with her laughter, and slung his arm over her shoulders, drawing her in for a kiss.

They strolled hand in hand, chatting, looking in shop windows, relishing the rekindled closeness of their courting days. Months of tiredness – endless rounds of feeding, changing nappies, playing, teething, all on very little sleep, had taken its toll on them. Ged's mam, in her infinite wisdom as mother, mother-in-law, and mother of twins herself, had decided to take charge. Beryl had already voiced her concerns to Ged about Julie's well-being. She could see that her daughter-in-law was on the edge of exhaustion, yet Julie refused to ask for help, either through pride or ignorance. Even Ged himself had recently lost his job through falling asleep at work. Enough was enough. In an effort to offer them some respite, Beryl had insisted on babysitting so that they could go out for the evening. It was the least she could do before she and Jud moved to Skegness.

It was a welcome break.

After setting Beryl into a taxi home, Ged and Julie checked in on the peacefully sleeping twins before heading towards their bedroom. As they neared the bedroom door, Ged took Julie by the hands and drew her towards him, his mouth searching for hers. Still heady from the pints of lager with their meal, she eagerly responded to his kisses and began to unbutton Ged's shirt. She stroked his chest, his dark hair silky to the touch. Her fingertips sensed the beating of his heart, and she could feel her own pulse quickening, fuelled by alcohol and endorphins. Ged deftly opened the bedroom door and led Julie inside. His hands expertly opened the buttons of her shirt, then eased his way inside to caress her soft skin and the curve of her flesh.

'Stop...' Julie forcefully pushed Ged away, the unexpected action causing him to lose his balance, his head narrowly missing the corner of the wardrobe.

'Wha...?'

'Stop. Please. I can't go through with this.' She backed away from Ged, her hands visibly shaking.

A bewildered look crossed Ged's face. 'But, I don't understand. I thought...' He sat on the edge of the bed, his legs unable to hold him. 'I thought that things were getting better between us...' His own hands started shaking with nervousness and adrenaline.

Feeling exposed, Julie closed the buttons of her shirt.

'I know.' Her voice became small and she hung her head, using her hair as a shield. 'But I just can't, Ged. I'm sorry...' She came and sat beside him on the bed and took his hand.

'Don't you love me anymore? Is that it?' Ged moved his hand towards her, to caress her hair, to look at her face.

To search for answers.

He recoiled as she slapped him hard across the cheek.

'I-said-don't-touch-me...'

'But...I just want to know what's going on. Why won't you let me make love to you any more? I don't understand.' He could feel the heat from tears building behind his eyes. 'We had a lovely evening together. I hoped we might...you know...get things back on track. Get our love life back on track...We've only made love once since...since...'

She hit him again. 'You just don't get it, do you? After what I went through – carrying the twins, the pain. Being torn apart. I can't go through that again...I can't...I can't take the risk.'

Ged's voice became taut with frustration and confusion. 'But you're back on the pill, aren't you? And I'm sure I've got some jonnies somewhere...'

Julie glared at him, answering through gritted teeth. 'I was on the pill last time. Or have you forgotten?'

Ged's shoulders sagged.

'I love you, Julie. I would never do anything to hurt you. But this is killing me. I want to touch you. I want to make love to you. I'm sick of having to toss-off in the bathroom...'

That got Julie's attention – she looked at him, taken aback. 'You do that? You toss-off?'

'Well, what else can I do? I'm only human. Look – I can understand your fears, but we can't go on like this. Why did you never say anything?' Ged hung his head, deflated. The ticking of the bedside clock seemed to fill the room, the only sound to be heard bar their breathing. 'What if I have the snip? So that I fire blanks. We can use all the protection you feel you need, Julie, but I want – *need* – to be able to make love to you. For us to make love to each other. Please...will you think about it?' Ged shuddered as his gaze met with Julie's hard stare.

She gave him a curt nod to signal acceptance of his suggestion, before standing at the bedroom door to encourage his exit.

'I think you'd better sleep on the sofa tonight...'

CHAPTER 25

Milestones

8th August 1986

Fat bees lazily bumbled their way through the delicately hanging trumpets of the foxgloves, their black and gold bodies a striking contrast to the purples and pinks of the flowers they were invading, while the brightly coloured wings of Red Admiral butterflies gently winked as they fluttered among the borders. The tall, red and yellow spike-blooms of the red hot pokers provided a striking backdrop to the blue of the cornflowers and vibrant pink of the peonies. A small lawn of bright green, neatly clipped grass added a foreground to the overall image. The cornfields beyond were ripe, at their golden peak, ready to be harvested. Ged stood at the top of the garden, his back against the cool stonework of the kitchen wall, and surveyed his kingdom, his handy-work. He inhaled the early evening air, just beginning to fill with the heady perfume from the hollyhocks and honeysuckle. All was well with the world. His sense of tranquility was broken by the sound of his father-in-law's voice as he came out of the kitchen, his arms laden with packs of chicken legs and burgers.

'Well, that's the coals ready on the barbecue, we can start putting the meat on. Where do you want the chiller for the beer?'

Jud appeared behind Frank, carrying the plastic bath belonging to the twins in one hand, and two large packs of ice-cubes in the other.

Ged looked around the garden to locate a shady spot.

'Over there, under the old lilac tree looks to be the best. It'll be in shade for the rest of the evening,' he instructed.

'Garden looks great, by the way,' Frank complimented. 'Perfect evening for the twins' first birthday party. Wow, time flies, eh?'

Ged smiled at his father-in-law, a smile laden with pride. 'Yep, it sure does.' Feeling puffed up, he returned to his task of setting out the little tables and chairs on the lawn, on loan from Frank's Rotary Club.

While Frank and Jud busied themselves with the barbecue, Jean and Beryl began laying out the accompanying food on the little trestle table at the side, choreographed, of course, by Jean, for looks and colour coordination. Her tables, no matter how simple, were a work of art. She fussed with the cakes as the centrepiece – two gloriously decorated, round cakes in the shape of Noddy and Big Ears, the twins' favourite bedtime storybook.

'There, all done. And just in time – here come the rest of the family.' Jean waved across the garden as her brother, Jack, and sister, Betty, arrived along with Frank's siblings, Eric and Babs, and their spouses.

Beryl noticed how highly polished the Halliwells and Bryants looked, with their fine clothes and jewellery. Even Jack, who was rarely seen out of his farming attire, looked smart in his corduroys and tweed. Old money. Beryl briefly wondered if she and Jud would ever get used to looking posh all the time, now that they had a bit of money…

Jean interrupted her thoughts.

'I hear from our Julie that the house-hunting went well in Skegness.'

Beryl smiled. 'Yes, we had a lovely ten days. Just got back last night. We've had an offer accepted on a four bedroomed detached bungalow.' Sensing Jean's underlying jealousy, Beryl couldn't resist adding a bit more spice to the conversation. 'Brand new, it is. Really swanky. The agent says that we'll be able to move in really quickly, with us being cash buyers.'

'How lovely. You must be really excited at the prospect?' fussed Jean.

'Oh, aye. Can't wait to move away. Get some clean, sea air instead of this mucky coal-dust.' Beryl was on a roll, eager to expel more information. 'Our Bren's movin' wi'us. She's already got a job lined up at Butlin's Holiday Camp. And we've managed to get the twins in at the local secondary school. It has a really nice sixth form. If all goes well, we should be in by the beginning of September, before the girls start school.'

'Really. Well, I do hope that you won't forget to come back and visit us,' laughed Jean, trying her hardest to sound sincere.

Beryl laughed along with her, then with equal faux-sincerity said, 'And you're always welcome to come and stay.'

Jean touched Beryl on the arm. 'Anyway, dear, better go and mingle and say "hi" with the family…'

'Aye, of course.' Beryl grinned to herself – would they have to start saying *"hi"* instead of *"ay-up"* now that they were money-folk? She shook her head in answer to her own question. 'Nah,' she muttered, as she rummaged in her handbag for her ciggies.

'Penny for 'em…'

Ged looked up to see a suitably chilled bottle of Newcastle Brown Ale being thrust under his nose. Col took a deep refreshing swig from his own bottle before pulling up a deck chair to sit beside his mate.

'Cheers.' The two pals clinked their bottles together.

Ged looked out across the garden at the birthday party, now in full swing. Even old Mrs Jessop from next door had joined the throng, bringing one of her famous apple and blackberry pies. His gaze settled on his wife, who was sat on a picnic blanket with Helena, her girlfriend, Lauren, and Ged's three sisters. They were all laughing, and playing a game with the birthday boys, Jon and Will, trying to get them to clap along to *Radio Ga Ga*.

'Who'd have thought it, eh – Gerald Steele, the scum of Castle Ridge, now has all this?' Col elbowed his best friend playfully.

'I know – I was just thinking that. Lucky bastard, aren't I?' laughed Ged.

Col pointed towards the group with his bottle. 'Do you think you'll have any more kids?'

'Nah, we've done our bit for the gene pool. Besides, I couldn't put Ju through that again. Going to have me balls disconnected.'

Col looked at him quizzically.

Ged mimicked a scissor action in the area of his crotch.

'I'm going to have the snip. And no, before you ask, it won't make me any less of a man.' He grinned shyly, aware that he'd perhaps divulged too much personal information.

Col laughed. 'I never said a word...Anyroad, congrats on getting the job at school. When d'ya start?'

'Next week. And no fuck-ups this time. Gotta keep me nose clean on this one. Plus, Julie's going to go back to work at the salon part-time – her mam's offered to look after the twins two days a week, and I can have them on Saturdays. So it's a win-win. We'll get some money coming in again, plus she'll get a break from the kids. These past few months have been a fuckin' nightmare.' Ged took a swig of his beer as if to wash away the mental burden.

'Gonna be weird wi'out yer mam'n'dad, though. But they deserve a bit o'good luck, eh?' Col smiled across to Beryl, and she waved to him.

'Aye, it's going to take some getting used to. But I'm happy for 'em. They've had an offer accepted on a rayt nice place, a bungalow. Besides, we'll get free holidays,' laughed Ged.

Col laughed along with him. 'Aye, free holidays to sunny Costa-del-Skeggy – life just don't get any better! By the way, there's a pool tournament on at The Cricketers on Sunday – are you up for it? We haven't been to the pub on a Sunday for ages.'

'Nah, soz, mate. Ju's been a bit out of balance lately. Think I'd best give it a miss...' Ged could see the disappointment in his best friend's eyes. 'But deffo next Sunday, eh? I'll try and make it for then.'

Col shrugged, fully aware that Ged would most likely find some excuse.

'Just whenever you can make it, eh. Family first. Anyway...' Col held his bottle aloft to clink it onto Ged's, 'here's to new beginnings, eh. Here's to the future...'

Ged returned the clink. 'Aye, here's to the future...'

*

'I saw you in the garden this evening. I saw you laughing with Col – mimicking having the snip. I suppose you think it's funny?' Julie busied herself with putting away the dishes and cutlery that Ged was drying, the ceramic and metal clattering as she rammed them into the cupboards and drawers.

'What? No! No, it wasn't like that at all...' Ged defended.

Julie turned towards him, and held the carving knife to his crotch.

'I hope not. Otherwise I can do it for free...'

Part 2

CHAPTER 26

Jon Francis Steele

08.08.1985 – 29.07.1990

*J*on died today.

  It was a tragic accident, they said. No-one was to blame.

A tragic accident?

  It wasn't Ged's fault. He was having a Sunday afternoon snooze after he'd been to the pub with Col – their 'best-mate' time.

  It wasn't my fault. I was busy in the kitchen painting my nails. The salon makes a mess of the nail varnish, you see. It's my 'me' time.

  It wasn't Will's fault. He was busy playing with his diggers and trucks in the sand box. He was just being a little boy.

  It wasn't the ice-cream van driver's fault. He was busy serving old Mrs Jessop.

  It wasn't the XR3i driver's fault. He was just out for a Sunday afternoon cruise around the lanes. Jon just ran out in front of him.

  And it wasn't Jon's fault. He just wanted an ice-cream, so he ran out into the road when he heard the dingle of Mr Frosty's ice-cream van. He didn't even have any money. Just went for an ice-cream.

  It wasn't anybody's fault.

A tragic accident.

Goodbye, my little one.
I love you, Jon.

CHAPTER 27

Downhill

*T*iny white finger tips clawed and scraped.

   Clawed and scraped and scratched.

Clawed and scraped and scratched.

Claw. Scrape. Scratch.

Frantic.

Blood.

Blood seeped from the tips, staining the white satin.

Claw. Scrape. Scratch.

Frantic.

'Mummy...'

Tiny white finger tips clawed and scraped and scratched their way through the satin, through the wood, through the earth.

Bones, mingled with blood, mingled with the cold, damp earth.

'Mummy...'

The surface was close now. Almost there.

Tiny white finger tips clawed and scraped.

Breaking the surface of the skin.

Breaking the surface of the earth.

Soft grass. Cool air. Fresh.

'Mummy!'

'*Jon!*'

Julie sat bolt upright in bed, her sleep tee-shirt drenched with sweat. She felt a tiny hand tugging at the bedding. She recoiled, disorientated, a scream rising in her throat.

'It's me, Mummy, it's Will. My bed's wet.' Will tugged again.

Roused by the commotion, Ged turned on the bedside lamp and ran his hands over his face in a vain attempt to wipe away sleep.

Julie pulled her knees up to her chin and locked her arms around them. She began rocking back and forth.

'Jon. Jon. He's trying to get out...I felt his hand. I heard him call my name.' She threw back her head and began wailing uncontrollably.

Unnerved and confused by his mother's outburst, Will took a step back and also began to cry.

'Mummy, it's Will. I'm wet.'

Ged leapt out of bed and scooped up his son, eager to allay his fears.

'It's okay, Will. Come on, I'll help you.' He took Will into the bathroom to wash him down, then went to get some clean pyjamas. Will was sat on the floor huddled under the towel when Ged returned.

'Mummy scared me. Did she see a ghost? Did she see Jon?' he asked.

'No. I think y'mam just had a very bad dream, Will, that's all. You know there's no such thing as ghosts, right?'

Will looked at his dad, unsure. He shrugged his shoulders.

'She's feeling really sad. We all are. But Jon can't come back. He's asleep with the angels.' Ged looked at Will, hoping that he understood. 'Anyway, let's get you back to bed. C'mon, we need to change your bedding.'

'Can I sleep with you and mummy tonight? Please?' Will's eyes pleaded with his dad's. Without waiting for an answer, Will went and crawled into their bed.

Their empty bed.

After making sure that Will was snug and settled, Ged went downstairs to look for Julie. Seeing the glow from the reading lamp in the living room, he pushed open the door. Julie was curled up on the sofa, gently cradling Jon's photo album, her fingers tracing the outline of his face. She looked up, her eyes manic yet her face serene.

'He is okay, isn't he? He can't feel any pain? He must be scared. It's dark and cold and lonely in the ground.'

Ged held out his hand in a bid to calm and reassure her. 'Yes, he's okay, Julie. He's with the angels, or whatever you think they are. They'll look after him.'

'You're lying! You're just saying that...' Julie set the album to one side on the sofa and sprang at Ged like a wild-cat. 'This is all your fault. You should have been there for him. You should have been with him in the garden instead of laying piss-drunk on the sofa.' With fists flailing, she laid into Ged. Blow after blow, pounding his head and his shoulders.

His defences kicked in, and he managed to take Julie by the wrists, then pin her arms by her side. He held her close, held her tight, all the while soothing her with reassuring words until her sobs subsided. He caressed her hair and kissed away her tears. Her eyes felt hot. Ged gently took her in his arms and carried her upstairs, laying her in bed beside Will. Exhausted, she was already asleep by the time he placed the covers over her.

Before turning off the lamp, Ged looked at his sleeping family. He felt a swirl of adrenaline run through his veins and pump through his heart, causing it to jag. Funny how sharp words hurt much more than pounding fists.

He glared heavenwards. 'Is there any fuckin' wonder I don't believe in you?' he hissed through clenched teeth.

Looking back, I thought I could pinpoint the exact moment when our life started going downhill. I thought it was after the twins were born.

But it was the exact moment when the Mr Frosty ice-cream van came around. That's when it started to go seriously downhill.

A squeal of laughter.

A squeal of tyres.

The scream of horror as old Mrs Jessop picked up the tiny, smashed body of our Jon.

The scream of horror as Julie saw Jon's tiny, smashed body...

Yep, that's when downhill started. At 16:05 to be exact, when the medics pronounced Jon dead at the hospital. There was no more that they could do for him, they said. They'd tried their best.

And of course, it's all my fault. She's even said as much.

If only I hadn't have been sleeping off a session from the pub instead of taking care of the kids in the garden while they played in the sandbox.

If only I hadn't been sleeping off a session from the pub instead of going and getting them an ice-cream like dads are supposed to...

If only...

FAB, that had been our Jon's favourite ice lolly, strawberry and vanilla, dipped in chocolate with hundreds of those coloured bits on. Bits that used to get stuck in the snot that constantly ran from his hay-fevered nose.

It isn't enough for Julie that we still have Will – being Jon's identical twin is a constant reminder that one is missing.

Yep, that was when life really started to go downhill...

Without brakes.

*

'Thanks for stopping by, Dr Wilson. Appreciate it.' Ged helped Dr Wilson slip into her coat.

'You did the right thing to call the surgery, Mr Steele. Grief and trauma can present themselves in many different ways. It's not unusual for someone to want to shut themselves away from the world – sometimes for days, sometimes for weeks.' Dr Wilson laid a reassuring hand on Ged's arm, then bent down to pick up her medical bag. 'All you can do is help her to get through one day at a time. Remain supportive – try and give her something positive to look forward to. I'm sure she'll soon get out of bed.'

'Thanks, Doc, that sounds like good advice.' Ged scratched his unshaven chin thoughtfully, the stubble making a rasping sound. 'I'll talk to her business partner – maybe she could visit, and encourage Ju to go back to work, even if only part time. Get back on the horse, so to speak. Plus, it's Will's birthday next week.'

'Well, hopefully these antidepressants will help. And I've also prescribed some sleeping tablets. She needs time to rest and heal mentally.'

Ged held out his hand to shake Dr Wilson's.

'She's lucky to have you, Mr Steele. And Will too. You're their rock.'

He closed the front door and leaned against it, then squeezed away the tears welling in the corners of his eyes.

Rocks don't cry.

They're not allowed to.

CHAPTER 28

Slash

D espite having left the windows of the Mini slightly open and parking it in the shade, the heat from the interior almost sent Julie reeling as she opened the door to get in. It had been a nightmare in the Co-op. Everyone was either hot or fractious, or both. Or bumping into her with their trolley. Or fawning over her after "her tragedy". The radio said that it was one of the hottest days so far this summer. *Yep, they got that one right…* She was looking forward to getting home, escaping from the pitying looks and intrusive stares.

She started the engine, wound down the window, and sat back in the seat with the blower on full-cold, allowing the chilled air to blow over her. She closed her eyes. It had been a tortuous few weeks since losing Jon. But mercifully since Dr Wilson's visit, she'd slowly been able to face each new day. One day at a time, that's what the doctor had said. Take one day at a time. The tablets had been a God-send – she'd been able to sleep through the night, and then make it through the day. And good old Helena, always there for her, had encouraged her to go back to work part time. Give her something else to think about. And, of course, Ged had kept the house in order, and taken care of Will. Talking of which, time to head home with the ice-cream and shopping.

Julie eased the car into gear, and pressed "play" on her radio-cassette player, not quite sure what tape she'd left in there. *Perhaps not a good idea to leave them in the player when it's so hot.* Julie immediately regretted turning up the volume as the opening guitar riff to *Sweet Child o'Mine* broke through the road noise – a track that cut deep into her fresh, raw emotions. It reminded her of Jon. She quickly ejected the tape and threw it over her shoulder onto the back seat. *Fuck you, Axl Rose!*

Ged moved his deck chair into the shade, accidentally knocking over his empty beer bottle in the process. It landed with a clatter on the paving stones of the little seating area just in front of the kitchen window.

'Shit!' He looked over at Will, who was languishing in his paddling pool, to see whether he'd heard his expletive. No reaction. Will seemed totally absorbed with something in the water. Ged pushed his sunglasses up the bridge of his nose and closed his eyes, allowing the warmth of the sun to wash over him. That was the beauty of his job as assistant caretaker at the Infants School – he got the same holidays as the kids and Will. And he was especially grateful that they were on holiday right now. Spending some quality time together was just what the family needed. All in all, it had been a shit couple of weeks.

Will observed his dad for a few seconds – the element of surprise was vital for his funny joke to work. Although Will couldn't see his dad's eyes from behind the sun glasses, he guessed that Ged was grabbing forty winks. Will quietly eased himself out of the paddling pool, dripping water onto the grass, making sure that the loaded water pistols were behind his back out of sight. He loved stalking things. He often stalked birds as they hopped between the rose bushes in the border, or foraged around the roots of the trees at the bottom of the garden. He was ace at stalking. He lifted the water pistols, and took aim...

'Argh! What the...?' gargled Ged, as the jets of cold water shot him in the face and chest. His deck chair toppled dangerously backwards as he jumped up in shock.

'Gotcha! Gotcha!' Will continued squirting his dad while running backwards out of arm's reach. Quick as a flash, Ged sprang towards the garden hose and turned it on, spraying Will.

'You want a water fight, you got one, buddy! Charge...' hollered Ged, as he continued his water barrage over Will.

Will made a run for the paddling pool and jumped in to refill his water pistols. He lifted the plastic pistols ready to shoot, when something caught his eye. His mother appeared around the corner of the house. A mischievous gleam twinkled in his eye. He couldn't resist – he just had to let both barrels go and shoot his mother with jets of water. Buoyed by Will's bravado, Ged put his finger over the end of the hosepipe to create a gentle shower of cooling raindrops over his wife. She threw her handbag and shopping out of harm's reach, and basked in the cool, refreshing impromptu garden shower, relishing the moment – her earlier mood washed away by the water. It was good to be home. The tablets were doing their job.

The evening air began to fill with the sweet smell of honeysuckle, its fragrance pungent and heavy. The honeysuckle vine covered a good portion of the rear of the cottage, making maintenance difficult, but no-one had had the heart to cut it down. The glue that held the house and its contents together. Julie sneezed lightly at the perfume. Ged put his hands together in mock-prayer, and bowed his head towards her.

'Bless you, my child!' He looked at her, his smile warm and broad. The honey-golden rays of the setting sun were acting as natural highlights in her dark hair. He reached across for her hand and kissed the back of it. He missed these moments of closeness.

'That was one mean chicken salad, Mrs Steele. It made a nice change to sit out here and eat tea. I think someone else enjoyed the evening too – look...' He nodded his head in the direction of Will, who had fallen asleep on the red and white gingham tablecloth spread out on the lawn, his thumb stuck firmly in his mouth. Remnants of their garden picnic were strewn all around him. Julie reciprocated Ged's kiss on the back of his hand and returned his smile with one of genuine warmth. She stood up from her deck chair, the tubular metal of the legs scraping on the pavers.

'Sshh!' She slapped the arm of the chair in fake chastisement. 'Don't wake the baby!'

Ged giggled, suddenly aware of his own light-headed disorientation as he knocked over their small collection of empty beers bottles. He addressed them with a stern finger-wagging. 'And you, sshh!' He looked at the still-sleeping Will, undisturbed by the noise. 'Time to get this little guy up to bed. I'll carry him inside, if you grab the tea stuff.'

After gently peeling Will out of his damp clothes and tucking him into bed, Ged headed downstairs to help Julie with the washing up. His journey was interrupted by the telephone.

'I'll get it…' he shouted, heading into the living room.

Julie froze at the sink, her heart pounding irrationally. *Oh my God, what if it's yet another reporter, or do-gooder? Don't they know when to leave well alone?* The telephone had become quite an intrusion this past couple of weeks. She strained to listen. The rise and fall of his tone sounded jolly through the muffle of the wall. *Probably Col.* She continued with the dishes.

Ged breezed into the kitchen, all smiles.

'That was me mam. She's invited us all to stay with them in Skeggy for the rest of this week. Will can celebrate his birthday there. Be great, won't it – few days away with the family? And you know how much Will loves to go to the seaside. Do us all good, after, you know...' Ged found it difficult to finish the sentence. He reached for the tea-towel. 'Stop us from being so maudlin.'

Julie abruptly stopped what she was doing, and stared at Ged. 'Maudlin? We've just buried our son, in case you didn't notice. I think we're allowed to be "maudlin". Anyway, didn't you think to consult me first?'

Her glare caused Ged to shudder, despite the summer warmth of the kitchen.

141

'Wha...no...I thought...'

'You *never* think...You just do whatever pops into your head...' Her face was inches from Ged's.

'I thought you'd be happy to go. Be great for Will to spend his birthday with his grandparents. For us all to go to the seaside,' he defended.

'Didn't you stop to think for one minute that it's also Jon's birthday? That I might want to go to the cemetery and wish him happy birthday? That I might want to spend some time with our dead little boy!' Her face was beginning to flush.

'No-one's saying that we have to forget Jon. But we have to consider Will. We have to make him feel special without dwelling on...you know...' Ged's voice was determined. 'It's the least we can do for Will...'

Julie slammed a plate down onto the draining rack. 'Well, you two go to Skeggy, if that's what you want...' She paused, her breath tight. 'But I'm staying here. I'm staying with Jon...'

★

The National Express coach pulled out of the town centre bus depot, its front display panel showing "Skegness". Ged and Will settled down in seats near the back. Will carefully set his red tartan duffle-bag stuffed full of sandwiches, sweets, pop and comics on the seat beside him. All his own. Didn't have to share them with dad. Dad had his own bag of goodies. Father and son. Off on their seaside adventure.

'Pity Mum couldn't get any time off from the salon. I bet she feels really sore 'cos we're going to be having fun at the seaside, and she's got to go back to work...' Will swung his legs, unable to yet reach the floor. Cigarette smoke wafted over their heads. Ged reached up to open the window, then ruffled Will's hair as he sat back down.

'Aye, lad. She really wishes she could've come. But, you know how it is, eh...'

'Aye, I know how it is,' Will replied, not sure if he really did. He snuggled up next to his dad. 'I wonder if Jon will have a birthday party in Heaven?'

Ged left the words hanging, unable to answer.

*

I don't know why people don't like graveyards, why they think they're spooky places. I think it's really quite nice here, in your little corner of the graveyard, in the Children's Garden of Rest. Green grass and all these lovely flowers. And the weeping willow tree. Quite apt really, to have a weeping willow. Bet you see parents weeping all the time. Anyway, Happy Birthday, my darling. Sorry Daddy and Will couldn't be here with you. They went to Skeggy, to visit Nanna and Grandad Steele. Wanted to celebrate your birthday with the living. Not the dead. Anyway, I'm here. I couldn't leave you – it's your special day too. I brought your teddy bear, look. Teddy wanted to say "happy birthday" to you. Are the kids going to have a party for you? A party without ice-cream…I see that a new kid has joined the garden. Little girl, I guess, with all the pink and white roses on her mound. Hope that you'll help to look after her. I miss you so much. There's another mummy and daddy, just over there, look. Come to visit their little one, I suppose. Why is life so cruel? Parents shouldn't have to bury their kids…

'Happy Birthday to you, Happy Birthday to you, Happy Birthday dear Wi-ill, Happy Birthday to you!' Ged's family sang with full, out-of-tune gusto for Will, who was happily perched on Ged's lap at the dining table. The birthday table was laden with sandwiches, buns, crisps, sausage rolls – all of Will's favourites. A cake in the shape of a castle, resplendent with turrets, castellations, flags and a wafer-biscuit drawbridge completed the scene. Almost like the castle back home. Will reached forward and blew out the five blue candles, then closed his eyes and made a wish, to the applause of his audience. Ged held his son tightly and kissed him on the ear, causing Will to giggle.

'Happy Birthday, son,' he whispered. 'Love you.' Will giggled again. Ged scanned the table – the family had kept their promise to put on a jolly face and make Will's day special. That said, he couldn't help but feel that something was missing. Jud caught his eye and gave him a knowing nod. Ged reciprocated with a similarly subtle nod, and gave himself a mental shakedown.

'Well, time to get the camera – better take some photos to show y'mam when we get back home.' He lifted Will from his lap and plonked him back down on the chair.

'And I'd better go and get something big and red!' boomed Grandad Jud. Will's face lit up in wonderment. Big presents were always good.

Ged returned with his Polaroid camera and took a couple of photos of Will with the cake while they waited for Grandad Jud to return. A scream of five year old delight rang out at the sight of a gleaming, fiery orange-red Raleigh Tomahawk bike, complete with stabiliser wheels. It was Will's dream come true. Ged quickly turned the camera on boy and bike to record the moment.

'I think he likes it…' laughed Grandma Beryl.

'You can take it home wi'ya. It's perhaps more use to you there than here,' Grandad Jud added. Will's face lit up at the prospect.

'Really? Aw, thanks, Grandad.' Will ran to his grandparents and gave them both a hug and a kiss. 'Can I phone me mam to tell her?' he asked, excited to share the news.

'Aye, course y'can, lad. I'm sure she'd love to hear from ya,' Beryl added, acutely aware that her daughter-in-law hadn't rung yet to wish Will a "Happy Birthday".

'And can I go for a ride on me bike?' Will asked, excited at the prospect. What to do first…? What to do first…? Ged bent down and gave him a hug.

'Tell you what – let's finish the party, then we can go for a bike ride along the seafront later. Lynette and Sharon want to buy you a new bucket and spade, and a kite. And your Aunty Brenda wants to take you for a donkey ride. How does that sound?' Ged stood up and walked over to the sideboard. 'By the way…there's another present here.' He handed a small box to Will. 'It's from me and y'mam. So that you can learn to tell the time.'

Will opened the little grey box to reveal his very first proper watch – a little Timex with a black leather strap. He looked from the watch to his dad, and back again to the watch. His mouth formed an 'O'.

'Thanks, Dad. A real watch…'

Ged noticed that tears were welling up in Will's eyes. A tiny voice came from the teary, snuffling face.

'I wish me mam were here. And our Jon…'

Ged took his son tenderly by the hand. 'I know. Me too. C'mon. Let's call her. Let's call y'mam.'

*

Restless. Julie prowled around the living room. Restless. Restless. Her visit to the graveyard had only succeeding in making her feel worse, not better. She picked up Jon's little teddy and held it closely to her, inhaling deeply. Jon's scent was still discernible. *Ged – Daddy – he should have been there too… And Will. We should have all been there for you.*

Still clutching the bear, she headed into the kitchen to make a mug of coffee. A tightness began to crawl its way through her stomach. Her hands flexed and clenched. Flexed and clenched. While she waited for the kettle to boil, Julie went to the bits-and-bobs drawer and found what she was looking for. Coffee forgotten, she grabbed the teddy and headed upstairs to their bedroom.

Julie sat the teddy down on her pillow then slowly, deliberately, went through Ged's side of the wardrobe. She picked out one of his denim shirts – the faint aroma of his favourite Denim aftershave pervaded the fibres, then threw it onto the bed. She rifled her way through his collection of beloved tour tee-shirts – Def Leppard, Genesis, Eric Clapton, Iron Maiden, Monsters

'83…her hand hovered over this particular one. Their honeymoon. The tee-shirt was no longer black, having been washed and worn so often. Faded. A metaphor for their marriage? She moved on, selecting his leather jacket. She threw this onto the bed to join the shirt then went to close the curtains.

Julie returned to the bed and laid the leather jacket out in a pose of supplication, its arms outstretched, the front open to expose the quilted, crimson-red satin interior. She kneeled on the bed before the jacket then inhaled deeply on his shirt. Ged's aroma filled her nose. *How could you not be with our little boy…today of all days?*

She reached for the item stuffed in the back pocket of her jeans. Julie slid the blade of the old Stanley knife forward and did a test prick on her index finger. A small, round globule of blood formed at the tip. *A bit like Sleeping Beauty before she fell into the one hundred year sleep…*She stuck her finger into her mouth and sucked away the blood spot. It tasted metallic. Slowly, purposefully, she unbuttoned the cuffs of her shirt and rolled up her sleeves, stopping just short of the elbow. Deep within her mind, Guns N'Roses were playing *Sweet Child o'Mine*. She glanced at the bedside alarm clock and checked its digital display.

16:03 She inhaled Ged's shirt, filling her senses with his scent.

16:04 She picked up the Stanley knife and held it tightly in her right hand.

16:05 *Slash…this is for you, Jon…*

Slash. Where do we go…?

Slash.

Slash. Where do we go now?

Slash.

Slash. Oh, Jon…child o'mine…Jon!

Julie stared down at the bed. The crimson-redness of the leather jacket's interior was now fluffed out with white, as the knife cut deep through the fibres, allowing the padding to escape. Her hands began shaking from the exertion and the realisation of what she'd just done. Of what she had become. She looked at the Stanley knife and launched it across the bedroom.

The jacket was a mess, irreparable. Another metaphor?

Jon...Jon...Ged...help me...please...somebody help me...

Please...

Then the telephone rang.

CHAPTER 29

Aliens

Why do I do it? Why do I hurt Ged? Because I can? Because it gives me pleasure?

I don't know – I don't have the answer.

I don't have any answers.

Only questions.

I just hurt Ged. Secretly. It's what I do, and I don't know why.

Have I always been mean to him? No. No, I haven't. I idolised him. Once upon a time – B.C. Before Children. Half the time I don't even know that I'm doing it. Something just takes over. I don't mean to hurt him. I don't mean to cause pain.

I don't.

Have you ever had your body invaded? Have you ever felt like an alien is growing inside you?

That's what it felt like to me. Aliens. Taking over my body, controlling my every move, my every action, invading my every thought. Every-bloody-thing that I did.

"Your skin will glow. Your hair will shine. Your pregnancy will be amazing. The birth will go like a dream if you remember your breathing exercises. The babies will be angels and feed by the clock, sleep by the clock."

Bollocks! Who writes this magazine bollocks?

Why did no-one ever tell me the truth?

This is the truth – the real truth: Your skin will erupt in boils. Your hair will fall out in handfuls. Your teeth and nails will crumble. Your hip joints and pelvis will scream for mercy. Your legs and ankles will puff-up like water balloons. Your blood pressure will go through the roof. Your belly will stretch to the point of splitting open. That's the reality the magazines don't tell you.

This was my truth. My reality.

Why did no-one ever tell me the truth?

There, there, dear. We've all been through it.

And then the aliens burst out of that over-inflated, over-stretched body, they tear you apart. And the bleeding won't stop.

And the room fills with panic. And the aliens scream and scream.

And then you panic. And then you scream and scream.

And the clinical wall-tiled echo screams back at you.

And then someone says "Congratulations, Mrs Steele, you've got twin aliens, but we need to take them from you because they're so tiny".

And you scream again – you want your aliens.

You've carried them for eight months. Eight long months of tortuous, bloated gestation. Even Officer Ripley didn't go through this much torture, this much pain.

Then the screaming finally stops.

The bleeding finally stops.

Finally.

Finally what?

You're finally a mum.

Battered.

Bewildered.

But everything will be alright. All will be okay.

But it wasn't. It still isn't. Not really.

There, there, dear...Aren't they adorable!

Life has changed. I have changed. Everyone around me has changed. Suddenly everyone has become a bloody expert on alien-care.

Why aren't you breast-feeding?

Why aren't they in a routine yet?

Why do they scream so much?

Why won't they sleep?

Why this? Why that?

There, there, dear. Chin up.

Why is no-one helping me?

Why is no-one asking me how I feel?

Why do I feel so alone in all this?

There, there, dear. Stop asking so many questions.

And then you lose one of your little aliens. One of those precious, dear little aliens that you carried, nurtured, lost. Dead.

There, there, dear. Sorry to hear that.

Here are some tablets.

Alone.

Afraid.

Abandoned.

In space, no-one can hear you scream.

Officer Steele, signing off.

There, there, dear…

CHAPTER 30

Mumbo-Jumbo

Julie ushered out the last of the day's clients, then dropped the latch on the door before closing the large, chromed "Silver Scissors" sign. She went to join Helena in the back room to help fold the towels from the tumble-dryer.

'Crikey, I swear the old dears come here on pension-day just for the free tea and biscuits. Do you know we got through three, *three* packets of Digestives today?' Helena laughed heartily, screeching emphasis on 'three'. She put the pile of folded towels onto the shelf then picked up the sweeping brush. Julie grabbed the cleaning cloth and disinfectant spray and joined her partner in cleaning the salon area.

'Hmm, but I think it's a worthwhile investment. Imagine all the Thursday gossip we'd miss if they went elsewhere,' Julie replied.

Helena imitated one of the gossipy old biddies, Les Dawson-style, causing Julie to splutter with laughter. She was glad to be back at work – she'd missed their camaraderie.

'Talking of which, who wins "Queen of the Gossip Award" this week?' Julie asked.

'Well, I think my nomination has to go to Mrs Fletcher. She was telling the whole salon about Dolly Sanderson. Apparently, she's been going to see some spiritualist in Langton. So that she can get in touch with her dear, departed Ernie.'

Helena rapped twice on the counter. 'Is there anybody there, woohoo, knock once for yes and twice for no...' She cupped her hand to her ear, listening for an answer.

'So you don't believe in all that then? Spiritualism, I mean?' Julie looked at her partner, slightly aghast at her mocking tone.

'Nah. Hokus-pokus, if you ask me. Mind you, Mrs Fletcher says that Dolly Sanderson usually has a right good natter with Ernie through the spiritualist. So who knows, maybe there is something in it?'

Julie shrugged her shoulders.

'Ged thinks that it's mumbo-jumbo too. He says they just fleece innocent people who are clinging to hope. He says when you're dead, you're dead.'

'Well, if it brings comfort to people, then I guess there's no harm in it.' Helena tipped the last of the hair sweepings into the flip-bin. 'Anyway, what's your gossip nomination for today?'

Julie scratched her chin thoughtfully.

'Well, I have two contenders – firstly, Mrs Carpenter was complaining that her three grandkids all have threadworm...'

'Eugh!' interjected Helena.

'But I think I'm going to go with old Mrs James. She was saying that her eldest grandson, who's only seventeen, has been seeing a married woman twice his age.'

'No!'

'Yes...And – the husband came home and caught them together...'

'No!' Helena's eyes were wide with shock.

'Yep. He's a long-distance lorry driver, the husband. Turns out that his lorry had broken down and couldn't be fixed, so he came home early. Found them in bed together. Apparently there was quite a kerfuffle, and he threw them both out, just wrapped in the duvet!'

'So, how did it end? Did Mrs James say?' asked Helena, curious to know more.

'Well, it drew quite an audience with the neighbours, as you can imagine. But it sounds like the husband has confessed to a few dalliances of his own while on the road. That said, the boy's parents have banned him from seeing the woman again. Not sure where it ended up between the woman and her husband. Can you believe these people?' Julie shook her head and shrugged.

'Well, I think you definitely win the "Queen of the Gossip Award" with your story about Mrs James. Honestly, the things we hear in this salon. You could write a book about it...' Helena could hardly contain her merriment as she began sorting through the tray of hair rollers, while Julie turned her attention to sorting the sterilised perming rods.

*

The house was bigger than Julie expected – an imposing double-fronted yellow sandstone house with tall Georgian windows framing the heavy front door. Then again, it was called "Langton House" – a sure sign of grandeur. The neatly manicured front lawn was framed by copper beech hedging, and divided by a central, yellow gravel pathway leading up to the front steps. Julie imagined that a spiritualist's house would look creepy. In fact, it looked rather welcoming, the sandstone glowing in the early autumn sunshine. A gnarled, old sycamore tree stood sentry in the front garden. Dozens of its little helicopter seeds swirled in the breeze, twirling gently to the ground, and falling alongside the growing carpet of autumn leaves. Julie reached across to the passenger seat for her handbag and to pick up Jon's little teddy bear. It was still wearing the yellow bow that Ged had made for it when the twins were babies. A wave of apprehension tingled through her, causing her stomach to flutter with inner butterflies. She looked at the little teddy bear then inhaled deeply. Although it had been a couple of months since Jon had died, it still carried a faint trace of his scent.

'I have to know that you're alright, my little one,' she whispered to the bear.

The dark blue front door was already opening before Julie had reached the front steps. Had the psychic sensed her coming? Nah, probably just heard the car, or the crunch of her footsteps on the gravel. *Stay realistic, Julie...*

Edith Pilgrim looked at the grandfather clock, its heavy brass pendulum rhythmically marking time. Almost eleven – the young lady, Mrs Steele, would be here any moment. She neatly folded *The Derbyshire Times*; an edition from a couple of months ago, dated 2nd August, 1990, which carried the news story about Jon's accident, and placed it on top of the one from a week later, which carried his obituary notice. She would cut out the articles after Mrs Steele had gone and glue them into a scrapbook, ready to be filed away with her collection of other past editions and notes. Having soaked up every detail, Edith now recalled the news article to mind. Such a tragic waste of a young life. She really hoped that she would be able to help. Parents who had lost young children were among her most desperate clientele, especially the mothers. Movement beyond the copper beech hedging caught her eye – she could just make out the roof of a little car parking in the lane. It must be her. She stood up and massaged her temples as she headed towards the front door.

'Good morning, my dear. Do come in. Mrs Steele, isn't it? I'm Edith Pilgrim.' She outstretched her hand towards Julie.

'Pleased to meet you, Mrs Pilgrim.' Julie took the psychic's hand, their handshake firm, bonding.

'Call me Edith, my dear. I find that the more relaxed and informal we are, the better our chance of "channelling" as I call it. Keeps the airwaves more conducive and receptive. Anyway, do come in.' Edith Pilgrim ushered

Julie into the spacious entrance vestibule before taking her coat and hanging it on a rack by the door. She discreetly observed Julie via a large gilt mirror, watching as Julie looked around and took in the classic splendour – black and white tiled floor, high doorways, and a wide, open-balustrade stairway off to the right. She saw Julie look at the small, round occasional table which stood in the centre of the square area, and was graced with a vase of simple white roses.

'A sign of purity,' said Edith, nodding towards the roses.

Julie jumped at the unexpected comment, then shivered at this woman's perception of her thoughts. One of the doorways was slightly ajar – Julie noticed a row of bookshelves along one wall. She presumed it was either a library or an office. The chequered shadow of a tall window could just be seen across the polished wooden floor, indicating that this room must have a view overlooking the front garden.

The psychic led Julie into what she assumed to be the dining room. An imposing dresser laden with fine chinaware filled one wall, and two winged armchairs faced the unlit Victorian tiled fireplace. Julie noticed a tweed trilby on the seat of one of the chairs, and a pair of polished brown brogues on the hearth.

'Belonged to my late Cecil,' Edith explained. 'We often sit and chat in the evenings. He also helps act as a guide. Here, take a seat,' she said, pulling out a dining chair for Julie, at the polished oval dining table. 'I'll just go and get us some tea, so that we can relax a bit first. You get comfy. I won't be a moment.' And with that, Julie was left alone. Although she was not sure what to expect, she was surprised to see that the room looked so "normal". It certainly didn't have the air of a fun-fair "Gypsy Rosalie" palm-reading tent. Silver framed photographs of Edith and Cecil hung on the walls – their wedding day, one of Cecil looking quite dashing in his Air Force uniform, one of them in their finery at Royal Ascot. Julie thought that they looked like a young Audrey Hepburn and Dean Martin. There was also another one of a young Edith laughing, standing shoulder to shoulder with another equally glamorous young woman. It looked like they were at a party or gala of some kind. Julie felt sure that she had seen the young lady before, although she couldn't quite place her face. Lady Someone? Or an actress, perhaps?

'He was quite a catch, wasn't he, my Cecil?' said Edith, as she returned with a tray of tea. Julie flinched. 'Sorry, my dear. I didn't mean to make you jump…' She laid the tray on the dining table and poured out two cups of tea. 'It will help us to relax, and open up the channels. Milk and sugar?' Edith passed the dainty sugar bowl and milk jug to Julie. 'I use teabags. Don't believe in all that "reading tea-leaves" nonsense,' she added.

After clearing away the tea tray, Edith sat opposite Julie. It was time to begin.

'I brought this teddy,' Julie explained. 'He loved this little bear. Had it since the day he was born. It even has his faint smell on it.'

'Good, sounds perfect,' said Edith. 'Right, put the teddy in your hands, and think of your little boy. I'll put my hands around yours. Keep your eyes open so that I can look directly into them. It's okay to blink.' She smiled at Julie. 'Don't be afraid – plates won't go flying off the dresser, or any of that horror film mumbo-jumbo,' she added.

Julie smiled nervously and did as she was asked. She could feel her hands getting really hot as the spiritualist encased her slender long-fingered hands around hers, the little teddy bear with the yellow bow at the centre. Edith's steel-grey eyes looked deep into Julie's as she began her soul searching.

'Your little boy died in a road accident. Tragic. Hit by a car as he ran out to get something – an ice-cream, perhaps?' Edith said, her voice low. She continued, 'He had a twin brother. Very different natures, yet very close. Four, maybe five years old.'

'Yes. Yes, that's correct,' said Julie, shocked by how much the spiritualist knew. Such small details. Moments passed.

Edith looked deeper, searching. 'His pain went away quickly,' she continued.

'Yes, he died...he died almost instantly...' Julie found it difficult to say the words. She bit her bottom lip to stem the tears that were building behind her eyes. Her hands were beginning to feel sweaty under Edith's. 'Can you hear him? Is he there?' Julie asked, desperate to hear her little boy's voice again.

Edith closed her eyes, her forehead furrowed in deep concentration.

'I don't hear a voice, but I get a feeling. I get a feeling of ...worry... agitation. There's someone there. I can feel a small sensation. But they're restless. Afraid of more pain. Stepping back...fading...' Edith opened her eyes and looked at Julie. She blinked, as if to clear away a vision.

Julie distinctly felt Edith's hands become cooler before she took them away from her own. She became aware of sounds returning around her – a clock ticking, birds fighting out on the front lawn, the distant sound of a car.

'May I keep the teddy? Sometimes they reach out to me when I'm alone. Sometimes Cecil helps guide them in...' Edith held out her hands to take Jon's teddy.

'Yes. Yes, of course.' Julie briefly wondered how she would be able to explain the disappearance of Jon's teddy to Ged, if he noticed its absence. But she had to make contact with Jon. She would never be able to find her inner peace until then.

'I'll call you if I get a message from your little boy. Jon, isn't it?' Julie flinched when she heard his name spoken. 'Otherwise, just let me know when you want to come over for another visit. When you feel that he's near. And we'll try again. It can take them a little time to find their way around their spiritual limbo,' Edith explained.

After leaving Edith's house, Julie sat in the car and cried. She questioned herself whether this was all for real. Was it all just mumbo-jumbo, like Ged thought? What was she expecting – for the room to go icy-cold and a ghostly fog to enter the room? To hear Jon's voice again? To hear him say that he loved her?

She checked herself for having these silly, horror-film thoughts. This wasn't *The Exorcist*! She took a few deep, even breaths to regain her composure.

But she would definitely be back for another visit to see Edith Pilgrim.

CHAPTER 31

Infinite Lies

Fingers of perfumed white smoke curled delicately upwards from the glowing tip of the joss-stick, filling Ged and Julie's bedroom with the oriental fragrance of sandalwood. Ged sauntered through from the bathroom, his body still damp from his bath. He pulled the pink and white floral towel from his waist, exposing all that lay beneath, and began to towel-dry the ends of his long hair. Despite having a hairdresser-wife, nothing and no-one had ever persuaded him to have it cut short. Just kept the ends neatly trimmed. He grinned at the provocative sight of his half-dressed wife, bent forwards while she scrunch-dried her hair upside down with the hairdryer to create fullness.

'Christ, woman, do you know how sexy your arse looks in those leather trousers?' He came and wriggled his naked body behind her, making her jump. She turned quickly and gave him a playful blast with the hairdryer. He took up the joke and began drying his chest hair seductively in the warm air. She turned the hairdryer back on herself, working her way slowly up her bra-clad torso, back to her hair. She pouted at him and licked her lips in a pseudo sex-taunt then turned around and wiggled her rear end.

'I'm not wearing any knickers…' she whispered huskily.

Ged grinned and looked at the bedside clock. 17:34. He shook his head.

'Sorry, babe – we're meeting the gang at The Greyhound in an hour. We've still got to finish getting ready, then catch the bus into town.' He play-slapped her on the backside, relishing the feel of the leather trousers.

'So, what's the plan?' she asked, turning off the hairdryer.

'Meet everyone in The Greyhound at half-six, swift pint or two, then catch the train into Sheffield.' He pulled the tickets out of his wallet to check the details. 'The City Hall opens its doors at 7:30. Wolfsbane's doing the warm up, then...' he drum-rolled '...Maiden!'

Julie grinned. 'It was really sweet of the guys to club together and get us these tickets. And in the stalls too – right underneath Bruce Dickinson and Steve Harris...' She made a seductive face, and looked at Ged to see if he'd taken the bait.

'Hey!' He feigned jealousy. 'What have they got that I haven't?'

She came and kissed him then continued her teasing. 'Hmm, money... good looks...fast cars...'

Ged turned away and sniffed, then stuck his nose in the air as if insulted. 'Well, go and run to the hills with them, you beast!' he mocked. 'Tell you what, though,' he said, his tone a little more serious, 'it will make a nice change to go out as "Ged and Julie" and not as Mum and Dad. We haven't done that in ages.' He carefully slid the tickets back into his wallet, taking notice of the date as he did so – 9th October, 1990. 'Wow. Do you realise that John Lennon would have been fifty today if that lunatic Chapman hadn't murdered him?'

Julie shook her head and laughed. 'My God, you're such a music nerd!'

Ged scowled, and pretended to be offended. 'Music, yes, that's what we need...' He selected Iron Maiden's *Seventh Son of a Seventh Son* album, and placed it onto the turntable of their mini hi-fi centre, choosing to avoid *Moonchild* and skipped straight to *Infinite Dreams*.

'Do you think Will will be okay? It's the first time that he's been away from us both since, you know...' Julie's voice was pensive.

Ged came and wrapped his arms around her, his hug strong and reassuring. 'A night at your mum and dad's – with that huge train set in the spare room to play with. I think he'll be fine.' He kissed her on the nose then walked over to the wardrobe and began scanning for something to wear as he buttoned up the flies of his jeans. 'I wonder what the new Maiden tour shirt will look like?' he commented absently. A small flutter of guilt tripped its way through Julie's stomach as the noise of the coat hangers scraped across the clothes rail. Ged selected his '88 Monsters of Rock tee-shirt – the tragic year that Maiden headlined, and slid it over his head, before picking out one of his denim shirts. His brows furrowed together, 'Hey, have you seen my leather jacket anywhere?'

Julie flinched as she privately relived the moment of its destruction.

'Isn't it there? Maybe you left it at The Cricketers?' she asked, her face showing fake concern.

Ged rubbed his chin as he thought for a moment. 'No, I'm pretty sure I haven't worn it since before summer,' he replied.

'Did you leave it at school? Or maybe it's at the allotment, in the shed?' she prompted. The image of the slashed jacket, hastily bundled into a Co-op carrier bag then unceremoniously buried at the bottom of the dustbin ran through her mind. 'I'm pretty sure it will turn up,' she lied. 'It can't be far away.'

Ged was still puzzled and perplexed. He continued searching as if it would miraculously appear before his eyes.

Julie bustled past him to get to her own side of the wardrobe and selected a white cheesecloth shirt and black leather waistcoat. 'Well, if it doesn't turn up, I'll get you a new one for Christmas,' she said, patting his arm.

It broke the spell of Ged's obsessive search. He moved away to brush his hair, still grumbling under his breath, and allowed the rhythm of the music to take over while he continued to get ready.

Julie also relaxed into the rhythm of the music, carefully putting together her outfit just as she would have done in the old days, or "BC" as she often called it – "Before Children". She carefully applied thick, black eyeliner, accentuating her dark eyes. Ged watched her as she slung her old studded belt around her hips, then laced up her black suede granny boots. Sure, she was a little curvier, but she looked all the better for it. He exaggerated using his hairbrush as a microphone and began singing along with the lyrics, emulating a classic Bruce Dickinson pose by putting his foot up onto the ottoman as though it were a sound monitor on the front of a stage.

Recognising the lyrics to the song, Julie blanched – "The Clairvoyant"… The lyrics were too close to home, penetrating the mind, seeing truth, seeing lies…Her hands and fingers began to flex and close, flex and close.

'I'm going downstairs to grab a beer. Do you want one?' she asked, making a swift, guilt-ridden exit.

'Sounds good,' Ged replied. And being the music nerd that he was, he realised what track was next. 'I'm almost ready,' he quickly added. 'I'll turn off up here and come down for it.'

Ged was pretty sure that Julie wouldn't want to hear *Only the Good Die Young*. He only hoped that Maiden wouldn't be playing it later that night…

CHAPTER 32

Turtles and Tinsel

T he fairy lights twinkled; colourful little stars of red, blue, yellow, green and pink, reflected in the baubles and tinsel, while the warming fragrance of pine mingled with the festive aroma of the Christingle orange and cloves that Will had made at school.

Julie picked up the last scraps of wrapping paper from the carpet and put them into a carrier bag, before bagging up the Christmas presents that she'd just wrapped for Will – a set of Teenage Mutant Ninja Turtles. They were the latest fad in children's toys – some kind of weird turtle super-heroes that ate pizza! Really! Where could she hide them? She knew that he'd already been poking around under their bed and in the wardrobe – someone in Will's class had started a rumour that Father Christmas didn't exist and that it was really mums and dads who hid the presents until Christmas Eve. She'd had a heck of a job convincing Will otherwise, such was his five year old logic. If Will would be a ninja turtle, he would be like the one with the orange mask – what was his name? Donatello? The smart one. He was way too perceptive for his own good. She looked at the clock – 4:20 p.m. Just enough time to finish cleaning up, and to hide the gifts before Ged and Will came home from school at five.

It was really convenient with Ged working at the Infant and Primary school – Will enjoyed staying behind at the end of the school day and helping his dad until his shift finished. Today had been a special day at school – it was the last day before the Christmas holidays. The kids had been to St. Lawrence's church for the Christmas Carol service, followed by a party in the Church Hall. They were going to have jelly, ice-cream, a magician, and games of musical chairs. Will was bound to come home on a high. Julie loosely wondered whether Will's suit had survived the day. He looked resplendent as he went out the door this morning in his navy blue corduroy suit, pale blue shirt, navy blue tie and his favourite blue-with-white-snowflakes tank top. He'd even combed his hair for the occasion, though the sticky-up bit by his crown had refused to lie flat, as usual.

Julie fingered the silver bow of one of the presents, a beautifully wrapped gift that wouldn't be hidden away. She looked at the gift tag – "To Jon, All our love in Heaven, from Mummy, Daddy and Will. Merry Christmas xxx". She had secretly bought a Turtle for Jon – she thought he might like the Michelangelo figure, the free-spirited joker of the group.

Just like Jon had been.

A tight feeling squeezed at her heart, and her hands began to shake as she read the words – words that had been so difficult to write. She looked despairingly at the tree, knowing that this gift would never go under it. Ged would think her "maudlin" for such behaviour.

There was one person, however, that wouldn't think her maudlin.

She picked up the phone.

'Wasn't that me mam's car?' asked Will, as he and Ged came around the corner towards Ridgeway Cottages. Ged squinted through the straggled ends of his limp, drizzle-soaked hair which was plastered over his eyes. He could just vaguely make out the numbers ...63 on the end of the number plate as the little red Mini headed off down Cornfield Lane.

'Looks like it. Wonder where she's going?' Ged replied, equally puzzled.

'Perhaps she's going to Nana Jean's.'

'Yeah, perhaps…' *Except that Nana Jean is busy in the shop with all the Christmas orders…*

'Does that mean you'll be cooking tea?'

'Yeah, perhaps…'

'Can we have fish-finger butties?'

Yeah…Perhaps…' Ged's mind was distracted by the direction that Julie's Mini was taking.

'Dad!'

'Okay, okay! Yep, we can have fish-finger butties for tea.'

'With ketchup?' asked Will, gleefully.

'Yep, as much as you want…let's go wild. Race you – last one home has to lay the table!'

'Hello, my dear. Do come in. Here, let me take your coat.' Edith Pilgrim welcomed Julie like a long-lost friend as she ushered her into the warm sanctuary of Langton House. A huge wreath of green cyprus, holly and pine cones, bound together with red satin ribbon and a huge bow, adorned the front door. The cavernous hallway was large enough to be graced with a beautifully decorated Christmas tree, colour-coordinated with classic red and gold lights and decorations, while a festive poinsettia stood on the central table. Julie's shoulders relaxed as she walked into the cosy, fragrant interior.

'What you need is an Irish Coffee to warm you up. Go through to our usual spot in the dining room. I've lit the fire for us. I'll join you in a moment.'

The dining room reminded Julie of an old-fashioned Christmas card, with the holly and ivy garland festooning the mantlepiece, while a log fire blazed in the hearth. Edith had already lit candles on the dining table.

'Here we go, my dear. I've only put a splash of Irish whisky into the coffee, knowing that you're driving. We don't want you getting into trouble, do we, dear? But this should warm and relax you. Let's sit by the fire and chat a while before we start channelling for Jon.'

Just hearing the mere mention of Jon's name caused Julie to jump, splashing some of the hot coffee out of the fancy Irish Coffee glass as she set it down on the little occasional table. *Relax, relax, otherwise he won't come through...*

Edith bustled around Julie. 'Oops, here, let me move my knitting out of the way. Don't want you sitting on those needles!'

Once she was settled into the armchair, Julie retrieved the gift from her handbag and set it on her knee. 'I want to give this to Jon. Can I leave it here with his teddy?'

'Of course, my dear. I'm sure Jon will love having something new to play with. To share with his friends. He's such a good boy with the other children, you know...'

'How do you know? Does he talk to you? Does he tell you things? Tell me!'

Caught off guard by Julie's outburst, Edith took her time to formulate an answer. 'The other children tell me. Sometimes I hear a happy "hum" in the air. It's the children playing...'

Julie stared at Edith, her mind a little fuzzy from the alcohol in the coffee. 'Yes, of course. I forgot that you can channel others. I...I...'

Edith sensed that it was time to move things along and reached to take Julie's empty coffee glass. 'The children are all excited,' said Edith. 'There's quite a bit of muddle in the airwaves to filter Jon through. But we'll try our best.'

Slightly unsteady on her feet, Julie stood up to join Edith at the table, the teddy between them, with the gift as a lure for their channelling. 'I hope that Jon will like it. It's *all* the rage with the kids this Christmas,' whispered Julie. 'I had to queue for ages to get them for Will and Jon.'

'Sshh, don't give the game away,' smiled Edith. 'Let's give Jon a surprise on Christmas Day,' she cautioned, her voice light-hearted.

They clasped hands around Jon's teddy.

Ged and Will had already eaten tea, washed the dishes, and Will was in his PJs sat on Ged's knee at the kitchen table playing a game of *Snakes & Ladders* when Julie came home. In an attempt to cover her tracks, she greeted her boys with an unnatural cheerfulness. Ged thought he caught a faint whiff of alcohol on her breath as she kissed him on the forehead and nose.

'My, you guys know how to live it up,' she laughed, noticing the empty fish-finger packet sticking out of the flip-top bin.

'It's all we know how to cook when you're not home,' Ged teased. 'Where y'been, anyway?'

Having already prepared a scenario in her head, Julie was ready for his questioning. 'Didn't you see my note on the table? "Gone shopping, back later." I thought I would pop to Makro to do a bit of last minute Christmas present shopping, in time to send things away to Santa,' she laughed, nodding and winking at Ged, knowing that Will was in earshot..

'Makro? Wasn't it busy?'

'Absolutely heaving, And the traffic on the M1 was a nightmare,' she lied, almost to the point of believing her own story. 'The car park at Makro was solid. I gave up in the end, and decided to come home.'

'So how come I can smell booze?'

'Oh, that. The car park attendants were bringing around chocolates for people to try while they were waiting to go in. I took a couple of liquors by mistake. What a sales pitch, eh!'

'Yeah, what a sales pitch...' replied Ged, playing along with her story.

Will rolled the dice for Ged, oblivious to the word-game going on between his parents. He manipulated his fingers as he added the two fives together.

'Dad, you got a ten. You've got to go down the big snake here. Oh no, you're back at the beginning...' He laughed, gleeful that he was winning against his dad.

And although Ged had noticed a faint streak of wiped-away mascara down the side of Julie's face, he never mentioned it. Nor did he mention that he'd seen her car heading in the direction of Cornfield Lane – the opposite direction to the M1 and Makro.

If she can have her secrets and lies, then so can I...

CHAPTER 33

What the Eye Doesn't See...

March 1991

'What the...What the bloody 'ell! Who's that? Is that you, Ged?' Ged awoke to find his leg being bashed with a coal shovel. Old Jim, the school caretaker, moved in for a closer look.

'It is you! Get up, y'lazy bugger!' he growled. The shovel clattered against Ged's knee.

'Okay, okay. Yes, it's me! Now stop hitting me wi' the bloody shovel, will ya.' The cobbles of coal shifted beneath Ged's feet as he tried to stand up, causing him to flail and stumble.

Jim moved the wheelbarrow to one side to allow Ged to walk out of the coal shed, catching a whiff of his breath as he did so.

'I think you'd better go to my cabin. We need to talk.' Jim's tone was firm, far removed from his usual joviality.

Ged hung his head and rubbed the sleep from his eyes. Coal dust from his hands streaked black marks across his face. He could feel adrenaline pumping around his system, causing his knees to jiggle. The last time that he'd had this feeling was when he'd watched his son's tiny white coffin being lowered into his grave.

Once in the cabin, Jim pulled out a chair for Ged.

'Sit.'

Ged meekly complied with the demand.

Jim looked out of the cabin window to see who was around before sitting down and joining Ged at the little table.

'What the bloody 'ell were you thinkin', lad? Asleep on the job. It's lucky for you that Miss Hanley didn't catch ya, otherwise you'd be out on yer ear!' He allowed the harsh reality of his words to sink in. Ged hung his head, not wishing to meet Jim's gaze.

'Have you been drinking?'

Ged nodded.

'Bloody 'ell. I could – *should* – throw the book at ya.' Jim sighed.

Ged took the sigh as a signal that Jim was softening. He took the chance to look up. A tear escaped, cutting a clean channel through his coal-dust streaked face.

'I'm sorry, Jim. Really, it's just...you know, what with...everything...' Ged attempted to explain himself, his voice low. His eyes welled, but stopped short of spilling over.

'I know, son. I know you've had a rough time. I can't even begin to understand what you've been through since losing your lad. But drinking ain't the answer. You've got to be careful. Jobs are few and far between these days.' He put his gnarly hands over Ged's and patted them. 'But what you've done is wrong. I can't let this go by, Ged. So you've got to accept this as an official verbal warning. No more drinking on duty, or sleeping on the job. Is that clear?' His voice was stern.

Ged nodded. 'Sorry for letting you down, Jim. I won't do it again. Promise...' He held out his hand towards Jim, to shake on his words.

Jim accepted the shake with a firm grasp. 'Now, go and wash yer face. We've got a school to prepare for the Easter break.'

It was so good to see the first of the spring daffodils – clusters here and there in the back garden were already showing their cheery golden and orange colours. Julie felt her mood brighten, as though the shadows of winter were being pushed away by the power generated by spring. She stood for a moment on the back door step, allowing the late afternoon sunshine to penetrate her soul, and erase some of the nagging guilt that seemed to cling to her. Guilt at being alive when others were not. She made a note to cut some of the daffodils and take them to Jon's grave this weekend – take some Easter sunshine. Maybe even give the gravestone a wash, do a bit of spring cleaning. Julie's train of thought was interrupted by the chitter-chatter of Ged and Will's voices behind her as they returned from school. She turned to greet them.

'Hey, how're my boys? Nice that we're all home at the same time.' She hugged Will and gave Ged a gentle kiss. 'I was just admiring the flowers, and thinking about taking some daffodils to Jon this weekend. Be nice – the family all together for Easter. What do you think?'

'I think it's a great idea, love.' Ged picked up on Julie's good mood. It made a change for her to sound so positive. Maybe the spring sunshine was helping to lift her spirits? He mentally decided to defer telling Julie about today's verbal warning. Did she need to know?

Not really…

Some things are best kept secret…

*

Will grabbed the red plastic bucket and set it in the middle of the kitchen floor. Julie verbally gave him a list of items to take with them to the cemetery.

'Cleaning cloths…'

'Check.' He put two cloths in the bucket.

'Green dish sponge…'

'Check.'

'Washing-up liquid….'

'Check.' Will tried picking up the bucket. 'It's heavy, Mummy, no more.'

Ged came into the kitchen with an armful of daffodils, some open, some still in bud.

'Is this enough?'

Julie laughed at Ged's lack of quantity-awareness. 'I think that's enough for the whole of the Children's Garden!' she laughed. 'Maybe you could take some of them to your Nana's grave, and Uncle Brian's?'

'Aye, that's a great idea.' Ged dropped them into the bucket with the cleaning materials.

'Da-ad...I can't carry it now,' complained Will.

'No problem – I'll take the bucket,' laughed Ged. He held out his hand to Will, something hidden inside. 'Here, you take these – one for you, and one for you to give to Jon. For Easter...' Ged handed two Cadbury's Creme Eggs to Will.

Will took the eggs and put them into his coat pocket, his face beaming at being given such an important task.

After the family had said hello to Jon's grave, Ged went to fetch a bucket of water for Julie, before heading off with some flowers for his Nana and Uncle Brian. Will sat on the grass of Jon's grave and ate his Creme Egg while Julie cleaned the headstone with the sponge and cloth. She then busied herself with arranging the remaining daffodils into the flower holder.

'Here, pass me the egg for Jon, and I'll put it by the side of the flowers.'

Will dutifully passed Jon's egg to Julie.

'Hey, make sure you put the wrapper in your pocket, don't leave any rubbish lying around,' she reminded him.

'I won't forget.' He held up his sticky hands.

'Here, wash them in the bucket...' She could see that Will was starting to get restless. 'Why don't you run off and find Dad? I'll finish up here, then come and find you.' Will didn't wait to be told twice, and disappeared to find Ged.

As Julie finished gathering the cleaning equipment together, she noticed something shiny lying between the edge of the grass and the base of the gravestone. She picked at it, silently chastising Will for dropping his rubbish after she'd reminded him not to. The piece of shiny foil was ravelled down below the grass line. It kept coming. It wasn't the wrapper to Will's Creme Egg. As Julie pulled the dirty but crumpled length of silver foil from the ground, she could see something attached to it. A dirty, soggy, Father Christmas shaped gift tag. The head came off as she gently tugged. Bile started to rise in her throat. Although the writing was no longer clear to see, she knew exactly what it was. Resisting the urge to scream, Julie placed the parcel ribbon and gift tag into the pocket of her leather jacket, her hands shaking uncontrollably as she pulled up the zipper. A tear escaped, then another, building into a choking sob. A sound came from behind her.

'Hey, are you okay?' Ged lifted her gently in his arms. 'C'mon, love. I think it's time to go. Our work here is done...'

*

After persuading Ged that she needed to "go for a relaxing drive", Julie stopped off at the telephone box at the edge of the village. She needed to make a phone call without anyone overhearing.

It was important.

Very important.

Edith Pilgrim hurriedly returned the scrapbook to its alphabetical location on the shelf above her desk when she heard the dull, thudding knock on the front door. She took a moment to compose her thoughts and straighten her pearl necklace before crossing the expansive hallway, the lining of her smart, peach-coloured suit rustling as she walked. The heavy, dull thump came again. Edith pensively opened the door, having taken a garbled phone call only a short while before. Her gaze was immediately drawn to a crumpled, dirty, yet still shiny length of silver foil ribbon with the remains of a Father Christmas gift tag hanging from it.

'Julie, my dear. What on earth is wrong? What is it? Do come in.' She ushered the still-shaking Julie inside.

Moments passed before Julie was calm enough to speak. 'I...I found this. At Jon's grave...' She held up the dirty scraps towards Edith's face. 'I... It's...it's...'

'Please, come through to the dining room, my dear. You've obviously had some kind of sign. A signal. Jon must be near.' Edith gently took Julie's coat then guided her into the room, where she sat her at the dining table. 'No time for chatting. Let's seize the moment, eh,' said Edith. She placed Jon's teddy in between them, then sat opposite Julie. Edith entwined the band and gift tag around Julie's fingers. As she did so, she noticed that Julie's finger nails still bore the residue of soil underneath.

They clasped hands around Jon's teddy. Edith's eyes bore deeply into Julie's searching, searching, before closing them. The atmosphere around them stilled; potent, save only for the rhythmic sound of their breathing. Edith broke the silence, causing Julie to jump slightly.

'I see the name of an artist. A great artist. From long ago. Michelangelo? Yes, Michelangelo. A free-spirit, roaming.'

Julie felt her hands being gently rubbed by Edith's thumbs, back and forth, as though feeling for energy, for information.

'I see the colour orange. A mask...and a creature. It's as though the artist is changing, he's mutating...'

Julie could feel her heart banging in her chest, and hear the blood rushing through her ears as she figured out Edith's cryptic ramblings. 'A turtle? Is it a turtle?' she whispered.

Edith remained still, silent, yet movement behind her eyelids showed much activity. 'I don't know. It's hard to see,' she replied. 'Yes. Yes, it's a turtle. How bizarre...The artist has become a turtle.'

Julie swallowed hard, compressing the bitterness rising in her throat. She wanted to speak. Wanted to say so much. But she knew that Edith preferred not to have the airwaves disturbed when she was channelling.

Edith continued, '..."Thank you, Mummy". I hear a voice, a faint voice, "Thank you, Mummy".' Her hands became vigorous again over Julie's. 'It's the label, it's the tag. It's drawing them here. Drawing Jon here.'

Julie's hands tensed around Jon's teddy at the mention of his name. She blinked away the tears that were forming at the corners of her eyes.

'The voice is near again. "Daddy, Will..." I can hear other children laughing, playing. He's fading, getting smaller... "Merry...Christmas... Mummy...".' Edith's eyes snapped open, causing Julie to jolt in her seat. She took a moment to regain her composure before removing her sweaty hands from around Julie's. 'I saw children playing with toys. Blurry, the vision was blurry. Jon was there. He had something in his hand. Green. I could make out the words "Christmas". I think he was sending you a message to thank you for his Christmas present.'

Huge sobs broke free from Julie, tears and slime ran freely down her face. Edith reached for the conveniently placed box of tissues and pushed them towards Julie.

'So he was calling me here? This tag – I found it at his grave today while I was there cleaning. It was somehow buried, poked down between the headstone and the soil. It's the tag from his Christmas present. The ninja turtle thing.'

Edith's face took on a serene, wistful mask as she took Julie's hands in hers, 'What a beautiful child. So thoughtful, so thankful.'

Julie nodded. Her brow furrowed as she held up the remains of the tag, 'But how did this get to the grave?' She looked directly at Edith.

'That I cannot answer, my dear. The spirit world moves in mysterious ways.' She paused. 'One thing is strange, though, now that I come to think about it. The box that you left when you came just before Christmas, I haven't seen it in quite a while...'

Julie shuddered. *Surely...no...*

'But I'm afraid I'm going to have to end our session for today,' said Edith, nodding towards the clock. 'Mrs Byfleet from the Ladies Circle will be stopping by any minute. We make things for charity, and she's picking up the scarves that I've been knitting. My knitting needles certainly keep me busy!'

CHAPTER 34

Burn

June 1991

*I*t was great finding the job of assistant caretaker at the local infants and primary school – it was a job that fitted perfectly around the kids and the allotment. Even the pub, if I managed to sneak for a lunchtime pint. Go in in the morning, get the boiler stoked, get the day started. Time for either a stroll to the allotment if it was sunny, or a swift pint in The Cricketers if it was raining. Then back in the afternoon to clean the school. And long summer holidays with the kids. Not a bad little number. Plus they were really supportive after we lost our Jon. The head caretaker, old Jim, was an absolute rock whenever I felt down. Mind you, the headmistress could be a stuck-up cow. Always seemed to have it in for me – Ged fetch this, and Ged do that, and Ged the toilets are blocked, can you go and see to them. It always felt like she was just watching and waiting for me to cock-up.

Okay, so Warning #1 was justified – Jim recently caught me snoozing on the job in the coal shed after I'd been for a lunchtime pint. There's just something about beer, coal and darkness that induces sleep. Jim gave me a verbal warning about that. A warning that I never told Ju about...

But at least I didn't get hauled before the headmistress like some naughty school boy.

That was for Warning #2. This time I was hauled before the headmistress. This time I had been truly naughty.

Not even a written warning. Just instant dismissal.

Lecture time, finger-wagging. Yes, of course I understood that stealing coal was a criminal offence, and yes, I realised how lucky I was that the police hadn't been called. The best Miss Hanley could offer was instant dismissal and nothing more would be said about the matter on account of my "recent tragedy". My eyes levelled with Miss Hanley's heavily mascaraed eyes. Locked in a 'who's going to back down first' battle, we were. Her eyelashes looked like a couple of big black spiders sat on her face. I swear that woman must have shares in Maybelline. Anyway, she won, smug bitch.

And I could see the look on Jim's face too – I'd well and truly let him down. Big time. He was the one who saw me hide the couple of sack-bags of coal behind the rose bushes. There was no way that he could ignore my wrong-doing. And now the poor old sod's been left to set up tonight's Summer Bingo all by himself. Worse still, he retires next year. I would have been up for his job – now he's got to train someone else. What a waste of nearly five years...

Daft thing is, it's not like I even needed the coal – we've got a gas fire these days. I was going to give it to Mr P at the allotment. His wife's got cancer, you see – she feels the cold. And his pension doesn't stretch very far.

Fuck, coal's been the bane of my life! First I lost my job and my coal allowance after being sacked from the pit. And now I've gone and lost this job. Fuckin' coal...

The interior of The Cricketers Arms pub was cool and dark. The lunchtime crowds were just starting to leave and go back to work – mostly groups from the local offices who had been for a swift pint and a bar-sandwich. The atmosphere felt jocular, friendly – quite the opposite to Ged's current mood.

'Pint of the usual, Cheryl love, and a Grouse chaser.'

'You celebratin' somethin', had a win on the horses?' enquired Cheryl.

'Nah, just trying to buy a bit of Dutch courage – gotta break some news to the wife when I get home.'

Too right I've got some news to break ...

Ged shakily aimed the key at the front door lock, then paused before going in. He took a deep breath. Although he had rehearsed what he was going to say, deep within he knew that... that...*Must paint this front door*, he thought, delaying entry. *But before that, I need a piss.* He nipped around the side of the cottage and nervously relieved himself behind the dustbin before daring to face Julie. He was pretty sure that there would be no time for a piss-break once she got started. *No, siree!*

Disturbed by noises in the periphery of her senses, Julie looked up from the mirror and listened for the cause of the disturbance. Mentally assuming it was Will upstairs, she went back to curling her hair – there was 'Summer Bingo' at Will's school this evening so she wanted to look her glamorous best, better than all the other mums. Because of her usual Monday closing, she had to do her hair sat at the kitchen table rather than at the salon. She glanced at the kitchen clock to try and calculate the time left for hair-curling and tea-cooking before having to head off to school by six. It was only four o'clock – plenty of time to get ready. A nip of fear bit into the pit of her stomach as she heard a scuffling noise by the dustbin and what sounded like footsteps. She gripped the curling tongs in defence. It was unlikely to be Ged at this time as he would be helping Jim put out the tables and chairs in the hall ready for the Bingo Night. Just to be sure, she double-checked the calendar on the wall – *Mon. 24th June, 6:00 pm. Summer Bingo.* Yes, she was right. She heard a key being poked into the front door lock, and then shoe-and-jacket removing noises in the hallway.

Ged entered the kitchen looking flustered and reeking of beer, immediately alerting Julie's instinct for trouble. With his head hung low and a desert-dry mouth, Ged leaned against the base-cupboards and nervously began recounting the events of his dismissal as assistant caretaker.

From the very same school where their son goes.

From the very same school where she was supposed to go later that evening and participate in the school's Summer Bingo night.

Julie remained deathly silent as she listened, her hand gripping the handle of the curling tongs, knuckles white. Although heady with the cocktail of emotions sweeping through her, Julie held her composure as she stood up and closed the kitchen-hallway door – young Will was playing upstairs with his Buckaroo and she didn't want him to hear their post-confessional *discussion*.

Having already played out a million different versions of the inevitable punishment-scenario in his head, Ged sat meekly at the kitchen table and awaited Julie's retribution.

She calmly unplugged the poker-hot curling tongs.

⋆

Not wishing to attract any undue attention or conversation from any other gardeners, Ged decided to go over to the allotment early so that he could get into his shed unseen. After all, he'd got nothing better to do... If it hadn't been for the pain throbbing in his left hand from yesterday's curling tong incident, he might have even felt like some stealthy spy sneaking through the gate and making sure the coast was clear before bolting into the shed. The familiar smell of potting compost reassured him that he was in his safe zone. He sat in the old deckchair and carefully began to unwind the bandage from his hand. Patches of dried yellow stains became visible the closer he got to the gauze dressing – he suspected it had stuck to the blisters. His heart sank; he knew it was going to hurt to peel it off – yet one more way Julie managed to hurt him. As carefully and slowly as he could, he lifted the dressing, the dead skin peeling away with the gauze.

He gritted his teeth, his face contorted to a grimace – it was the only way he could stop himself from crying out loud. A long red weal lay across the palm of his hand and into the crook of his thumb where the main blister had skinned open, framed by a few smaller open wounds. Small pools of clear liquid were already reforming to replace the crusty scabs. His hand throbbed, and he could feel the raw new skin below beginning to tighten. *Why, Julie, why...?*

Ged reached under his workbench for the old catering-size Bisto tin to retrieve his hidden Polaroid camera. He reminded himself to find a new hiding place – a curious young Will had almost found it on his last visit to the allotment. He slung the carrying strap over his head and positioned his hand on the workbench to take a picture of the damage. The camera flashed and whirred before spitting out the evidence. He carefully took the photo and began to waft it around to allow the picture to develop.

'Hallo, hallo – is somebody in there? Hallo.' The handle of the shed rattled, followed by hammering on the door. Ged recognised the voice – *shit, Mr Poulter!* He quickly put the camera under the bench, behind some sack-cloth bags.

'It's okay Mr P – it's me, Ged. I...' he said, trying to defer the old boy from entering. But it was too late, the door opened.

'Uff, thank goodness, I thought it was one of those young ruffians from the estate, like. I...' Mr Poulter suddenly took note of Ged's hand.

'What the bloody 'ell you been up to? That looks nasty.' Mr Poulter made a move towards Ged to get a closer look.

'I was helping the missus cook dinner last night – burned me hand on the oven shelves, tch!' Ged explained, rolling his eyes upwards to exaggerate his bare-faced lie. It was the same lie that he'd told Will when he asked why his daddy's hand was bandaged while cooking fish-fingers and oven chips for the two of them. Julie had declared that she "simply couldn't eat anything" and elected to still go to the Summer Bingo at school, to "salvage whatever dignity she had left".

'Your missus lets you help in the kitchen? Uff. Mrs P won't let me anywhere near, sick or not. You modern couples, eh! Good for you two.' Mr Poulter looked at Ged, wistfully thinking about his wife. 'Aye, I dread the day when she goes. I don't have a bloody clue how to boil an egg! Probably have to live off raw veg from the allotment.' He laughed, shaking his head at the thought. 'Anyroad, where's your First Aid tin? Let me help you fix that.'

Ged suddenly noticed the photograph lying on the workbench and intercepted Mr Poulter as he reached for the tin of bandages. 'Here it is, here's the First Aid tin,' said Ged, thrusting it under Mr Poulter's nose, covertly diverting his attention away from the evidence. With calloused yet gentle hands, Mr Poulter cleaned and dressed Ged's wound. Ged hung his head, his long hair hiding the truth in his eyes…*if only Mr P realised the irony…*

And with any luck, Mr Poulter hadn't realised that it was only 10:00 o'clock and not the usual 11:00 am when Ged had his usual morning stroll to the allotment on his break from school. Otherwise, that would be another lie that he would have to tell the old boy.

CHAPTER 35

One Year On

29.7.91

S o came the day that the family knew they would have to face: the one-year anniversary of Jon's death – the painful memory of putting their little boy in the ground. A job no parent should have to do. The plan was for the family, together with both Ged and Julie's parents, to visit Jon's grave and spend some time together in remembrance of this little life, cut short by tragedy. Will had chosen to take a toy car and put it on Jon's grave – a little blue sports car of some kind. He thought Jon might like something to play with in heaven. He thought toy cars more useful than flowers.

Julie was solemnly quiet, sat alone at the kitchen table with her head downcast, when her parents called to collect her and Will. Her once-glossy black mane hung in limp strings around her alabaster-white face, giving her a manic appearance. No amount of soothing words could get Julie to break her silence, yet her eyes held a strange, foreboding emptiness. Ged had already gone ahead in Julie's Mini to pick up his parents from the Castle Hotel and was going to meet up with Julie, Will and her parents at the graveyard.

Afterwards, it was agreed that Will would go and stay with Nana Jean and Grampy Frank, so that Ged and Julie could talk, grieve, reminisce and help each other to get through the day, devoting their time to Jon's memory without making Will feel pushed out. Ged dropped his parents back off at the hotel before returning home to Julie.

The home atmosphere hung heavy and silent. Julie returned to her position at the kitchen table, head down, fists opening and closing. Her polished nails dug deep into the palms of her hands, drawing spots of blood.

'Shall I make us a cuppa? Coffee? It was surprisingly cold up there today. A warm drink's what we need. Or would you rather have a brandy?'

No reply.

Ged turned his back to her, and busied himself with filling the kettle, then flicking the switch to 'on'. In the moment it took to reach up and grab two coffee mugs and the jar of Nescafé, Ged found himself reeling from blow after blow as the tubular metal chair legs smashed across his ribs and flesh, unbalancing him. More blows rained down on the side of his head and ear, then his forearm as he held it up in defence. His head collided with the open cupboard door as he lost his balance, stumbling, but not quite falling. Momentarily stunned, he heard the smashing of crockery and glass, sensing the light tickle of instant coffee granules and debris brush over his socked feet. Pain seared through his ribs and the soft, fleshy part below, his head and ear felt tender. He heard the kettle starting to come to the boil, steam rising into the air. *What the…?*

Slowly, slowly, one by one, his senses returned. As he refocused his vision, he caught sight of the kitchen chair back in its place, and the kitchen-hallway door slamming closed. Open-mouthed, confused, he attempted to absorb what had just taken place. He gingerly touched his ear and right side. Pain akin to a thousand volts of electricity seared through his torso causing him to draw a deep but painful breath. Lifting his shirt, he could see deep red lines starting to swell up and bruising already colouring his skin. Bewildered, Ged looked around him, taking in the scene. 'CLICK'

– the kettle switched itself off, the sound resonating around the kitchen, breaking the unearthly silence. The muted, surreal tones of TV laughter filtered through from the sitting room. If it wasn't for the reality of the pain and debris, he would swear he was dreaming.

Ged cautiously navigated a pathway through the broken glass and crockery towards the cupboard under the sink in order to retrieve the dustpan and brush. Hot tears pricked the corner of his eyes as he reached inside. Despite willing himself not to cry, one defiant tear escaped. It carved a salty path down his left cheek and landed on his knee. A myriad of emotions tore through his heart and spun through his head as he slowly and painfully swept up every last shard of glass and every last coffee granule from the tiled floor, tipping them into the flip-bin in the corner.

Why? Why? Julie, what's happening to you? To us? Questions in his head that he couldn't find the answer to, nor explain. Questions that he wanted to ask Julie but knew there would be no answer. It was over. It was all over. This was the tipping point of no return, the tipping point that caused him to feel sick. Was there any way back for them? Would she ever stop blaming him for Jon's death? As he finished cleaning down the work-surface of stray coffee granules, his hand inadvertently brushed against the kettle, still hot from its recent boiling. Another wave of emotion threaded its way through the pit of his stomach, causing it to lurch – the heat from the metal casing jolting his memory of the curling-tongs. He felt strangely grateful that it was 'only' the kitchen chair that had been used as punishment and not a kettle-full of boiling water. He retched into the kitchen sink.

It was over.

Trembling, Ged sat down at the kitchen table as noiselessly as possible, not wanting to attract any undue or painful attention. Like a wild animal on high alert, his senses became primed to every sound, every movement, every shadow. He became acutely aware that the kitchen clock ticked in rhythm with his adrenaline-fuelled heartbeat, like some kind of battery-powered metronome, keeping time; tick-tick, tick-tick, tick-tick. His shaking hands told him that he needed a calming brandy, but the dull ache in his side told him that he needed to stay alert.

4:35 He weighed up his options – fresh air, a walk? But what would he come home to? Irrational images of boiling kettles, sharp knives, chairs, tumbled through his thoughts. Irrational – yes – but given Julie's state of mind? Her cathartic behaviour was becoming too unpredictable. Ged shuddered involuntarily. Go to the allotment, his bolt-hole? Like a rabbit transfixed by headlights, he remained rooted to the spot.

4:42 Tick-tick, tick-tick.

4:43 Muted TV mumble – theme tune to Blue Peter? He wasn't sure.

4:45 He heard the burbling warble of the Trimfone, then Julie's muffled voice as she answered. He couldn't make out any conversation, but a moment later he heard a jangle of car keys, and rustle of jacket and shoes. The front door slammed, rattling the frame. Ged caught sight of Julie's Mini reversing off the driveway as if in a hurry, and then she was gone. To where, and for how long, he had no idea.

Was she seeing someone else? This wasn't the first time that she'd received furtive phone calls then shot off without explanation. He recalled one time – a Monday, it was – when she'd taken one of these strange calls. Monday was normally the day she went to the wholesalers in Sheffield, and although she'd used this as her cover story, she strangely came back without any stock. There was also clear evidence that she'd been crying and was very subdued and withdrawn. And then there was that time just before Christmas...

A deep, foreboding silence enveloped him. He closed his eyes and took shallow yet painful breaths. Then quite without warning, a flood of grief, pain and shock hit him, racking his body and soul, draining every last drop of his reserves.

*

Edith Pilgrim held her hands around Julie's, Jon's teddy bear at the centre, her face slack, her steel-grey eyes vacant, withdrawn. Her lips started moving but no words came forth. Slowly, hushed sounds, parts of words – unintelligible at first – began to take shape.

'H..hu..hurt. No more. Hurt no more.'

Julie's dark eyes began brimming with tears, spilling over to create mascara-streaks down her face. Although she knew Edith preferred no interruptions during their sessions, Julie couldn't hold back.

'Jon, Jon, is that you? Mummy's here...' Her voice trailed off to a whisper, 'What are you trying to tell me? Talk to me, Jon...I miss you so much...' She found herself squeezing the little teddy, as if to squeeze out a response. 'We came to visit you today...'

The old woman's head lolled forward to her chest, and she inhaled and exhaled deeply, allowing Jon's 'voice' to channel through her again.

'Tell Mummy. Not hurt.'

Julie could feel a sense of frustration tying her in knots. What did Jon mean? What was his message?

Edith evoked Jon's 'message' again. 'Hurt. Not hurt. I not hurt...Tell Daddy...' Her voice trailed away, leaving an unfinished air of silence, permeated only by Julie's racking sobs. The clairvoyant lifted her head, fixing her gaze deep into Julie's eyes.

'He's gone for the moment, but I sense he's very frustrated, confused.' She massaged the bridge of her nose before speaking again. 'I sense that Jon's no longer in pain. Maybe this is why I sense frustration – maybe he's ready to move on. Perhaps this is why he called you here tonight.'

Julie could feel her heart breaking all over again as she relived the painful horror of Jon's death.

'But I don't want to let you go, Jon...I can't...I need you...' She hung her head. 'Try again, Edith. Try and reach him again...'

Edith clasped her hands around Julie's and gently rubbed Julie's skin. 'Look at me, Julie, allow your mind to focus on Jon. Let me reach into your mind...' Her eyes glazed over, then closed. She remained stock still. 'I sense him, but from a great distance. Perhaps we have to try again another day, my dear. It's been a traumatic year for him too, stuck between our world and his. Let him rest for now...' Edith's eyes flickered open, and she smiled sympathetically at Julie.

It was too much for Julie. She snatched up Jon's teddy bear and headed for one of the armchairs, curling up into the foetal position, and clasped her arms tightly around her legs. Her voice became tiny, childlike.

'But now I'm hurting. It's me that's in pain. I lost my baby Jon...Why does he want to leave me?' She threw her head back and allowed the floodgate of tears to open.

Free from the burden of her channelling, Edith stood and stretched, then walked stiffly over to Julie. She tenderly moved strands of hair away from Julie's wet eyes.

'There, there, my dear...I understand.' She patted Julie's head like one would pat an obedient puppy, 'Let me make you a cup of hot, sweet tea. You're in no fit state to drive home yet. Then we can talk some more.'

It had already gone dark when Ged awoke, groggy and disoriented, at the kitchen table. He listened – no peripheral noises barring the ticking of the kitchen clock came to his ears. Ged noticed that Julie's Mini was still missing from the driveway – 10:45 pm and no sign of her. Where did she go? Was she seeing someone else? A knot formed in his stomach as he flashed back to earlier events, causing an involuntary shudder. There was a fine line between love and hate. Perhaps hate was too strong – fear? Yes, fear. The fine line had moved, his love now clouded by fear. Ged realised that his mouth was dry, his tongue almost welded to the roof of his mouth. He went over to the sink and let the water run cold, splashing his face. He poured himself a glassful and drank it down in one, the coolness of the water engaging his survival instinct. He poured a second glass, this time drinking it more slowly, helping to wash down three paracetamol tablets.

Think, think, think…what to do? He realised the gravity of the situation and suddenly felt very alone. If he went to get help, for either him or Julie, then questions would be asked… questions he couldn't face giving answers to. What man readily admits to being beaten up by his wife? Thinking time was needed. And he certainly didn't want to be around if and when Julie came home. Not tonight.

Exhausted, Ged made his way upstairs, first stopping off to pee before going into Will's room. There was no way he was going to risk sleeping in his own room – their room. He flicked the switch on the bedside lamp, casting a cosy glow over everything. The smell of Will hit his nostrils and instantly soothed him. A photo of the twins splashing in the sea on their first holiday to Skegness set a seed of determination – he knew that he had to get through this for Will's sake, if nothing else. Grampy Frank and Nana Jean would be bringing Will home around teatime tomorrow – that gave Ged some time to think, some time to get his head together. In order to give him some overnight security, Ged pushed Will's set of drawers across the bedroom door to block Julie out. God knows what she could be capable of given her current mood. And with that in mind, he lay down on top of Will's bed, deeply inhaling his scent from his young son's pillow, and allowed sleep to take him. It came surprisingly quickly.

CHAPTER 36

Revelations

The chatter of the morning bird-chorus and drone of a distant tractor seeped into Ged's aural sense. He slowly opened his eyes. As the rest of his senses returned, he was acutely aware of the deep, dull throbbing pain in his side and head. He gently raised himself up from the bed and padded over to the wardrobe mirror to assess his injuries. The underside of his right forearm was bruised, obviously from where he'd held up his arm to protect his head. A red mark was clearly visible on the top arch of his ear, and was tender to the touch. But it was when he lifted his tee-shirt that he reeled in shock. Wine-red welts, framed by blue and purple bruising, lined his ribs and soft flesh. Ged gingerly touched the bruising on his ribs and winced. Was anything broken? He shook his head in disbelief – his own wife, his love, his Lady Juliet, had done this to him. He moved over to the window – Julie's Mini was on the front pull-in. She had obviously returned sometime during the night, though he never heard anything. He stood stock-still and listened. Faint noises permeated up from the kitchen – water running, crockery clattering. He assumed that Julie was getting ready to go to the salon.

Hmph! Like nothing's happened…

He sat on the edge of the bed while he patiently waited for Julie to go, before venturing out of Will's room. He was not ready to face her yet.

Once the coast was clear, Ged headed for the bathroom to freshen up, then into their bedroom for a change of clothes, selecting his favourite old jeans and Meat Loaf tee-shirt. He gingerly tidied up Will's bedroom, each movement causing pain, before heading down to the kitchen. Though he wasn't in the mood to eat, he fixed himself a light breakfast of Weetabix, and a glass of orange juice. He had a lot of thinking and a lot of planning to do, so needed to nourish his mind, fuel his thoughts. Ged found himself gagging with every mouthful, but willed himself to keep it down. He couldn't risk going to the doctor's or hospital with his injuries. Questions would be asked, suspicions would be aroused. Child services might even become involved, and Will put into care. Not an option. But what options did he have? Try and talk to Julie? Surely she was aware of what she was doing? Run away with Will – go to Skeggy to his parents? No, Will shouldn't be a pawn in all this. His mind bounced back and forth until he felt dizzy with the effort. He decided on a slow walk in the fresh morning air, and a visit to the allotment. If nothing else, he had to take Polaroids to catalogue the injuries. Photos that would join the numerous others. He grabbed his Wrangler jacket and headed out.

The town was already starting to bustle with activity when Ged called off at the newsagents to pick up a Daily Mirror and a strip of Anadin tablets before going over to the allotment. Old Mr Poulter, who had the allotment across from him, was already there, tending to his plants. He looked up from his weeding when he heard the gate squeak open and smiled broadly when he saw Ged,

'Morning, son. Thought I'd come early today, before it gets too hot. Forecast to be a scorcher today.'

'Aye, it's good weather for the garden. Tomatoes are ripening a treat. Getting some good crops,' Ged replied. As much as he enjoyed chatting with the old boy, today was not the day for it. He just wanted to get into his shed and be alone. Ged politely shared a few more minutes of conversation, then made his excuses to get into his potting shed, saying he had some mower blades that he needed to sharpen.

The interior of the shed was cool and dark, a welcome relief from the rising heat outside. It wouldn't take long for it to warm up, though, once the sun had moved from behind the apple tree and began streaming in through the window.

Old spider-web covered plant pots lined the shelves, together with cans of oil, nuts and bolts and old seed packets. Two large weed-killer tins sat high on the top shelf out of harm's reach – 'Warning: Poison' signs stark reminders of their toxic harmfulness. He always warned Will not to touch them when he came to the allotment to help. Heaven forbid if anyone got a hold of the contents...

Ged painfully reached up to the tins, choosing the one on the right. The Polaroid camera rattled inside as he lifted it down and put it onto the workbench by the window. An array of family photos, pebbles, shells, and a little stash of money – winnings from bets on the horses – sat in the bottom of the tin together with the photos from his catalogue of injuries. The money was going to be a surprise for Julie and Will so they could have a little family holiday. Somewhere different from Skeggy – somewhere for just the three of them. Maybe the money would now be his escape?

Ged positioned the camera so that he could take instamatic photos of the injuries to put with others. And like the others, they would be carefully dated and labelled. Was this the evidence he needed to get custody of Will and leave Julie? It was the only way anyone would believe the abuse.

But did he want to leave Julie?

Could he leave her? Could he break his vows?

He remembered once, when he and Julie were out shopping together not long after they'd buried Jon, some old biddy came up to them in the Co-op. She took Julie by the hands, and told her how sorry she was to hear about Jon, that there was "no pain like that of a grieving mother". Did she think that dads don't have a right to grieve and feel pain too? Why was it always the mother that 'suffered'? Couldn't anyone see that he was suffering? His head began to pound, and uncontrollable tears poured from his eyes, from his heart.

Sobbing for himself. Broken.

Sobbing for Will. Innocent.

Sobbing for Jon. Dead.

Sobbing for Julie. His Lady Juliet. Guilty. Unhinged. Depressed. Vulnerable.

Unpredictable.

Dangerous.

As the sun moved from behind the apple tree, dappled light filtered through the leaves, casting an ever-shifting leopard print pattern on the workbench. The mercury in the thermometer began a steady upward journey as the heat in the shed began to rise. Depleted of tears, Ged returned the weed-killer can of secrets to its top-shelf location.

Time to plan.

He turned on his battery-powered radio-cassette player and rummaged in his box of cassettes, selecting his all-time favourite, *Bat Out of Hell*. One of the best concerts they'd ever been to, seeing Meat Loaf at Donington back in '83 – their honeymoon! He pressed 'play' and settled down into the stripy deck chair, allowing the music to wash over him. He knew every word, every chord…each one resonating with raw passion, with raw emotion. It was almost too painful to listen to – the lyrics like a play-script of his life with Julie. He rubbed his temples and turned off the cassette player. Meat Loaf wasn't helping.

Ged noticed a Cornish pasty and a can of Lilt on the workbench. Ever the sucker for a Cornish pasty, he hungrily tucked into it – though if he was honest, he couldn't exactly remember how long it had been sat there. Two days? Three days? A week? He washed down the warm dryness of the flaky pastry with the tepid Lilt, and threw in four more Anadins for good measure. Ged closed his eyes and slowed down his breathing – the allotment was a good place to be, a tranquil sanctuary away from the madness of life, a place where the soul could connect with nature. A hippie-philosophy, but it worked for him.

He picked up the Daily Mirror and scanned the news stories. Maggie Thatcher was still creating mayhem in the mining industry as her legacy, as more local pits were to close. Doom and gloom. Ged tutted in disgust, and turned to the sports pages at the back in an effort to lighten his mood. There were some good horses running today, so a bet was in order.

And he had reached a decision…

Mr Poulter had already left his allotment when Ged emerged from his shed. The building heat was evident, creating a surreal, quivering haze over the tarmac pavement as Ged strolled steadily back into town and headed for the bookies. After placing his bet, he kissed the ticket for luck before stuffing it into the top pocket of his jacket. A familiar voice hollered across to him as he exited – Col.

'Nah then, y'ugly bugger. Where you been hiding?'

With an air of apprehension, Ged responded, 'Shit, man, long time no see.'

They shook hands, cautiously at first, before clapping each other on the back, Ged careful to avoid contact on his bruised side. It was good to see his old best friend – he'd missed him terribly after their recent bust-up.

'You look like crap, what's up?' Col noted, as a looked Ged up and down. Not ready to divulge the truth, Ged deflected Col's comment.

'I'm ready for a refreshing pint, that's "what's up". Fancy one?'

'Sounds good. *Black Bull*?' Col replied. The *Black Bull* was one of the quieter pubs, located on the far side of the Market Square, and had picture-postcard views over the ridge, castle escarpment and the valley beyond. The two friends headed towards the pub, happy to be reunited. Ged wasn't sure if mixing Anadin with lager was a good idea, but what the hell. It was all pain relief.

The pub wasn't busy, just a couple of old codgers sat in the corner playing dominoes, and a group of teens around the pool table. After ordering their pints, the two friends elected to sit outside in the shade of the beer garden. There was a welcome breeze blowing up from the valley. Ged took a long draught on his lager before speaking first.

'Sorry about how things ended up. I guess Julie just got a bit pissed off at our Sundays together. I've missed you.'

'Same here, pal. We've been friends for too long. I...I...' They shook hands again, and filled each other in with the gaps since their falling out.

'Anyroad, I'm glad I've seen you. I heard that you lost your job at school, so I've got a proposition for you.' Col continued, 'Old Ernie is retiring at the end of August, so if you want his job on the coal lorry, helping to bag and deliver coal, then it's yours. I could do wi'a bit o'young blood on the team – me old man's not in the best of health these days since he hurt his back. Be like the old days...' Col slapped Ged light heartedly across the belly, indicating that he would need to shape up if he was going to be able to shovel coal and carry bags. Ged winced in pain.

'Sorry, pal, are you okay? It was only a slap,' said Col, apologetically.

Ged couldn't hold back his emotions – his head was starting to pound, and his stomach was beginning to feel queasy. It was all too much.

'Come wi'me...' Ged grabbed Col by the hand and dragged him inside towards the men's toilets.

'What the f...?' Confused, Col had no choice but to be led indoors. It took a moment for their eyes to adjust from the brightness of outdoors to the shade of the inside.

Once in the men's toilets, Ged made sure that no-one else was around before taking off his jacket and lifting his tee-shirt. Col stared open mouthed, stunned and speechless at the purple vision before him.

Ged simply said, 'Julie'.

'But, I don't understand, what do you mean "Julie"?' asked Col.

Ged took a cautious, yet painful deep breath before answering. 'Julie beat me senseless wi'a chair last night...' and then he began to sob uncontrollably.

Col came over and hugged Ged the best he could without hurting him, then handed him some cold, wet paper towels so that he could cool his face and wipe his eyes. Once Ged had calmed, Col guided him through to the Snug and went to get two cold, fresh pints of lager.

They needed to talk.

Ged began pouring his heart out to Col, starting with the events of this most recent attack. Col merely nodded, sensing his friend needed this confessional to be uninterrupted. Ged continued to divulge the behind-closed-doors revelations of his marriage,

'Looking back, our relationship started to go downhill after she became pregnant wi'twins. Just little things back then: sullen silences, sniping comments, temper tantrums – things I put down to hormones. The birth left her virtually traumatised. She wouldn't let me touch her for nearly a year – she was terrified of getting pregnant again. It can wear a man down. Mercifully that side of things improved once I'd had the snip. At least we got some closeness back.'

Col nodded. 'Aye, I remember you talking about getting it done.'

'But it was after we lost Jon that things really got out of control.' Ged paused, as if gathering his thoughts and strength to continue. 'Remember not long back when my hand was bandaged, and I fed you some bullshit story about having burned my hand on the oven shelves? Well, it was just that – bullshit. Julie had burned my hand with the curling tongs. Punishment for losing the job at school. And, of course, she's tried to keep us two apart.' Ged took a sip of his cold lager before continuing. 'She's cut me, beat me, she's thrown things at me. I could go on, but...' Deflated, he looked up at Col.

'All this time...why did you never say owt? I'm your best mate, for God's sake,' Col asked, shocked by what Ged had just revealed.

'What was I supposed to say? Oh, by the way, my wife beats me, but other than that life's just fine and dandy.'

'But...I don't know ...couldn't you stop her?' asked Col.

Ged sighed, taking his time to reply. 'C'mon, Col, you know me better than that – I'm a lover not a fighter. Anyway, I love her too much to hit her back. No matter what, you can't just turn that off, it's not that simple. "For better or for worse" and all that. So, I take it. I don't really have a choice – I have to shield Will from all this.'

Col slowly wiped the condensation from his pint pot while searching for an inspirational reply. 'And didn't Julie also make vows? "To love and to cherish"? Not "I promise to beat my husband".'

Ged winced. It sounded harsh, hearing it spoken. He nodded, then lowered his head before speaking again. His hair flopped over his face, a useful shield to avoid eye-contact with his best friend.

'There's summat else...I reckon she's seeing another bloke...'

Col coughed on a mouthful of lager as it stuck in his throat. He suppressed the sudden urge to bad-mouth his friend's wife, choosing instead to ask why Ged thought this.

'She keeps getting strange phone calls,' Ged explained. 'Then she goes out. Sometimes for hours.' Col looked at him quizzically, his eyebrows furrowed together. Ged continued, 'She's always in a rayt bad mood when she comes back. Distant...'

'And have you asked her where she's been? What does she say?' Col asked.

'I've only ever asked her once. She just screamed and screamed, and said that I wouldn't understand. Then she threw the nearest thing – a vase of flowers. Shattered everywhere.'

'And that's it? You just accept it?' Col's voice was tight.

Ged shrugged his shoulders in vague affirmation.

'How long's it been going on?' enquired Col.

'Started a couple of months after we lost Jon. Maybe she just needs something to fill the void. Something I can't give her,' he said, in an attempt to justify his wife's behaviour.

'For fuck's sake, Ged! The way I see it, she needs help. Big time. You both do.' Col laid his hand over his friend's – an act of solidarity and unity.

'But I just don't know how. I don't know where we go from here.' Ged began to cry again.

Col shook his head. 'Why did I never see the signs? I'm so sorry! Look, if there's owt I can do to help, let me know, yeah?'

'Thanks. Just chatting has helped. And the job offer. But please…' He grabbed Col by the arm. 'Not a word to anyone. I need to figure this out so that Will isn't affected by our mess.'

Col looked at his friend then nodded. 'Aye…' There was nothing more he could say.

Ged and Col both looked up as the door to the Snug opened – it was the same two elderly gentlemen who had been playing dominoes earlier, each carrying what looked like the same glass of Guinness. They asked if it was okay to turn on the Snug's TV to watch the afternoon racing, and settled down by the unlit fireplace.

Ged nodded towards the two old boys, and said to Col in a low voice, 'That will be us two in forty years' time…' He took out his betting slip and together they began checking over the horse-racing bets that he'd placed earlier. If felt just like the old days.

Almost.

'Well, would you look at this!' exclaimed Col, poking at Ged's ticket. 'Your horses have all romped home. I bet you've got a fair few quid to come.'

In a vain effort to try and sound positive, Ged said, 'Aye, and I've just been offered a job at my favourite coal yard. Thanks, pal. Life can only get better, eh.' He smiled weakly – his head was swimming and he was beginning to feel nauseous again. Heat was coursing through his veins, and he could feel rivulets of sweat starting to roll down his back and dampen the waistband of his jeans. Perhaps everything was catching up with him. Shaking, he picked up his pint then put it back down again, unable to finish it.

'Y'know what, I'm gonna call it quits for now and head off home. I need some fresh air – I feel like I'm going to puke.'

'Aye, perhaps that's best. But you stay in touch, d'you hear? We've been mates since we were kids – you don't have to go through this on your own. Julie doesn't need to know that you've talked to me. But a problem shared is a problem halved, eh. Call me when you're feeling better,' said Col.

Ged stuffed the betting slip back into his jacket pocket, and shook Col warmly by the hand before leaving, promising to stay in touch. He stepped out of the pub into the bright afternoon sunshine and made his way along the Market Square, his gait unsteady. But Col was right – opening up about the problem had lightened some of the burden that he'd been shouldering all this time. Could he convince Julie to do the same?

Christ, he felt dizzy. His stomach began to lurch as shooting pains gripped him.

Quick, where can I go...?

Don't ...feel...well...

Co-op...doorway...quick...qui...

CHAPTER 37

Bitch!

The *swish* of the door opening to the Family Room caused everyone to break their shock-induced reverie, all looking up expectantly in the bid for news. A sleeping Will wriggled dream-like in Grandad Jud's arms, blissfully unaware of the drama unfolding around him. He'd already lost his twin brother to a car accident, so the family had done their best to play down the seriousness of his father's predicament. An efficient looking nurse holding a clipboard entered the room, her kind eyes searching around for Julie.

'Could you come with me, please, Mrs Steele? Mr Steele is out of surgery. The consultant is ready to see you now.'

Frozen to the spot, dreading what she might hear, what she might have to face, Julie began trembling uncontrollably. Seeing his daughter in distress, Frank Bryant held her in his arms.

'Would you like me to come in with you, love?' he asked gently, offering his support. She shook her head, and meekly allowed the nurse to guide her out of the door towards the ICU room where Ged had been put.

Although the nurse had pre-warned Julie that Ged was heavily bandaged and hooked up to machines, it didn't really prepare her for the assailing sensory overload as she entered the ICU. The orange and white blinds had already been drawn to close out the evening darkness; the only splash of colour against the clinical creamy-white walls. Harsh fluorescent lighting made the room seem stark and un-naturally bright in comparison to the serene lamp-lighting of the Family Room. The cloying smell of sterility and anaesthetic hung heavy in the air. It was as if time was standing still, punctuated only by the rhythmic bip-bip of monitors and steady air-flow of the ventilator. Tall metal frames holding bags of fluids and blood stood like sentinels guarding over their patient, drip-feeding Ged's veins with liquid life. Tubes and wires snaked around him, finding entry, helping to keep him sedated, to keep him breathing. Another nurse was bustling about quietly and efficiently, checking levels and readings. She looked up and smiled sympathetically at Julie.

'Oh my God, Ged…' Julie reached out towards him, her hand shaking. The nurse allowed Julie a brief moment to look at Ged before gently guiding her to a chair, where the consultant was waiting to explain the extent of Ged's injuries. He was still in his green scrubs, which added to the urgency and severity of the situation. Julie could barely look towards the consultant, her eyes transfixed on the machines, tubes and fluids surrounding Ged. She noticed that Ged's left leg was lifted in traction, a metal cage-like contraption clearly visible, pinning his femur together. Another row of pins was visible on his jaw. The consultant's voice was soothing, despite the grim list of injuries he was spelling out to Julie – a couple of broken ribs, fractured jaw, internal bleeding, fractured hip and broken thigh. It was going to take Ged quite a long time to heal and recuperate – he'd taken a hell of a hit from the delivery van. Julie absorbed the words, though their meaning was not yet sinking in. This was all so surreal. Was history about to repeat itself?

The consultant looked over Ged's chart and tapped it with his pen, then looked up quizzically at Julie, before continuing.

'Eye-witness reports say that Mr Steele appeared drunk and disorientated when he stepped out into the road. However, the toxicology results show that he'd barely consumed any alcohol. It does seem, though, that he has food-poisoning. There was residue of stomach fluid and food splashes around his mouth and on his clothing – like he'd been vomiting – so we were able to take swabs for analysis.'

Julie nodded, unaware of the run-up to Ged's accident. She explained how the family had been gathered in a memorial for Jon the day before, but that she and Ged had spent the night separately "for their own reasons". She hadn't seen him this morning, so had no idea about his whereabouts over the day. She had gone to work with having the salon to run. It was only when the police came that...that...Her shoulders trembled as she began to cry. *Why is all this tragedy being forced upon me...?* The nurse that had brought Julie into the room handed her some tissues, so the consultant could continue. He had more questions.

'Had your husband been in a fight recently?'

Julie cocked her head on one side, feigning puzzlement. 'Well, he had a big bust-up with his best friend a few weeks ago...'

The consultant took a deep breath before continuing. 'No, this is fresh damage. There's some rather severe bruising to the right side of his torso, right forearm and the side of his head, but the van struck him on the left side. The impact and the way he fell wouldn't have produced these injuries. Do you have any ideas how he could have gotten these bruises?'

Julie shook her head and gave a noncommittal shrug,

'I'm sorry, no. He often comes back with injuries after he's been up to his allotment. Cuts and bruises. And burns. He can be quite clumsy...' Her pulse started to race.

The consultant paused, raising his eyebrows. 'Hmm, these are not conducive with "clumsy" injuries – these are from a heavy blow rather than a fall. Plus, they seem quite fresh.' He looked directly at her.

'Like I said, I'm sorry, I don't know.'

The consultant rubbed thoughtfully at his chin, but said nothing. Julie felt sweat beginning to run down her back. She seized the opportunity to steer the conversation towards Ged's treatment, and estimated length of stay.

'Will he make a full recovery?' she asked.

'Hmm. Well, I anticipate that he will make a full recovery, but as I said earlier, it's going to take quite a while. He's going to be in hospital for many weeks. And I anticipate that walking could be difficult or uncomfortable. He may need the aid of a stick.'

Julie felt a selfish air of relief – this would buy her some time. She could feel the net closing in – surely it was only a matter of time before Ged would speak out, so she needed to be ready. She knew this was the make or break point in their relationship. Her eyes filled with tears.

Make or break...

'Well then, shall we go and get the rest of the family?' He offered Julie a hand to help her to her feet. The nurse who was tending the machines came and took the clipboard to hang it at the foot of Ged's bed, while the other nurse opened the door ready to follow the consultant and Julie. They stepped out into the silence of the corridor to head over to the Family Room.

'You bitch! You absolute – fuckin' – bitch!' Having recognised Julie from the other end of the hospital corridor, Col strode purposefully towards the trio as they exited the ICU room. He continued his verbal tirade, his pace quickening to an almost-run.

'This is all *her* fault, the bitch...' He spat the words out venomously, pointing an accusing finger towards Julie as he neared them. 'My best mate's lying in there because of her!'

'Sir, I must ask you to refrain from this shouting, otherwise I'll have to call for one of the porters to escort you out,' implored the consultant, as he stood protectively in front of Julie. But Col wasn't letting up.

'Did she show you the bruises, eh? Did she show you what she'd done to him? He showed me this afternoon.'

The consultant looked perplexed, and was about to speak when the door to the Family Room swung open. The disturbance had attracted the attention of both Ged and Julie's families, who slowly filtered out into the corridor.

'Col, love, what are you doing here?' asked Ged's mam.

'I heard the news about the accident so I came straight over. He is my best mate, after all,' replied Col, visibly distressed.

The two families gathered around Julie, the consultant and Col, expectant, waiting for answers.

'What do you mean, "it's all her fault"?' asked the consultant, directing his question towards both Col and Julie.

'She knows! She was the one that drove him over the edge to this. Did she show you the bruises? It was her that done this to him. Beat him senseless wi'a chair, she did. His own bloody wife beat him senseless wi'a chair. And it's not the only thing...' He looked directly at Julie, his eyes burning with accusation and anger. 'How could you, you bitch!' The stinging words hung in the air, waiting to be absorbed by the familial audience.

Ged's mother spoke up first.

'Is this true, Julie?' She looked her daughter-in-law directly in the eyes, then at Col.

'I...I...' Julie paused, her voice small. 'I love Ged. I could never hurt him.'

Col felt stung by her bare-faced denial. He had known Ged since they were kids, and if there was one thing he knew about his friend's character, he was no liar. All hell broke loose as the two families began screaming for answers. The consultant bellowed for them to stop, and ushered them back into the Family Room. Will crept out from behind Grandad Jud's leg, having witnessed all the commotion and everyone screaming at his mother.

He tugged at his grandad's trouser leg, and asked, 'Why is mummy crying? Is Daddy dead? Why is it Mummy's fault?'

Grandad Jud took Will tenderly in his thick arms, 'No, Daddy's not dead, he's just been in an accident. The hospital is doing all it can to make him better. Daddy's asleep at the moment.' Jud, this big rock of a man, found it hard to contain his emotions as he spoke to his young grandson. But he was sure as hell going to get to the bottom of Col's accusations that his only son was lying in a hospital bed because of his daughter-in-law. 'You run along wi' Sharon and Lynette and see if you can find a vending machine. Bring us all some drinks and Mars bars, yeah?' He urged Ged's younger twin sisters to take their little nephew out of the situation. They understood, and took the proffered money from Jud, along with Will's hand.

Voices, accusations, questions were all hurled in Col and Julie's direction –

Is it true?

Why?

How could you tell such lies?

Bitch!

Julie's head began spinning...*voices*...*spinning*...*voices*...*bitch*...

Is it true?

Why?

How could you tell such lies?

Bitch!

She could feel herself buckling under the questioning, the accusations, sinking to her knees; *make them stop, make them stop...*

She screamed; a howling primal scream from deep within. The consultant caught her as she swayed over, preventing her from hitting the hard floor.

'Quick, nurse, help me to get her to a chair,' he barked, jostling everyone out of their way so that he and the nurse could assist Julie. 'And you lot should be ashamed of yourselves – this is a hospital, not a three-ring circus,' he admonished.

The cacophony died down, with the two families taking seats on opposite sides of the Family Room.

'This lady clearly needs help. The last thing she needs right now is to be surrounded by this behaviour. I'm not saying that I condone what she's done, *if* what you say is correct,' he pointedly spoke to Col, emphasising the 'if'. 'But from what I gather, she's had a huge amount of personal trauma to deal with. You all have.' The consultant's eyes travelled compassionately around the room as he continued to address them all, his tone authoritative, professional. 'Now, I'd like you all to calm down. The nurse will talk to you before taking you in to see Mr Steele.' He softened his voice as he turned towards Julie, 'Meanwhile, I'm going to take Mrs Steele to my office and make arrangements for a colleague of mine to come and talk to her. In fact, I think you all could do with some trauma counselling. There's a long road ahead for all of you, and now, more than ever, you *all* need to support each other. Mrs Steele is in too fragile a state to cope with this alone.'

Col spoke up first. 'Sorry about earlier, I...I was in shock...I think I should go.' A ripple of murmurs ran around the Family Room as he stood up to leave.

'Don't you want to see Ged?' Beryl asked, taking him by the arm.

'Not tonight – I don't think I can face it now. I'll stop by tomorrow after work.' Unseen by the others, he locked eyes with Julie – she read his message loud and clear.

This was perhaps not the way that Ged would have wanted the abuse to come to light, least of all while he was unable to take part in the discussion.

But the seeds were sown.

And they would grow.

Both she and Col knew it was just a question of when and how big.

CHAPTER 38

Aftermath

Although the nurse had prepared the two families for what to expect, they returned in silent shock to the Family Room after seeing Ged unconscious and hooked up to machines in the ICU. Frank Bryant took out a neatly folded white handkerchief and began cleaning his glasses – a dramatic tactic he usually employed in court when defending a client. Except this time it was his daughter that he was defending in a pseudo kangaroo-court in the hospital's Family Room.

'Well, I'm sorry, but I still find it hard to believe Col. I really can't imagine that Julie is capable of doing these things to her husband, to Ged.' He remained standing for good effect.

'I can.' All heads swivelled towards Jean Bryant. 'I can. I've seen it myself. Maybe not the physical stuff, but I've seen what she's like when she can't get her own way.'

'Rubbish, woman,' Frank retorted.

'Rubbish? Is it? Have you ever seen her when she's been told that she can't have something? Have you ever had to duck a flying hairbrush? Have you ever been screamed at, face-to-face?' A tear escaped, belying her usual demure composure.

'No, but...' Frank tried to defend his daughter, but Jean intercut him,

'No. No, you haven't. Because you've always been the "yes" man to her, while I've had to be the one saying no. The bad guy.' Jean took out her own neatly folded handkerchief and dabbed her eyes.

Ged's mam noticed how Jean's diamond cluster ring caught the light and sparkled. Frank obviously liked to treat his ladies to expensive stuff. She looked down at her own simple diamond ring and remembered how hard Jud had scrimped and saved to buy one for her. Strange, she'd always taken Julie's parents to be Mr & Mrs Perfect, the couple who had everything – money, businesses, nice house, two cars, holidays abroad. She looked intently at her own husband and took his hand. She gave it a grateful squeeze.

Frank squared up his shoulders to make himself appear taller, imposing – another one of his courtroom tactics. 'Well, I'm going to stick with the maxim of "innocent until proven guilty". And if it turns out to be true, then we'll just get her whatever help she needs.' He paused briefly, having suddenly realised that this wasn't just about his daughter. 'Whatever help *she and Ged* need to get through this.'

The room fell silent, expectant. Julie's parents were suddenly aware that they had an audience to their exchange. The door opened, breaking the tension, as Will and his two young aunties returned with cans of Coke and Mars bars for everyone. Jud scooped up his grandson and lavished him with grateful kisses, making Will giggle.

It was the break they all needed to close the discussion.

The consultant guided Julie towards his office. His desk, though covered in stacks of folders, looked neat, orderly. He ushered Julie into one of the comfy chairs and handed her a glass of water. He sat beside her in a matching chair, elbows on the arm rests, his fingers steepled under his chin, waiting for Julie to compose herself. Breathing sounds filled the room, the air pensive. Julie spoke first.

'It's true. What Col said is true...'

'Yes, I figured it must be, but knew it wasn't the right moment to pursue this. You do realise that what you're doing is very wrong? That you need help.' His gaze fixed on her intently. She lowered her eyes, unable to match his eye contact.

'But how can I get help without this affecting our little boy, Will?' asked Julie. 'I don't want him to be drawn into this mess. Will child-services have to get involved?'

The consultant thought for a moment before replying with a question. 'Have you ever hurt Will, or as he ever witnessed you hurting Mr Steele?'

'No,' she said simply. It was true, he hadn't.

'Then let's start by getting some psychological help for you. In fact, I think the whole family would benefit from some trauma counselling. We can work on this while Mr Steele is recovering in hospital. He will also need support – lots of support. Not just medically, but emotionally.'

'And Col?' asked Julie.

'Yes, we'll need to speak to him too. It sounds like your husband has already opened up to his friend – Col seems quite aware of what's been going on. We need to smooth things over for him too,' said the consultant.

Julie recalled Col's stinging attack on her. *But what did he mean by "it's not the only thing"?*

The consultant's voice softened. 'You also have a lot of healing to do.'

Julie was relieved by the consultant's empathetic tone. It was the first time that anyone had really offered her a non-judgemental helping hand, and she was grateful to reach out and take it. She picked nervously at an invisible thread on her sleeve,

'Will I get into trouble?'

'Only if your husband decides to press charges. That's up to him,' replied the consultant.

Julie felt slightly relieved at the consultant's answer, and asked, 'Just one final question – when and how should I admit everything to the family?'

The consultant stood up and stretched, 'Not tonight, my dear. Let's speak to the psychologist first. Get her guidance on the matter.' He opened his desk diary. 'I'll see you again at two o'clock tomorrow afternoon. That will give me a chance to call the psychologist and get this ball rolling. Now, my dear, I think it's high time we all went home to get some sleep – it's almost midnight.'

Julie began to cry again, tears of relief, fear and anticipation, now that it was partially out in the open. But acknowledgement was only the first step to healing.

She hoped Ged would find it in his heart to forgive her.

Make or break…

The atmosphere in the Family Room was heavy and tense when Julie and the consultant returned. She got the distinct feeling that there had been a heated discussion, and that she had been at its epicentre. Will was curled up in Grandad Jud's arms, sucking his thumb – something Julie hadn't seen him do in years,

'Can we go home now, Mummy? I'm tired.'

Julie looked at Will – *how could I have been so stupid? How could I have risked throwing all this away?* 'Sure, we're all going home now, we're all tired, sweetheart. Let's say "thank-you" to the doctor, eh.'

The families shook hands with the consultant as they left, and thanked him for all that he'd done for Ged.

He in turn reminded them that now was not the time for family divisions.

Now was not the time.

CHAPTER 39

Saints & Sinners

Before heading to the hospital, Julie dropped off Will at her parents' house. She sensed a distinct fake jolliness from her father when he scooped up Will to greet him, and her mother seemed distant, almost nervous, around her. Julie's mother always adopted this kind of reaction toward her if she sensed any looming embarrassment to her world. But her father's reaction was something new – she'd never witnessed this kind of cold-shouldering from him. He was the one person she'd always been able to depend on, to be by her side. Frank always knew how to counsel her out of a tricky situation. Now she felt that her one true ally was switching sides. They were treating her differently.

She could feel it.

Next stop was the Castle Hotel to pick up Ged's parents so that they could all go down to the hospital together. Ged's twin sisters had chosen to stay behind rather than see their brother "smashed to pieces". A shift in their mood towards her was similarly evident; the conversation in the car felt animated, the atmosphere fragile. Julie noticed that Beryl's eyes were puffy and red; every fibre of her clothing exuded the cloying smell of cigarette smoke – a sure sign of a tearful, sleepless night.

'Col stopped by at the Hotel this morning and had coffee with us. He wondered if he could have the keys to the shed so that he can look after the allotment while Ged's in hospital. He didn't want to call round at the cottage, you know...' commented Beryl, her tone emotionless. Julie noticed that her mother-in-law couldn't even look at her directly when she spoke; her head was turned towards the car's side window.

'That's really kind of Col. Yes. Yes, I'll bring the keys to you later so that you can give them to Col this evening. I remember him saying that he was going to stop by the hospital after work. Perhaps it's best if I keep out of the way while he's there.' Julie could feel her heart kick up a gear as she recalled the venomous accusations being blasted at her by Col last night. She guessed that's why her in-laws were being frosty with her today, and could well imagine that her name had come up a few times over their morning coffee.

Trying to make conversation was futile – Julie was beginning to feel unwelcome in her own car. She wound down the window and allowed her mind to wander, to escape. There was no doubt that Ged and Col had a rock-solid friendship – she loved hearing stories about their antics as kids; damming the little stream that ran by the side of the estate, making mud bombs, terrorising the estate on their bicycles, 'penny-for-the-guy' pranks near Bonfire Night. Never clean, but always happy. Beryl often said that Ged's clothes were held together by mud and grass stains. And Ged had been there for Col when his mum had died of cancer a couple of years ago. She felt a pang of guilt over her fight with Ged a few weeks earlier when she's banned him from seeing Col, accusing him of spending more time with his mate than with her. Enough was enough. So, how come Ged had met with Col yesterday? Had he gone against her wishes and still been hanging out with Col behind her back? She squeezed her eyes together and pursed her lips, miffed. But she had to admit, it would break Ged's heart if the allotment went to rack and ruin while he was incapacitated – that allotment was his passion. Col would do his mate proud by taking it on for a while, of that she was sure.

A shudder ran the length of Julie's spine as she noticed that they were already at the motorcycle showrooms opposite the entrance to the hospital grounds. She must have been driving on autopilot, having no recollection of the journey. Helena often commented about that – there were many occasions when she's been trying to have a conversation with her in the salon, but Julie was clearly zoned out. That said, Helena fully understood that Julie had been through a lot these past few years, she had a lot on her mind. She was a good friend, Helena. She let Julie have her space, but was always there for her when and if the need arose. And, of course, Julie had been there for Helena when she'd chosen to 'come-out' and tell her parents that she was a lesbian. That she had a girlfriend, Lauren, and they were going to move in together. Those had been tough days for Helena. Friendships were indeed a precious commodity.

The ICU unit gently bustled with an air of calm yet purposeful activity as the duty nurse checked charts and monitors. The room already felt stuffy and airless. Julie noticed that the nurse had pulled back the cotton sheet so the oscillating fan could waft a cooling breeze over Ged's torso. The extent of Ged's bruising and life support equipment became more vivid in the harsh light of day, causing Julie to recoil. *So they're the bruises that Col was talking about...*

She caught sight of Jud putting a supportive arm around Beryl, her shoulders shaking with silent, racking sobs. It was evident that they had also absorbed the extent of their son's injuries as he lay prone before them.

A different consultant to the one last night greeted them, and proceeded to explain that Ged had passed a peaceful night. Ged appeared to be responding well to medication, but they thought it best to keep him in a medically induced coma or state of unconsciousness for a short while longer. That way, his body could heal without him having to suffer any undue pain and distress. The consultant's voice was soothing yet authoritative, and they felt no need to question his reasoning.

After the consultant had left them, neither Julie or her in-laws seemed willing to move from the bedside. Ged looked so vulnerable. Julie noticed early signs of grey in Ged's sideburns; something she's never noticed before. She recalled having read an article in one of the salon's magazines that a sudden shock could sometimes induce temporary grey. It suited him.

'Did-you-hurt-my-son?' Beryl's direct, staccato questioning caught Julie off guard. 'Did you?'

'I…I…We fight sometimes. Sometimes it gets physical.' It was Julie's best explanation. Neither woman looked at the other.

'If I find out that you did this to my son, this will be one case your *daddy* won't be able to win for you.' Beryl's words were clear, decisive.

'Are you threatening me…?'

'Threatening you? No, Julie, I'm not threatening you. I'm *promising* you.'

Though they were only stood centimetres apart, the chasm that had opened between the two women felt immense. Julie willed her legs to move, but they wouldn't. She felt trapped. Her mind raced, searching its darkest recesses for a viable answer.

'I admit we've been having some problems. I have an appointment to meet the consultant from last night at 2 o'clock today. He was going to find a way of helping. Counselling, and such like.' It was the only answer she could come up with, without a full-blown confession.

Beryl neither acknowledged nor disregarded Julie's marital revelation. She simply said, 'We can catch the bus back to the Hotel. There's a regular service between here and Castle Ridge. Don't forget to leave the allotment and shed keys at the Hotel's reception so that we can give them to Col later.'

Julie suddenly felt very alone. Very isolated. Trapped. She exited the ICU without looking at, or speaking to, Ged's parents. It took her a moment to get her bearings as she searched for the ladies' toilets. She could already feel the bile rising in her stomach as she pushed open the door, before throwing up all over the floor. She crumpled to her knees, drained of all fight.

Her mother-in-law was right – this was one battle Daddy couldn't fight for her.

CHAPTER 40

Moving Forward

The therapist's office was surprisingly bright and cheerful – Julie had pre-imagined it to be gloomy, with overstuffed, well-worn leather chairs, and shelves filled with musty, leather-bound books. Instead, the décor was a calming pale green and white. Tropical yucca and rubber plants battled for floor space, and sunflower pictures graced the walls. A vase of yellow gerbera added a bold splash of colour to the white desk, while inviting white linen-cloth armchairs had soft yellow blankets draped over the arms, and plump yellow cushions were strategically placed for style as well as comfort. Gold-framed certificates confirmed that Dr Amanda Sheldon was more than qualified to do her job. Julie's preconceived image of a grumpy old therapist was similarly dispelled – Dr Sheldon was young, her demeanour warm and approachable as she held out her hand to greet Julie.

'Good morning Mrs Steele, Julie. Lovely to meet you.' She guided Julie towards one of the armchairs. 'How can I help you?'

Julie felt instantly at ease. She felt like she could open up…

'I've been bad. Very bad.' Julie's voice began to waver, to falter. 'I…I need help. I desperately need help.'

'I'm not here to judge you, Julie. I'm here to help you.' Dr Sheldon lay a reassuring hand on Julie's arm. 'Now, why don't you begin by telling me what you've done that *you* think is so bad…'

Although Julie felt extremely exhausted, both physically and mentally, after the first session with Dr Sheldon, she felt like she had taken the first positive step towards resolving all what had gone wrong in her life, and consequently her marriage. It was agreed that Julie would continue working with Dr Sheldon, then Ged would start trauma-counselling sessions with her once he was well enough. Dr Sheldon also recommended Ged and Julie have joint marriage-guidance sessions with a counsellor from Relate. The therapist had warned Julie that there was no "quick-fix" – they had many years of pain and grief to unlock and work through.

The first thing Julie did once she got home was to make herself a cup of calming peppermint tea. While she waited for the kettle to boil, she looked around the kitchen, the heart of the home. Food battles had been won and lost, pictures finger-painted, babies bathed in the sink…Her eye was drawn to the crescent shaped dent in the wall and chipped corner of a wall tile – a reminder of her first real moment of anger when she'd thrown a mug of steaming hot coffee at Ged. Luckily, it hadn't hit him, having smashed into the wall instead. She shuddered, guilt at its core. Prompted by her feelings of remorse, she went upstairs to the twins' room. The poem that Ged had written for them just after they were born still hung on the wall – a daily dedication to the passion he felt for them as a father. She reached out and touched the glass, finger-tracing the words as she read the poem to herself. Here was a man so caring, so passionate…

All the best writers were called William…Oh, Romeo, Ged…We were once inseparable lovers…

His Lady Juliet owed him one hell of an apology.

She only hoped that he would accept it.

CHAPTER 41

Insurance

Col eased his Ford Escort van onto the cottage driveway behind Julie's Mini. Good, Julie was at home. As he went around the back of the van, he sensed someone creeping along the side, edging slowly towards him.

'Halt, who goes there? Friend or foe?'

A mini spaceman was directing a fully loaded water pistol and a red plastic space laser gun towards him. Col held up his hands submissively,

'I come in peace. Take me to your leader,' he reassured his would-be captor. Will the spaceman still couldn't resist squirting Col with the water pistol before being absolutely sure that the Earthling was as good as his word. Col played along with the game and faked that he'd been shot.

'Ay-up, Will. I've got some stuff for yer mam. Is she at home?' The spaceman nodded his affirmation. Col handed Will a trug full of delicious looking soft fruits, freshly picked from Ged's allotment. 'Here, take this.' Col then picked up two sack-cloth bags from the back of the van and followed Will into the kitchen.

Julie stiffened, having recognised Col's van when he pulled onto the driveway. She had only been home from work a short while; her legs ached and she was in no mood for any more of Col's pointed accusations. The therapist, Dr Sheldon, had recommended Julie return to the salon part-time, in order to restore some "routine and purpose" to her recovery. She allowed herself to relax a little once she saw Col bearing fresh produce from the allotment, ably assisted by Will the spaceman.

Col accepted an invitation to sit down at the kitchen table. In his childlike innocence, Will decided that the invitation also extended to him and sat with them, munching on strawberries from the trug.

'Good harvest,' commented Col. 'Everything's looking great up there. Here's a bagful of other stuff too. Cabbages, peas, carrots, new potatoes and the like.'

'They look fabulous, Col. I wanted to thank you personally for doing this, but, you know, it's...' Julie let her head fall forward so that her long hair shielded her eyes. She heard Col clear his throat, then address Will,

'Here, why don't you go and take this trug next door to Mrs Jessop. I bet she'd love to make lots of jam with all this lovely fruit. But I would take that space helmet off first, eh. You don't want her to think that Castle Ridge has been invaded by alien spacemen.'

Will collapsed into fits of giggles, and could be heard muttering, 'I come in peace. I come in peace...' as he made his way next door with the basket. Once he was out of ear-shot, Col lifted another bag onto the table and began rummaging around inside.

'I found Ged's insurance policy up at the allotment, when I was helping old Mr Poulter clear some weeds.'

'Insurance policy? But Ged has one with the Co-op Insurance. Why would he want another one – a secret one?' Julie looked at Col, puzzled.

Col placed the weedkiller tin on the table in front of him. Julie looked from the tin to Col, and then back to the tin.

'Weedkiller? Do you think he was going to top himself? I don't understand – how is this insurance?'

Col opened the lid. 'Oh, this is a fully comprehensive insurance policy – I can assure you of that.' He lifted out a camera and laid it to one side. Julie's eyes flickered with confused recognition. He then lifted out a Polaroid photograph, and read the date and description. He repeated the process again and again, each time holding the photographs closely to him until he had a fan resembling playing cards in his hand. He turned the pictures to face Julie so that she could absorb the cruel, vivid images – bruises, cuts, burns – before carefully putting them back into the tin, making sure that it was out of her grasp.

Next, he lifted out Ged's gardening diary, in which Ged had meticulously recorded many of the occasions when Julie had said or done mean things without causing physical harm. He waved the book slightly.

'Makes interesting reading. Well, perhaps "interesting" isn't quite the right word. Made me feel sick, to be honest. This is emotional carnage…'

Julie sat in stunned silence, frozen.

'Like I said – fully comprehensive insurance. Imagine the damage this little lot could do…' Col let his words hang in the air, volatile, threatening. He noticed a single tear escape and roll down Julie's cheek, splashing onto the kitchen table. Seconds passed, the silence loaded.

Julie spoke up first, her voice barely audible.

'When you came to the hospital and accused me of all those things, I knew exactly what you were talking about. I knew you were right. But I just couldn't face the truth in front of everyone. I…my God, I'm such a monster…' She looked at Col with pleading eyes. 'I'm truly sorry. You have to believe me…'

'Why should I believe you? Why should I trust you?' He waved the tin under Julie's nose, causing her to recoil.

'I know what I've done is wrong. And despite what you might think, I do love Ged. And I do want to stop – get back to how life used to be.'

Col mimicked her words, unconvinced.

'It's true!' she defended. 'I spoke to the consultant – told him everything. He put me in touch with some therapist, some shrink, and she's working with me. Helping me to talk it through and get to the root of everything. She said that asking for help is not a sign of weakness, but a sign of courage. We shouldn't be ashamed to ask for help. She says that I have some form of severe depression connected to the bad pregnancy and shock of birth – something called "post-natal depression". It can be quite bad for some women – it can last for years.' Her voice became small again. 'And, of course, the trauma and grief from losing Jon. I've never gotten over that...I don't think I ever will. Unfortunately, Ged was my emotional release. My emotional punch-bag...someone to blame.' Her voice trailed off. Seeing the pictures, hearing the words – affirmation of her appalling cruelty – was akin to pouring acid on an open, festering wound.

'Oh, I know everything. Ged told me all about it. I bumped into him on the day of the accident, so we went for a pint and a chat. To patch things up, like. I was in shock – still am...' Col explained. 'He showed me the bruises. Told me all about this abuse.' He tapped the tin. 'And how you've been seeing someone else behind his back.' He stared hard at her.

'Seeing someone else? No! No, I've never done that!' Her voice became raised, defensive. And then she suddenly realised what Col was referring to – the secret visits to the clairvoyant. Ged had obviously misunderstood and assumed that she was having an affair. Knowing that Ged thought this kind of thing was spiritual clap-trap or mumbo-jumbo in order to prise money out of vulnerable people, she had never tried to explain it to him, but rather fended off his questioning with violent outbursts. Now it all made sense.

'No, Col. I'm seeing a spiritualist. She helps me to stay in touch with Jon...'

'But you know that Ged thinks it's a pile of shite. A money-making racket,' Col retorted, with a little too much growl in his tone.

'Yes, I know. But it helps me – I'm just not ready to let go...' Julie could feel tears brimming in her eyes. 'Anyway, the therapist also wants to meet with Ged once he's well enough. You know, to help him talk through the different traumas. And then she wants to put us in touch with Relate for some marriage-guidance counselling.' She paused to dab away the tears. 'I really want this to work, Col. You have to believe me. I want things to get back to the way they used to be.'

Col took a deep breath and stretched, regrouping his thoughts.

'Well, I'm glad to hear it, Julie. I hope you realise that even with all this...' he rapped hard on the tin, 'that Ged still loves you. He's shit-scared of you. But he still loves you. He just doesn't know how to fix it. He especially doesn't want Will to get messed up in all this.' Julie hung her head in shame, as Col continued his tirade. 'Ged's mam's well pissed off with you an'all.'

'Okay, okay, I get the message...' Julie paused, and fiddled with her fingers. She was extremely relieved to hear that Ged still loved her. At least she now knew that there was some hope of working through their difficulties. 'Would you explain everything to Beryl? About the therapy, and stuff. That I'm trying to get help. And tell her that I'm sorry...'

Col softened a little. 'I don't really think that it's my place to tell her, Julie. You have to tell her yourself. Tell it to her like you told it to me,' he encouraged. 'Invite her and Jud for Sunday dinner – it'll save all this veg from going to waste. Cook one of your famous roast pork and cracklin' dinners.'

Julie looked up, sparked by Col's wave of positivity, and wiped her eyes. 'Would you come too? I'd feel better if you were there,' she asked.

Col nodded his head in confirmation. 'Aye, I will. I'll go and talk to Beryl and Jud, and I'll let you know what they say. I've offered Ged a job at the coal yard, by the way – old Ernie is retiring at the end of August. The job's there for Ged as soon as he's fit and ready. I'm sure he'll be able to use the bagging machine, even if he can't help us with heavy stuff.'

A ray of light was beginning to shine at the end of Julie's tunnel. 'Thanks, Col. You're a good friend.' She put her hand on Col's arm. 'The doctors are happy with Ged's progress over this past ten days. They've taken him off the ventilator, and he's now breathing unaided. His reflexes are responding, so the doctors are planning to bring him out of the induced sleep.' Julie managed a weak smile. 'Please don't stop visiting. I think it will help Ged to recover if he hears your voice.'

'Aye, I would like that, thanks.' Now that Col was privy to what had been going on, there was no way he could abandon his best friend. He would be there to watch his back. Col stood up ready to leave, and put the tin of weedkiller 'insurance' back into the sack. 'I'm going to hang on to this tin for now.' He held the cloth bag closely to him, a physical wedge of ruinous proportions. 'I hope you'll be as good as your word, Julie. I hope you're not full of shit...'

'Why is Mummy full of shit?'

Col and Julie froze on the spot. How much had Will seen and heard?

'Er, your mum's full of shit because, er, because...she's been eating lots of cherries from your nanna's fruit shop, and it's given her tummy ache,' stammered Col.

'I know what you mean. They make me full of shit too,' giggled Will, knowing that he shouldn't say 'shit' because it was a grown-up word.

Col stared at Julie. Both were trying to stifle a laugh, momentarily easing the tension between them.

'Well, I'd better get going,' said Col, as he headed towards the hallway and front door, accompanied by Julie.

Before she let him out the door, she held him by the elbow and whispered, 'Are you blackmailing me...?'

'Yes, Julie. Yes, I am blackmailing you. This is Ged's insurance, and you need to pay him back in full – with interest. Otherwise...' Col patted the tin, and gave her a knowing wink. 'I'll let you know about Sunday,' he said, as a walked towards the van.

Julie closed the front door and leaned with her back against the wall. She thought about the tin of photos and book of notes. Ged had all the evidence he needed – evidence of her physical and emotional vandalism, should he choose to press charges against her. And now Col had her backed into a corner with his knowledge of everything. She massaged her eyes and tilted her head slightly upwards as she took a few deep breaths to help slow her pulse. Julie felt a small hand slip into hers.

'Are you okay, Mummy?' came a concerned little voice.

She squeezed Will's hand reassuringly. 'Yes. Yes, I'm fine, sweetheart. Mummy's just feeling a little tired – it's been a long day.' Julie deftly changed the subject. 'Well, Mr Spaceman – what shall we have for tea?'

But Will was already galloping away on his imaginary space horse. He was on a mission to save the world, and didn't have time to stop and give answers.

Julie sighed and headed for the kitchen – *fish-fingers it is, then.*

CHAPTER 42

One Door Closes

1992

Edith Pilgrim looked up from her knitting, her gaze drawn to the little teddy bear with the yellow bow. She went over to where it was sat and gently picked it up – she inhaled deeply then held it close to her heart. 'So, your mummy and daddy are happy now. That's good news, eh. I think we can let your mummy know that Jon's finally at peace and you can go home.'

Mrs Steele was by far one of her easiest clients – she was from a wealthy business family who were quite well connected in the local community, so moved in similar circles to herself. She often heard titbits of gossip about Mrs Steele and the family.

Edith reflected on Mrs Steele's most recent visit. She had felt more like a confessional listener than a clairvoyant. They'd gotten through two cups of tea and had a good chat before Edith could begin her "channelling" to search for Jon. And when she found him, the news was only good. Jon sensed that the family were moving on and that meant that he could move on too – finally. It was the first time that Edith had seen Mrs Steele's face look truly relaxed. And it had been, what, maybe two years since she started visiting? Yes, it must be at least two years since the little boy was tragically killed. Edith recalled that Mrs Steele used to visit quite a lot in the beginning, desperate for news about her little boy, but the visits gradually faded over time. There were even times when Mrs Steele had visited but Jon never came through. But then again, Edith never offered any guarantees of making contact. So, maybe it was time to close the book on this client?

She looked at the clock – 10:30 pm – it was too late to call Mrs Steele this evening. She would call her tomorrow and let her know.

Teddy could go home now – Jon was finally "at peace".

Time to close the book, in more ways than one.

CHAPTER 43

Jonah no more

1993

G ed put down *The Derbyshire Times*, not liking what he'd just read – Castle Ridge Colliery was on the "imminent" closure list, with neighbouring Markham earmarked for closure within the next few months. Still, they'd managed to keep the collieries going for another eight years or so, since the strike ended. He sighed. They'd been lucky to hang on this long – most of the other local pits were long gone. The closures would surely signal the death-knell for his friend's coal haulage company; a company that had been handed from father to son since being founded by Col's granddad. Then the company's reins had been handed to Col a couple of years ago, after his dad had incurred a back injury from the constant shovelling and hauling of heavy coal bags. Even though Ged himself was on lighter duties at the yard – a throwback from his accident a couple of years ago, it was becoming increasingly difficult to use the coal bagging machine, then help Col load the bags onto the lorry. He seriously doubted that his weak hip and leg would be able to take the strain of manual work for much longer. It would provide the perfect excuse for giving up work at Col's haulage yard without him having to say as much.

Perhaps the nearby Smokeless Fuels plant would negotiate a haulage contract with Col? But what was the point? Why flog a dead horse? Maggie, in her infinite wisdom, had made it clear that the future of fossil fuels was dead. This would be a serious blow for his friend, as well as the community.

Ged briefly reflected on his own history around coal – he'd often laughingly called himself the "Jonah of Coal", such was his bad luck around the damned stuff. But if the truth be known, the pit closures could be a blessing in disguise, even if only from a health point of view. Maybe now was the time to return to his qualified trade of electrician? Perhaps set up his own company after a bit of retraining? Time to break the Jonah spell.

Julie came into the sitting room and immediately took note of Ged's furrowed brow. 'You look deep in thought. What's up?'

Ged poked at the front page of *The Derbyshire Times*. 'Castle Ridge Colliery is due for imminent closure, with Markham to follow. I was just pondering the future, for Col and for the business. And for us.'

Julie came and sat beside him. She thought back to the miners' strike, and how hard the industry had fought to delay the inevitable. Hard times were once again on the horizon for the local community. 'So what are you thinking?' she asked.

Ged put forward his idea for setting up his own electrician's business, starting by going back to night-school to retrain – something light, based on the way his hip and leg were aching.

'I think it's a great idea, Ged. Be your own boss. People will always need electrical work doing,' Julie encouraged, in a bid to conceal her fears over Ged's now uncertain future. She was hit by a sudden wave of angry wasps stinging around in her stomach, a feeling she hadn't encountered in quite some time. It caught her off guard.

Ged could feel a sense of pride growing. Yes, he – *they* – had suffered some major traumas along the way, but, ironically, he felt all the stronger for it. *They* seemed all the stronger for it. He took Julie's hand. 'But what about Col? I can't really return the favour and take him on,' he said, shaking his head and shrugging his shoulders in a genuine show of disappointment.

Julie had always functioned under a cloud of guilt since Col had presented her with Ged's hidden stash of Polaroid photos, and she'd confessed about secretly seeing the clairvoyant. But she had remained as good as her word and got her life back on track with therapy, and worked with Ged on renewing the strength they once had in their relationship and marriage. Even the clairvoyant had said that Jon was able to move on because he knew that his mummy and daddy were happy. Jon had also found peace. Col had similarly kept his side of the bargain – the tin of photos had been carefully put back in the shed before the keys had been returned to Ged, and he had never said anything about the clairvoyant. In fact, on a recent trip over to the allotment, Julie couldn't even see the tin in the shed. Maybe Ged had moved it out of the way? Or even destroyed it? She would never know. And in a bizarre kind of way she would always be indebted to Col for exposing one secret and keeping another – it forced her out of the shadows of depression and into the light of support.

'I could have a word with Uncle Jack up at the farm. Maybe he needs a haulier for the wholesale market? Or maybe a farm-hand, driving the tractor or harvesting machinery? I'm sure we can help Col to find something,' said Julie, trying to add a ray of hope. 'We know that the pit closure is imminent, so we can at least work towards helping Col wind down the haulage yard, if that's what he wants. We haven't even talked to him about it.'

'Aye, maybe it's time for us all to move into a new chapter, eh. There's going to be changes afoot for many families.' Ged sighed at the bleak prospect for the local people yet again. The Conservatives had certainly produced a lot of unrest and uncertainty in this decade. It certainly wouldn't be remembered as a time of prosperity for the majority of industrial communities.

'I suppose the main blessing for Col is that he stayed a bachelor. He doesn't have a wife or family that depend on him,' said Julie. *Unlike you do...*

'True. That would make losing the coal yard an even bigger pill to swallow,' Ged acknowledged.

Driven by the need to feel secure, Julie wriggled under Ged's arm and snuggled up close, her legs over his, childlike. Ged gently took a handful of her hair and twirled it through his fingers, relishing its softness, rekindling memories. He stole the opportunity to kiss her on the nose, savouring the sweet fragrance of his wife's perfume. 'Well, I'm sure we'll work something out – a Steele never gives up without a fight,' he said, drawing her head towards the crook of his shoulder.

Julie felt herself meld into him. 'Especially if it's worth fighting for,' she whispered, returning his closeness. She closed her eyes and put her free hand over her stomach.

So why are there still a few wasps of nervous apprehension buzzing around, stinging?

CHAPTER 44

A Cloud Appears

"A woman was arrested on Tuesday morning on suspicion of conspiring to defraud the public. Edith Pilgrim, aged 68, of Langton House, Langton, was arrested after one of her clients exposed her as a charlatan clairvoyant. The client became suspicious after Mrs Pilgrim made a number of claims about the client's deceased relative, which the client knew to be untrue.

A search of Langton House has revealed a large hoard of local newspapers dating back years, together with a number of journals and scrapbooks relating to her so-called clients. Speaking in her defence, her solicitor, Mr Frank Bryant, of Bryant & Harding, said that Mrs Pilgrim had only wished to bring comfort and succour to her clients, she had never wished any ill-will.

Mrs Pilgrim, a former starlet and socialite, fell heavily into debt after the death of her husband, Cecil Pilgrim. At the risk of losing Langton House, she allegedly chose to use her acting skills in the form of clairvoyancy. As a member of many local committees and community services, Mrs Pilgrim had discreet access to a great deal of local knowledge, which, the client claims, Mrs Pilgrim used to her advantage.

Police have taken away the scrapbooks and journals as well as details of Mrs Pilgrim's bank accounts, for further investigation. The true extent *of her alleged fraudulence has yet to be assessed. Any persons who think they might have been affected by this are encouraged to report to their local police station. All reports will be dealt with in the strictest confidence."*

Julie put *The Derbyshire Times* to one side on the sofa, still open at the page that she'd just been reading. A huge ball of angry wasps formed in the pit of her stomach, causing bile to rise to her throat.

Edith Pilgrim was a fake.

She had kept scrapbooks and journals on her "clients". She had snooped; she had pried; she had blagged her way into people's grief and confidence. And Julie was one of those gullible people.

She had been sucked in by the mumbo-jumbo.

By needing to know.

By needing to be close to her baby.

And ironically her own father would be defending the woman.

Ged was right.

It was all a con.

Julie recalled her first visit to Edith and shuddered with the ease that she'd been taken in by this woman's convincing charm and dialogue. The elegant surroundings. The seeming perceptiveness of reading Julie's thoughts. She remembered a picture on the wall with a face that she could never pinpoint – Edith looking glamorous at the side of some other young, equally glamorous lady. Now it all made sense – the starlet days, the budding actress days, waiting for the big break that never came. Instead, she was whisked off her feet and charmed by an older gentleman, and started moving in the circles of landed gentry. Yes, it suited Edith well, until it was all so tragically cut short by Cecil's untimely death. Guess she had to make a living somehow without getting her well-manicured hands dirty. Julie looked at her own chewed and chipped nails – no longer long, lacquered and elegant. She realised that her hands were shaking. It was just one thing after another...

Was there a journal or scrapbook on her? On Jon? What if the police tried to contact her? What if the truth came out?

She felt the sting of bile in the back of her throat. She could feel the blood pounding in her temples. An immense pressure descended on her – more than when Col challenged her about the Polaroid photos of Ged's injuries. Somehow this felt even more degrading. Deeply personal.

She felt raw.

She felt exposed.

She felt defiled.

Julie closed her eyes and took a deep breath.

And another.

And another.

In. Out. In. Out.

After allowing her mind a few brief moments of clarity, she grabbed some bits from the cupboard of the pine dresser, and the keys to the Mini.

*

'Well, I think your mam's going to be well impressed now that you've got your woggle. You look really smart in your uniform.' Ged proudly held Will's hand, while Will held the bag of fish-and-chip take-away in his free hand. 'C'mon, race you...' teased Ged, his walking stick clattering in step with his bad leg in a bizarre kind of three-legged race.

As always, Will took up the challenge, going as fast as his little eight year old legs could carry him. Will knew that he would win on account of his dad's bad leg and hip, but Ged still insisted on pretending to race.

'Don't look like me mam's home yet,' Will announced, seeing the driveway empty. 'She'd better hurry up, or else her fish n'chips'll get cold.'

On entering the hallway, Ged noticed that her jacket and shoes had gone, yet the house felt as though it had only recently been vacated. There was still a faint air of warmth and smell of coffee lingering in the air.

'I'm sure she's not gone far. She knows Thursday is chip-night after you've been to Cubs. C'mon, let's lay the table ready.'

*

Ged paced the sitting room, trying not to let his nervousness show. Julie's fish and chips had long since dried up in the oven, then been taken out and gone cold.

'Let's put the telly on, eh, and then I'll call Grandma Jean. Maybe Mummy's gone there, and forgotten to leave us a note.' Ged turned on the television and found a repeat of "George and Mildred". Will loved watching this programme – he seemed to identify with the little boy, Tristan.

'…Oh, so you haven't seen her today. No, I tried her mobile, but it was turned off. Yes, okay, I'll give Helena a try. Maybe they've gone to Makro together. Yes, okay, see you Sunday for lunch.' Ged disconnected the call, then dialled Helena's number.

'…left the salon at 5 o'clock. Oh, okay. Yes, I can see that she's been home, it looks like she was sat reading the DT, then went out. No, I tried her mobile, but it was turned off. Yes, maybe she's gone shopping. Okay, cheers, Helena.'

A knot was beginning to form in Ged's stomach. He looked out of the window into the darkness before drawing the curtains, then sat on the sofa next to Will and gave him a reassuring cuddle. 'I'm sure she won't be long, eh.' He picked up *The Derbyshire Times* and began to read the page that had been left open. The headline "Clairvoyant Charged with Fraud" caught his attention. He read it.

While the headline and news article might have caused a dark cloud to descend for Julie, the cloud had just been lifted for Ged. He had a feeling that this story was somehow connected to his wife. It was certainly connected to his father-in-law. Is this where Julie had been going? All the weird phone calls and equally inexplicable departures suddenly made sense. Julie was certainly vulnerable enough to be sucked in by something like this. He felt Will wriggle by his thigh.

'C'mon you, let's get you up to bed.' Ged gently nudged his snoozing son, and carried him upstairs. As he retrieved some PJs from Will's drawer unit, something caught his eye. Jon's old teddy had suddenly reappeared in among the collection of soft toys. Ged's eyes narrowed as he tried to recall the last time that he'd seen it. Or even if it had been missing. He shook his head, unsure of his own memory. Perhaps it had just been hiding under the pile of toys, and had been brought to the fore when Julie last cleaned the room. He gently eased Will into some pyjamas then covered him over with the duvet. 'Night, night, Will. I'm sure Mummy will be back soon,' he whispered to his sleeping son before kissing his forehead.

Ged headed back to the sitting room and looked at the clock. It was after 10:00 pm. He suddenly felt very alone. He called his in-laws again to see if they'd heard anything from Julie. Now equally nervous, her parents agreed to come over.

Within ten minutes or so, Ged saw the muted sweep of headlights through the curtains and heard the distinctive diesel clatter of Frank's Discovery as they pulled onto the driveway. But instead of feeling relieved, a wave of nervous energy began coursing through his veins.

After filling his in-laws in with what he knew, what he'd just read, and what he now surmised, Ged wondered if they should call the police and report her missing.

Frank could see that Ged's eyes were full of panic. 'Tell you what, Ged – let me go for a drive over to Langton House. Maybe Julie's there?' suggested Frank. 'If, like we assume, our Julie is one of these so-called "clients", maybe she's gone there for some kind of retribution. Although Edith Pilgrim isn't there. I can't really say any more than that because of client confidentiality, you understand.'

Ged nodded his mute agreement.

'I have my mobile with me,' Frank continued. 'I'll call you and let you know what I find. And if she isn't there, then I'll call the police and report her missing. Okay?'

Ged nodded again. 'Thanks, Frank.' He smiled wanly at his father-in-law.

Julie wasn't at Langton House.

EPILOGUE

We waited all night, with no news.

It was some poor old bloke having an early morning walk with his dog that found Julie's Mini parked up at the back of the old railway sidings on Quarrystone Lane, partially hidden by the copse and old wagons. He'd heard an engine running and thought someone must be there nickin' stuff. Poor bloke got the shock of his life, seeing the windows all fogged up like that. He tried to open the door, but she'd locked the car from the inside. And although he pulled out the towels blocking the top of the window, it was too late. The exhaust gases had done their damage.

Ironically, the closest house that he could go to for help was Col's. His coal yard backs onto the old sidings and the copse. It's actually quite a pretty area considering the old pit head and winding gear are its neighbour – there's even a little fishing pond nearby. Serene. Col recognised the car straight away and called the police. Imagine that, finding your best mate's wife. He was able to give them an informal identification. We never saw the Mini again – we had it scrapped and crushed. Frank took care of that. And, of course, Frank had to step aside from handling the Edith Pilgrim case.

The moment that I saw Col get out of the police car, I knew something was wrong. They allowed him to break the news to the family. Jean was hysterical – reminded me of when we lost Jon. The pain of losing a child. A mother's pain.

She'd left two notes. One note clearly outlined her intentions – that she'd meant to do this. She'd never really got over the death of Jon, only to be cheated by that *damned Edith woman. It was too much for Julie to bear. And although I don't believe in all that spiritual mumbo-jumbo, I hope that she found the peace and solace she so truly sought. I hope that she found Jon. Talking of which – and I've never told anyone this – I swear that I saw Jon reaching out to me when I had my accident. As though he was trying to guide me towards him. So, who knows?*

The other note was in a sealed envelope, addressed to me. This is a very private confessional that only I will ever know the words of. I read it every night before I go to sleep. The letter was bound to her Dire Straits 'Making Movies' CD with a black satin ribbon. She especially loved the 'Romeo and Juliet' track – said it was "our song". There was also her old school copy of Shakespeare's 'Romeo and Juliet'. She'd put a bookmark in Act V, Scene III – the scene where Juliet dies.

It helps me to understand the many layers of pain, guilt and grief that my love, my Lady Juliet felt. Even with the eventual help and support, there was still so much that she kept locked inside. Could I have done more? I really don't know. Sadly, it's a question that I'll never know the answer to. Strangely enough, I still have the Polaroid photos of my injuries, of the abuse. It was all part of our life together, good and bad. A reminder that, even with all the help and counselling we finally received, there was always something haunting her.

She never really got rid of all her inner demons.

You think you know someone, eh?

I have a suspicion that someone found the photos. I always placed the tin in a certain way on the shelf, with the label facing the wall, and when I finally got back to pottering about at the allotment, I could see that the tin had been moved. The photos were jumbled too, no longer in date-order. Perhaps it was Col, when he looked after things for me? He's never said 'owt about it, and I've never asked him. Anyway, they're a funny green colour now, faded. Maybe one day I'll burn them. Finally let go.

Get rid of my own demons.

It helps me to understand that, for her, it was the only way out.

But I'm sick of all the endless paperwork – legal this, and insurance that. I'm sick of all the pitying looks, and whispered gossip. Will and I need to heal in peace, so we're moving to Skegness to be near my family. Make a fresh start. I don't even have any plans to start work – gonna have a bit of quality time with Will first. We need it. Anyway, the removal van's loaded up and ready to go – we're just here to say our last goodbye to the cottage before we hand the keys in to the estate agent. We plan on finding a little house by the sea. I know the "experts" say never to do anything rash in the first year of loss, let alone in the first months. But it's hard to be in the cottage, for both me and Will. There are memories everywhere we turn – in every room, in the fields at the back where Julie and I courted.

It all tells a story – our story.

To lose one person is bad enough, but two...

Besides, I have the letter from Julie, and Jon's little teddy. So I don't need a physical space to remember them. Wherever I go, they go with me.

And I still have Will.

We went to the graveyard this morning to say our goodbyes to Julie and Jon. Julie has a gravestone now. We chose a white marble heart with gold lettering. We're going to come back once a month to visit them, and to see Frank and Jean. Will asked me if his mum loved Jon more than she loved him – because she'd chosen to be with Jon. How do you explain that to a kid, eh? I told him that she was just worried about Jon being on his own, so she chose to go there, knowing that Will would be safe with me. Perhaps that explains why Will has started to wet the bed again. Poor kid, he's had so much to deal with.

I've told him not to bottle anything up – that he can always talk to me. And I've promised to do the same with him. I think it's good for us to talk things through. We've learned the hard way, that holding in your pain is the worst thing to do. It helps no-one.

But while-ever I have my mind I have my innermost memories.

Of meeting my girl.

Of dancing together.

Of eloping.

Our moments of joy.

Our moments of passion.

Our moments of pain.
And yes, our moments of grief and sorrow.
Memories of Jon.
And of my Julie.
My Lady Juliet.

Acknowledgements

Golding, W. (1954), *Lord of the Flies,* London, Faber and Faber Ltd.

Guns N'Roses, (1989), 'Sweet Child O'Mine', *Appetite for Destruction,* Geffen Records (UK).

Harris, S, (1988), Iron Maiden, 'The Clairvoyant', *Seventh Son of a Seventh Son*, EMI, Capitol (US).

Knopfler, M. (1980), 'Romeo and Juliet', *Making Movies,* Vertigo Records.

Rossi, F. & Young, B. (1974), 'Down Down', Vertigo Records.

Shakespeare, W. (2005 [1599]), *Romeo and Juliet*, London, Penguin Books Ltd.

Steinman, J. (1977). Meat Loaf, 'Bat Out of Hell', *Bat Out of Hell*, Epic/Sony Records.

44301288R00148

Printed in Poland
by Amazon Fulfillment
Poland Sp. z o.o., Wrocław